A THOUSAND TINY DISAPPOINTMENTS

SARAH EDGHILL

BLOODHOUND
— BOOKS —

www.bloodhoundbooks.com

Print ISBN 978-1-914614-40-8

1

Martha's mobile rang as she was running across the car park.

No Caller ID. She shoved the phone back into her pocket; it was bound to be someone trying to sell her something.

Rain was hammering against her face and by the time she got to the car she was soaked, strands of hair slicked across her cheeks. She was sliding into the driver's seat, when the phone rang again. Some people just didn't give up.

'Hello?' she snapped, her wet fingers fumbling to get the key into the ignition. She didn't have time for this: she was already going to be late picking up Joe. She could picture the look on the face of Sue, the nursery owner: the almost imperceptible eye-roll as she handed over Joe's bag and twisted her wrist slightly to make Martha aware that, although she wasn't exactly checking the time, she wanted to hammer home that Martha was one of the last parents to pick up. Again.

'Is that Mrs Evans?'

'Yes?'

'Mrs Martha Evans?'

'Yes! Who is this?' It was a woman's voice; not one she

recognised. The car's engine roared into life, and Martha flicked on the wipers, reaching for her seat belt as the windscreen cleared, revealing the grey exterior of the office, its sliding glass doors disgorging more people out into the car park. She registered a flash of turquoise: Janey in her new skirt; then close behind her was the guy who'd just started in sales, his jacket open and flapping behind him in the wind. This downpour hadn't been predicted. No one was dressed properly.

'I'm calling from the accident and emergency department at the Royal Surrey. It's about your mother.'

Martha's breath caught in her throat, trapped there as suddenly as if she'd been punched in the stomach. The woman was still talking, but all Martha could focus on were the wipers flicking across the windscreen ahead of her. She closed her eyes and pushed the phone against her ear. It was hard to make out what was being said, over the percussion of the rain on the roof of the car and her own heartbeat roaring in her ears. Her brain registered disconnected words: fall, x-ray, fracture.

'I'll come at once,' she said, her voice coming out as a whisper. For a few seconds she sat, staring down at her phone, running her thumb across the dark screen. She was struggling to process what she'd been told, and now there were questions rushing into her mind, important things she should have asked. Where had it happened? *When* had it happened? She could picture her mother's face, as clearly as if she was sitting beside her in the car: the slightly lopsided smile, her lips their trademark fuchsia pink, a stray speck of lipstick on her front teeth.

The rain had nearly stopped, but the windscreen wipers were still skimming backwards and forwards, squeaking as they dragged across the dry glass. There were fewer people coming out of the office now. Many of the cars around her had pulled away and a straggle of people were walking down the side of the building, taking the shortcut to the station. How long would it take to get to Surrey? On a good day it was a two-hour drive, but it was now rush hour, traffic building up on the main road beside the car park.

She dialled his number, her finger trembling. 'It's me,' she said. 'Listen, I've had some bad news.'

'Really?' Simon was distracted, his voice distant; he was probably in the car, her voice must sound equally tinny through the speakerphone at his end.

'I've had a call from a hospital. Mum's had a fall. She's in A&E. I've got to go there straight away. You'll have to collect Joe.'

She closed her eyes and listened to the silence on the other end. 'I'm leaving now, but I don't know how long it's going to take,' she went on, aware of the wobble in her voice. 'It's the worst time of day to be on the motorway.'

'Jesus, Martha. Look, I'm sorry. That's awful about your mum. But I can't just drop everything, I'm on the way to the club. You know I've got a game this evening.'

Football, bloody football. Her jaw tightened. 'That's too bad, Simon. I've got to go to Surrey. I need you to pick up Joe.'

There was a muffled sound, as if he was swearing under his breath. Then a sigh, clearly intended to be loud enough for her to hear. 'This is bloody bad timing. What am I going to tell the guys? I can't just drop out at the last minute like this. I'll let the whole side down. The away team are coming from Worcester.'

'Please, Simon? This isn't my fault.'

Her temples had started to throb and she felt light-headed, as if water was flooding around her body instead of blood. There was silence on the other end of the phone.

'For God's sake, Simon. Did you even hear what I said? My mother's in hospital – sod your football.'

'Can't you wait? If you go later, you'll miss the worst of the traffic.' There was a hopeful edge to his voice. 'Think about it,

Martha, if you leave now, you'll just sit in jams on the motorway. You know you hate that journey at the best of times. Do yourself a favour and wait a couple of hours, then you'll get there more easily.'

Maybe he was right? It would be a less stressful drive if she let the traffic die down a bit. That would mean she could go straight to the nursery and pick up Joe; Simon could go to his football and take over at home later. It would make everything less complicated. But her mother was hurt; how could she carry on as normal for the next few hours, as if nothing had happened?

She took a deep breath, pressing her lips together to stop the lower one trembling. She was damned if she was going to cry. Part of her couldn't believe her selfish bastard of a husband wasn't prepared to give up his Wednesday night football to help her out in a crisis. A larger part felt guilty having to ask him to do it. He had a right to be pissed off.

'Simon, please just go and get Joe,' she said. 'I'm leaving now. I'll call you later.'

The hurt stayed with her as she edged out of the car park and into the slow-moving string of red tail lights on the main road. It was still there half an hour later, when she finally accelerated down the slip road onto the motorway. By that time there was worry mixed in as well. Would Simon remember Joe needed a bath tonight? Would he find the chicken she'd put to defrost on the lower shelf of the fridge? She tried to call but there was no answer; they were probably upstairs. She'd try again later; the recycling needed to be put out tonight as well.

She stopped at a services on the M4 to buy a sandwich, her legs wobbly when she stepped out of the car. She dialled his number again, but it went straight to voicemail. *For God's sake, Simon – just pick up!* If he did, he'd be short with her, but she was desperate to talk to him. To anyone, come to think of it. Maybe she would try Claudia? It was a bad time: she'd be getting the kids ready for bed. But Martha needed to hear a friendly voice.

'Hi,' she said. 'It's me. I'm so sorry, I know you're in the middle of things...' She couldn't finish, her voice cracked and the sobs forced their way up into her throat without her realising they were coming.

'Hey, you, what's the matter?' Claudia's voice was so full of warmth that it made Martha cry harder.

'I'm sorry,' she whispered. 'It's just that my mum's in hospital, she's had a fall, and I'm on the way there now. I just needed to speak to you.'

'God, that's awful!' In the background Martha could hear running water, splashing, a child's voice counting to ten. Everything was echoey. 'Do you know what happened?' Claudia was asking. 'Has she broken anything?'

'I'm not sure. I didn't ask the right questions.'

There was a squeal and a thud, then Claudia came back on the line. 'Sorry, dropped the phone. Listen, I can't talk right now, but call me later. Okay? I'm sure everything will be fine. Drive safely.'

Looking at her reflection in the mirror in the ladies' toilets, Martha ran her hands through her hair, trying to drag it back into some kind of shape after the rain had wrecked it earlier. In the harsh glare of the overhead lights, the bags under her eyes looked grey. She grabbed a lipstick from her handbag and ran it around her mouth, before frantically scrubbing most of it off again with the back of her hand. It was too bright, almost cheerful. She couldn't arrive at the hospital looking like that – what was she thinking? She never usually worried about her appearance, so God knows why it suddenly mattered now. She pictured nurses standing in corridors, holding clipboards, hair pulled back into utilitarian ponytails that would weather stressful twelve-hour shifts. The people who were busy dealing with emergencies and saving lives really wouldn't care what frantic relatives looked like when they turned up.

It was already dark by the time she arrived, and it had started raining again. The red and white accident and emergency sign shone out across the ambulance bays, familiar though Martha had never been to this hospital before. But they'd had their share of visits to local A&E departments over the years, mostly with Joe, once with Simon after he'd fallen off a ladder and broken his elbow.

That had been a nightmare: Simon with one arm in plaster, not allowed to drive, unable to help get Joe out of bed in the morning or carry him downstairs. To start with, Simon hadn't even been able to get himself dressed; they'd laughed about it during the first couple of days, as Martha knelt by the side of the bed and pulled on his socks, squeezed a slug of toothpaste onto his toothbrush, knotted his tie before she dropped him at work. But the novelty had soon worn off. All she remembered now was the bad-tempered bickering, her exhaustion, his frustration and their combined relief when the plaster was finally sawn off.

An ambulance pulled away from the front of the building as she walked towards it. She glanced at her watch; she wanted to try Simon again but suspected he wouldn't pick up. *Please let him have got Joe into bed by now.* Her boy would be fractious without her there, disturbed at the change to his routine. She sent a text:

Just got to the hospital. Is J ok? X

As the glass doors swooshed open to let her through, she passed a pregnant woman smoking, her free hand grasped around the stem of an IV stand, a bag of liquid swinging from a hook, a tube running into the back of her hand. She was muttering to herself, staring at the ground, stepping gingerly from one foot to the other. Martha wanted to grab the cigarette from between her fingers and throw it to the floor, crushing it beneath her heel.

'My mother's here,' she said to the receptionist. 'Judith Cook. She had a fall.'

The woman nodded and tapped something into a keyboard. 'Bay 4, through those double doors and right to the end,' she said. She looked exhausted; worn down by the crises in other people's lives. She pressed a button on the desk in front of her and buzzed Martha through the doors. Ahead was a wide corridor, with a nursing station and bank of computers to one side, a row of curtained cubicles stretching away on the other. A man in blue scrubs was on the phone, a nurse was writing on a whiteboard on the wall and a paramedic was resting his elbows on the high desk. He turned and smiled as she walked past.

It was quiet; eerily so. Martha had been expecting chaos, frenzied noise; people lying on trolleys, stressed medics racing to save lives. But the click of her heels rang out as she went down the corridor, louder than the voices coming from behind drawn curtains and the bleep of machines. Her mouth was dry and there was a fluttering in her stomach. How would her mother look? Would she be bruised? Would she even be conscious? There were so many questions she'd been afraid to ask earlier.

Martha saw her mother immediately, as she passed a cubicle at the far end. She was lying on a trolley, her eyes closed and her head tilted slightly to one side. Most of her face was covered by a transparent oxygen mask, and a thin tube was running into her right hand, a plaster covering the point where the needle had been inserted, purple bruising flowering across the skin beneath it.

'Mum,' Martha leant down and whispered. 'Mum, it's me. Can you hear me?'

Her mother's eyes flickered, then opened. She gave a little cry and the mask moved as she smiled. 'Hello, darling,' she said, her voice croaky, not her own. 'What are you doing here? You shouldn't have come all this way.'

Martha leant down and kissed her cheek; the skin was papery but reassuringly warm. 'Don't be silly,' she said. 'How are you? What are the doctors saying?'

Her mother shook her head slowly from side to side and closed her eyes again, as if the effort of talking was too much.

'Don't worry, I'll find someone,' said Martha, running her hand across her mother's head to smooth the tousled hair. Thank goodness she couldn't see herself: she'd hate looking so dishevelled. Judith had never been the type to check her appearance as she passed a mirror, but she liked to look smart. Her long hair had been replaced with a short bob years ago, when she stopped dying it, but the cut was always stylish and neat. Now it looked as if it hadn't been brushed for days.

The man in blue scrubs appeared at the end of the cubicle, carrying a folder. 'Hi,' he said. 'Are you a relative of Judith?'

'Her daughter,' nodded Martha. She was expecting them to exchange pleasantries, giving her the chance to apologise for being so late and explain her long journey. But he didn't even look at her, flipping through the printed pages in front of him.

'I guess you've been told the basics?' he said. 'She's had a nasty fall and a scan has confirmed a fracture of the right hip. She's also got severe bruising on her right arm and a couple of broken ribs. The scan has shown there's no head injury or swelling on the brain, although she has been drowsy and there's a chance of concussion.'

Martha was watching his mouth as he spoke, listening to words that seemed too clipped and clinical. She was suddenly dog-tired. For hours she had been focusing on getting here, staring at the cars in front of her, concentrating on the road ahead and pushing away thoughts of Joe, worries about what she might find when she got to the hospital. Now it was as if someone had pulled out an imaginary plug and allowed every ounce of energy to flood from her body. She leant against the side of the trolley, slightly dizzy.

'We'll operate on the hip as soon as possible, but need to stabilise her first,' the doctor was saying. 'At the moment her lungs are a concern: there's a pulmonary contusion. We can't administer a general anaesthetic and a spinal isn't ideal for someone of her age.'

Martha nodded. This doctor was possibly only in his twenties, but his face was drawn and pale, and he still hadn't met her eye. The high-pitched shriek of an alarm exploded into the corridor, and he moved away, raising a hand in apology. Martha turned and saw her mother staring up at her, terror in her eyes.

'It's okay.' She forced a smile, aware of the raised voices at the other end of the corridor, but not able to make out what was being said. 'I'm here. We'll be fine.'

Her phone pinged: finally, a reply from Simon. A one-word text: *Yes.* There was no x at the end.

2

_____

It was 2am by the time Martha got back to Judith's bungalow. With no lights on inside, and the nearest street lamp throwing just a faint pool of brightness onto the pavement, she stood outside the front door, struggling to find the right key.

She jumped as something thumped against the other side of the door and there was a sudden, frantic barking. The dog! How could she have forgotten him? As she finally pushed open the door, he launched himself at her, his tail wagging furiously, his claws scrabbling at her tights in his eagerness to reach higher than her knees.

'Nipper, get down!'

The young doctor had told her Judith fell while she was at the local post office, mid-afternoon, so the dog must have been shut in here for hours. There was a wet patch on the hall carpet, and another in the middle of the kitchen floor. She opened the back door and chased him into the garden, before dropping to her knees and scrubbing at the carpet with handfuls of kitchen roll.

He trotted back in and sniffed at her fingers as she blotted up the worst of the stain. She'd never been keen on dogs, but he was a sweet little thing: a squat, wiry haired Jack Russell her mother had found in a rescue centre, three years ago.

'It's madness to have a dog, at your age,' Patrick had said. 'You can't walk it properly and it's a tie if you want to go away. What is the point?'

But Judith had insisted. 'He's going to be company for me,' she'd said.

Oh God, Patrick! Martha sat back on her heels, suddenly realising she hadn't let him know what had happened. It was too late to call now. Where had the last few hours gone? She had waited with Judith until a bed was found for her on a ward, just after midnight, and held her mother's hand as the trolley was wheeled back along the corridor to the stack of lifts at the far end of A&E. It had then taken another hour for the ward staff to log her details and set up the necessary drips and monitors. By that time Martha had been exhausted; all she'd been able to think about was getting back here and going to sleep. But she should have remembered to call Patrick; she would phone him first thing in the morning. Not that he'd drop everything and rush down to help out: she doubted her brother had been to see Judith for months, even though he lived less than an hour away.

Back in March, Martha had come here to take Judith out for lunch on Mother's Day. It had meant a lot of driving and it hadn't been easy persuading Simon to look after Joe for the day, but she hadn't minded making the effort. When she arrived, the hall table had been hidden beneath an extravagant arrangement of pink roses and speckled Stargazer lilies.

'Look what Patrick sent!' her mother had gushed. 'That lovely boy, he spoils me!'

Martha had smiled and made appreciative noises as she handed over her own, rather insignificant, bunch of garage roses. How much easier it was, she'd thought bitterly, to rattle off a credit card number over the phone, than to take a few hours out of your life to visit in person. She'd been sure that, deep down, Judith must be upset her son couldn't fit her into his busy schedule but, if so, her mother had become expert at hiding the hurt.

Martha wandered through the bungalow, opening doors, drawing curtains to hide darkened windows, even though it would soon be morning. The sitting room looked cold and unwelcoming under the harsh glare of the overhead bulb. There was no sofa, just a pair of upright, old-fashioned armchairs, which Martha had always disliked. They were from an era when people sat to attention – even while relaxing; back then, there was no lounging around on soft, squishy sofas, watching outsized flat-screen televisions. She lowered herself into one of the chairs now, kicking off her shoes. It felt strange to be sitting here without Judith in her usual place in the one beside it, their mugs balanced on the table between them as they stared at the small television in the corner of the room.

She realised she had never been in this bungalow without her mother. She and Patrick had grown up on the other side of the town, in a cavernous family home with high ceilings, draughty windows, creaky floorboards and an attic running the length of the house, which the children had been convinced was haunted. But when their father died, ten years ago, they'd discovered there wasn't as much money as they'd all expected: he and Judith appeared to have spent most of what he'd earnt on luxury holidays and endless maintenance. The money pit of a house had been sold to a developer, who promptly began to convert it into flats, and Judith had seemed relieved to move into this bungalow. So much had happened in those ten years, and her mother was happy and settled here, but Martha still felt like a stranger every time she walked through the door.

An excess of furniture in the little sitting room made it dark and oppressive, and there was so much clutter, you couldn't see the bare bones of the place. The wooden shelves, the side tables and the windowsills were all hidden beneath the ephemera of Judith's life: every surface laden with decorated plates and bowls, china figurines, tarnished photograph frames and pots holding forgotten safety pins, hair grips and elastic bands.

Martha's own house, where she longed to be right now, contained hardly any clutter. No trinkets, no ornaments, no decorative knick-knacks. She always joked that she couldn't be doing with the dusting.

As she reached out to switch off the light, her eyes were drawn to the photo on top of the bookcase. Simon had taken this picture of her and Joe a couple of years ago and she'd loved it so much that she'd had a print framed and given it to Judith on her birthday. Joe was sitting on her lap and Martha was holding him tightly round the waist, leaning forward slightly. They were both laughing, his eyes wide as she tickled him. She picked up the frame and studied it more closely under the light, smiling despite herself. Looking at this picture now, she could still hear her son's shrieks of near hysteria, could still remember him squirming to get away from her fingers as they tickled the soft skin on his tummy. She really loved this photo.

Further along the bookcase, there was another, smaller picture in a cheap wooden frame. Martha hadn't noticed it the last time she came to visit her mother; it must be new. It was of Judith, sitting out in the garden, with a little girl on her lap. The sun was shining in their eyes and they were both squinting slightly as they looked at whoever was taking the photograph. Judith was laughing and looked relaxed. It was one of the best photos Martha had seen of her. She had no idea who the girl was, possibly the granddaughter of one of her friends.

Nipper was sitting in the hall, staring up at her. Martha led him back into the kitchen and patted the fleecy blanket on the dog bed until he trotted over and curled up inside it, his eyes never leaving her face, although his head was resting on his paws.

'Sorry, Nipper,' she said, stroking him. 'I know this is all very weird.'

She didn't want to sleep in her mother's bed – that wouldn't have felt right – so found some linen in the wardrobe in the back bedroom and made up the single bed in there. Everything smelt stale, even though the sheets were clean and patterned with a grid of ironed folds.

She sat down on the bed and checked her phone again; there was no way Simon would contact her at this time of night, but she still longed for the glint of a waiting text. She could imagine his voice telling her to stop being paranoid, but worry was eating away at her. She just wanted reassurance that Joe had eaten some tea and had enough to drink, that he hadn't played up during bath time. She wanted to be able to fall asleep herself, knowing her son was safely curled up in his bed. She pictured him lying there: his arms around Fluff, the brown teddy they'd bought for him before he was born. When she washed it, she had to do it at night, prising the sticky fur out from his fingers, desperately hoping he wouldn't wake up until the washing machine cycle had finished.

As she started to peel off her clothes, the dog scurried into the bedroom and flung itself down at her feet.

'Not a chance,' she said, pushing him towards the door. 'Sorry, Nipper, but I need to get some sleep tonight.'

The last thing she was aware of, as she lay down on the bed and dragged the duvet across her shoulders, was the dog's persistent low whine on the other side of the door.

3

There was a heavy thump, then a clatter.

'Judith?' someone called.

Martha started, sitting up in bed so suddenly that her breath caught in her throat. For a second she didn't know where she was but, as sunlight streaked across the yellow walls of the small bedroom, it all came rushing back. The drive down the motorway, the glaring overhead lights in the A&E department, her mother's pale, panicked face.

'Judith, are you here?' called a woman's voice. 'Hello, Nipper!'

What the hell? Martha threw her legs over the edge of the bed and pushed herself up, pulling open the bedroom door in time to see someone walking away towards the kitchen. The girl turned and they stared at each other. Martha's brain was so fuggy with sleep that she struggled to remember her name. 'Alice!' she managed, finally, her voice croaky. 'Sorry, I didn't know you'd be coming today.'

The girl's mouth had dropped open, and Martha suddenly aware she must look a sight: standing in the bedroom doorway wearing one of her mother's faded Marks & Spencer floral nighties, her hair flattened to the side of her head, pillow marks streaking down one cheek.

'Oh, hello.' The girl looked confused. 'Where's Judith? She doesn't normally sleep this late.'

'No, she's not here,' said Martha, running her hand through her hair and moving forward. 'She's in hospital. She had a fall yesterday.'

'Oh no! How awful. Is she okay?'

Martha had forgotten how pretty this girl was. She was Judith's dog walker, and they'd met briefly on two or three occasions, but without having more than a passing conversation. 'She's got a broken hip and some cracked ribs,' said Martha. 'She's not great. I got called down here last night.'

The dog was yapping and jumping up and down, biting at the lead hanging from the girl's hand. 'Nipper, stop!' Alice bent over and grabbed his collar, clicking the lead in place. 'Poor Judith. I'm so sorry. How long will she be there?'

'I don't know. I'll find out more when I go in again today.' Martha was suddenly impatient to get going, aware she must have overslept. 'What's the time?'

'It's nine o'clock,' said the girl. 'I always come now, to take Nipper for a walk so he doesn't bark at Judith all morning. She then takes him out for a shorter walk in the afternoon.' The dog was straining on the lead, dragging her towards the front door.

Martha was horrified; how had she slept so late? She should have called Simon hours ago, to check he'd packed everything Joe needed for the day; the nursery opened an hour later on Thursdays, because of staff training – would Simon have remembered that? Probably not.

'Thanks for taking him out, Alice. Look, I need to put on some clothes and go. I didn't get back here until the middle of the night, otherwise I wouldn't have slept in like this.' Why did she feel the need to justify herself to this skinny girl? 'How long do you usually take Nipper out for? I'm not sure I've got any cash on me – I'm afraid I've no idea how much Mum pays you.'

She was embarrassed not to know the details of this arrangement. Judith might have told her, but she'd never paid much attention. Alice had been coming to walk Nipper for a couple of years now; the girl's mother cleaned for Judith and had introduced them. At the time, Judith had insisted it was just a temporary thing, until the weather improved; but the spring of that year had turned to summer, then to autumn, and Alice had been coming ever since. She had a daughter who was a similar age to Joe. Looking at her now, Martha wondered how old she was: possibly early twenties? She must have been very young when she got pregnant.

Alice was shaking her head. 'Don't worry. Judith pays me weekly, but we can sort it out another time. I can come more than once a day if that would help? What do you think?'

Martha didn't know what she thought. She was tired and stressed and the last thing she wanted to have to worry about was Nipper. She suddenly realised Alice had let herself in, so she had a key. It was probably sensible, in case Judith wasn't there, but it was unsettling that this stranger was so familiar with her mother and the home where Martha herself didn't feel comfortable.

But it would be useful to have one less thing to worry about. 'Maybe that's a good idea,' she said. 'Could you manage to come in the afternoons as well? I'm not sure how long I'm going to be here, or when Mum will come home, but let's see how things go.'

Alice was nodding and had dug her phone out of her pocket. 'Of course. Let me take your mobile number, so we can keep in touch.'

Martha rattled it off, hugging her arms around her chest as Alice tapped it in.

'Right, that's done,' said the girl, looking up. 'I'll text you with mine. Can I go and visit Judith? Which hospital is she in?'

Martha was cross with herself for not being the one to suggest they exchange numbers, and even more irritated that this girl wanted to go and see her mother. 'I'm not sure she can have visitors,' she said. 'I'll let you know. Anyway, she's in Guildford, which is miles away.'

'I could get the bus,' said Alice. 'Please tell her I'd like to come and see her. We were planning on going out later in the week. She'll be upset to miss that.'

Martha frowned. 'Going out? Do you mean you were helping her with shopping?' She couldn't imagine why her mother would have needed help: Judith had certainly slowed down, now she was in her seventies, but she prided herself on being independent and still drove everywhere – her white Fiat was parked outside – and she'd never mentioned needing any help. Paying for someone to walk Nipper had struck Martha as being an indulgence rather than a necessity.

'Oh no, nothing like that,' Alice was saying. 'We were going out to lunch, or maybe even to the cinema. We hadn't decided yet. We often do something together on Fridays. It's my day off and Gracie's in nursery – that's my daughter – so it suits both of us.'

Martha felt a stab of something – she wasn't entirely sure what. 'Right, well I need to get dressed,' she said. 'Thanks for dealing with Nipper, Alice. I'm not sure what time I'll be back here later, but let's keep in touch.'

She smiled: a stiff smile that didn't feel natural, but which probably wouldn't seem strange to this girl who hardly knew her. She opened the front door and stepped back as Nipper pulled Alice through it, almost choking himself as the collar bit into his neck. 'Nipper, slow down, you crazy animal!' The girl laughed.

After closing the door, Martha went into the sitting room and peered through the gap in the curtains; Alice was walking down the path, talking to the dog as he jumped up at her knees, barking with excitement. Martha stood at the window, watching them, until they disappeared around the corner at the end of the road.

4

'But are you sure he had enough to eat this morning?'

'Yes, Martha, he bloody well ate loads. I'm his dad, for God's sake – I know you think I'm useless, but you can trust me to feed my own child. Look, I need to go, I've only just got into work and I'm *trying* to get on with it. I haven't got time for all this.'

The line went dead. Simon was right: she *was* being overprotective. But if he hadn't always made such a big deal out of doing his share of the childcare, she wouldn't be so worried about leaving him to look after Joe. He should be capable; he *was* capable, but there was always something else he was on the point of doing; he would sigh deeply, close the newspaper, put down his phone and do whatever it was she'd asked. But, as he fed Joe his tea, he'd have one eye on a live Premiership match on the television in the corner. Or, as he strapped his son into a chair, he'd have his mobile propped under his chin, arranging to meet a friend later, for a beer. He seemed permanently distracted and she always felt guilty for having asked him to help.

She pushed her phone back into her pocket and buzzed to

be let back onto the ward. There were more questions she wanted to ask: did Joe sleep okay? Did he have Weetabix or Cheerios for breakfast? It might smooth things over if she called back and apologised for nagging but, judging by the way Simon had reacted just now, he wouldn't answer. She had to be here with Judith: it was her duty as her daughter. But at the same time, it was so hard being away from home. It produced an underlying sense of panic in her, as if all the plates she usually kept spinning in the air were toppling to the ground, and the carefully orchestrated routines she followed to make sure their lives stayed on track, were cracking apart, so that at any moment one of them – most likely Joe – might end up falling through the gaps.

She forced a smile as she sat down beside Judith's bed.

'Everything all right?' her mother asked.

Martha nodded and reached out to put her hand on top of the pale fingers, trying not to touch the bruised skin where the intravenous drip was still attached. 'Everything's fine,' she said. 'Simon got Joe sorted this morning, and now he's at work.' *Pissed off and feeling nagged by his horrible wife*, she was tempted to add.

'I'm so glad Alice is looking after Nipper,' Judith said. 'I can't bear to think of him all on his own.'

'Well, he's not going to be on his own, I'll be back there later,' said Martha, fighting down a prick of irritation. Why did Judith seem more concerned about her dog than her grandson? 'I'll make sure he's fine.'

'Yes, but he doesn't know you!' Judith was shaking her head. 'He knows Alice and she's so good with him. You should see how excited he gets when she arrives to take him out for his walk.'

I have seen, Martha itched to say. *I was there this morning, holding the fort.*

'She's a real tonic, that girl,' said Judith, wheezing with the effort of speaking. 'I'm as happy as Nipper when she gets there!

Do you know, she walks dogs for other people as well, not just me, and she does some gardening in the summer – she sorted out all my pots for me last year. She does some shifts in the canteen at the leisure centre, then on Saturdays she works in a care home on the other side of the station. Do you know the one I mean? I can't remember what it's called but it's got a long drive with flower beds running all the way up. I really have no idea how she does it all, with Gracie to look after. She's a sweet little thing, such a pretty child. She calls me Nipper's Granny – isn't that lovely?'

A nurse came up to the bed and pushed a button on the monitor. 'How are we doing, Judith?' she asked. 'Is that breathing getting any easier?' The machine started bleeping and the nurse leant across and adjusted the tube running down Judith's arm and into the back of her hand.

'Alice left school at sixteen,' Judith was saying. 'She got pregnant so couldn't stay on to do A-levels. But it's such a waste because she's got a real spark about her. She wants to go into nursing, working with children with learning disabilities, so she's going back to college to get herself some qualifications. Isn't that impressive? I helped her look up how to go about it – she has to do a diploma to apply to university.'

Martha smiled and nodded. Right now, the last thing she wanted to hear was how wonderful Alice was. The promised ward round still hadn't materialised and she'd been sitting here for nearly two hours. Life in hospital seemed to move at its own pace: there was clearly a lot happening behind the scenes, but if you had to wait this long to get questions answered in any other work environment, someone would be yelling blue murder. She'd phoned the office earlier and left a message for Clive, explaining what had happened and that she'd need to stay in Surrey for a couple of days; she knew he'd be sympathetic when he called back, but there were apologies she had to make to other people as well, meetings and deadlines which needed to be rescheduled. Frustratingly, she couldn't get on with any of that because there was absolutely no doubt that if she left Judith's bedside the consultant would pick those minutes to visit.

What she could really do with, was some support from her brother. When she'd phoned earlier, to tell Patrick about their mother's fall, he'd sounded preoccupied.

'So, what's the prognosis?' he asked. 'When can they do the op?'

'I don't know yet,' Martha said. 'I can't get any answers from anyone. I don't think she's well enough to have an anaesthetic – there's a problem with her lungs. But they haven't said how long it will take to sort that out.'

'Jesus, this is all I need,' Patrick had said. 'I'm closing on a big deal today, so it's going to be hard for me to get down there, if that's what you're saying.'

It wasn't what she'd said, but it was what she'd been working up to.

'Then I'm flying to Paris for a meeting tomorrow, so you'll have to handle it, Martha. This really couldn't have come at a worse time, bloody inconvenient. Got to go, there's someone on the other line. Keep me posted.'

Afterwards, Martha realised he hadn't even asked how his mother was doing, or sent his love. 'You're a prize shit, Patrick,' she'd muttered, into the dark screen of the phone.

It was late morning before the consultant finally swept into the ward, white coat-tails flapping behind him, along with a posse of young, nervous junior doctors.

'Mrs Cook!' the man beamed, grabbing the chart from the end of her bed. 'What have you been up to then? Late-night dancing with a handsome stranger?'

Judith's laugh was muffled by the oxygen mask.

'Now, we need to give you a shiny new NHS hip joint,' the consultant was barking. 'But we can't do that until you're feeling a bit more chipper. Those cracked ribs are causing you a few problems, making it hard to breathe, aren't they?'

Martha watched as her mother nodded; she was giggling like an infatuated schoolgirl and staring up with wide-eyed awe, as if George Clooney had arrived at her bedside.

'So, the plan is to monitor you,' he boomed. 'See if we can get you stronger and ready for surgery. That means you'll be with us for a while I'm afraid. But these pretty young things on the ward will do a marvellous job of taking care of you.'

The nurse standing beside the group of young doctors raised her eyes to the ceiling.

'Do you have any idea how long that will take?' Martha asked.

The consultant turned and stared at her, his brow wrinkled, as if she'd just asked whether her mother might be fit enough to fly to the moon on Friday.

'It's just that it would be quite helpful to know...' she stuttered, '...how long she'll be in hospital, I mean. I have to make plans.'

The man was now looking disdainful. 'It's not an exact science,' he said. 'I'm afraid the NHS can't work to order. We will take it hour by hour, day by day, and you and your social life will just have to bear with us.'

Martha's mouth fell open but, in a clatter of clipboards and swoosh of white coats, the team was gone, moving on to see the patient behind the curtain in the next bed. Before the nurse turned to follow them, she winked at Martha. 'Don't mind him,' she whispered. 'He's very, *very* important!'

'Mrs Beech!' Martha heard the consultant bellow, in the next cubicle. 'What have you been up to then? Late-night dancing with a handsome stranger?'

Martha slumped back in her chair. Well, that had been pointless. After all the hanging around, she still didn't know any more about what was likely to happen, except that it was going to take time. Which was the last thing she had to spare. Her social life indeed – the bloody cheek.

A nurse appeared and gently lifted the oxygen mask away from Judith's face. 'Let's have a break from this for a while, shall we?' she said. 'Give you a chance to have some lunch.' She moved around the bed, tucking the sheet beneath the mattress with swift, practised movements. 'We inserted a catheter last night when you arrived at A&E,' she explained. 'That's going to stay in for the time being I'm afraid.'

'But I need to wash my hair,' Judith said. 'I'm sure it looks dreadful. Doesn't it, Martha? I really want to go to the bathroom and freshen up.'

'Mum, you look fine. You can't move until you have the operation on your hip. You just have to stay in bed.'

'We'll do everything for you,' said the nurse. 'We'll give you a wash in bed. That's not a problem.'

Judith looked horrified, and Martha felt so sorry for her. The indignity of it all was hard to bear. Less than twenty-four hours ago, her mother had been self-sufficient, living in her own home and more than capable of taking care of herself. Now she was confined to a hospital bed: her bones were broken, her breathing was restricted, her urine was being drained out into a transparent bag and someone was promising to come at her with a flannel and a bowl of warm, soapy water.

'I know it's awful,' she said, taking her mother's hand. 'But it won't be for long.'

That was probably a lie. People had told Martha similar lies, five years ago before Joe was born. *It'll be a breeze! You'll be fine. Childbirth is the most wonderful thing. You'll bounce back in no time.*

She had believed it when the first twinges of labour deep in her belly made her gasp, her heart racing with excitement. She believed it when the pains became stronger and more frequent and Simon helped her into the car and threw her suitcase onto the back seat. She still almost believed it when an entire day had gone by on the maternity ward and she'd lost all sense of how long she'd been moaning and writhing in pain. By the time the midwife called in a consultant, Martha didn't care anymore whether or not those things were true. The news that she needed an emergency caesarean to save the baby had been so shocking that much of what happened in the next few hours was a blur.

She never forgot all those lies she'd been told: that she'd be fine, she'd get back to full fitness, she'd be able to do everything for herself again soon, her baby would thrive. Like Judith, she'd loathed being dependent on other people. She hated not being allowed to drive or lift up her own baby. It made her furious that she couldn't walk without wincing, or look at her newborn son without bursting into tears. Shortly after Simon brought her and Joe back home, Claudia had arrived clutching flowers and Prosecco and radiating confidence and happiness. Just two weeks after having Barney, Claudia was already back in her jeans, and her perfect baby was sleeping, feeding and flying through all the health visitor's tests.

Martha had sat and watched as her best friend collapsed onto the sofa, tucking her tiny son under her T-shirt to feed, all the while chatting and laughing, passing on gossip about a mutual friend, looking across at Joe and telling Martha how gorgeous he was.

Everything had gone right for Claudia, as usual. But for Martha it had all gone wrong. Nearly five years later, she was still so angry. She had never told anyone – even Simon – how scared she'd been or how useless she'd felt. She had never been able to admit that, although she loved the tiny scrap of a baby whose traumatic birth had led to all this, at times she almost hated him too.

Judith coughed and winced with pain, putting her arm across her ribs. A smell was drifting onto the ward, a fusion of overcooked meat and stewed vegetables. There was a clattering from the corridor, and an orderly wearing a plastic apron appeared beside the bed, beaming and holding a tray in front of him, as if it contained a precious gift. He put it down and lifted up a plastic dome to reveal a plate of brown food.

'Chicken tikka!' he grinned. 'Then there's pears and custard for pudding.'

The smell was so reminiscent of school dinners, it turned Martha's stomach. 'Mum, I need to pop out and call the office,' she said, picking up her bag. 'Can I get you anything from the shop while I'm down there?'

'Oh, Martha, you work too hard!' her mother was tutting. 'It's not good for you. When you were young, I stayed at home to look after you and Patrick.'

'Well, that's not how we do things nowadays,' said Martha. 'I need to work – you know how expensive things are with Joe. Anyway, I love my job.'

'Your father wouldn't have it any other way,' muttered her mother. 'He was insistent that I stay at home with you. I'm sure Simon would feel the same if you let him.'

'Simon is very supportive of what I do. He knows how important my career is to me.'

Judith was shaking her head, reaching forward to pick up the knife and fork on the tray. Martha's pulse was racing, hands clenched by her sides. Why did being with her mother always do this to her? She was forty-two years old, yet one remark or judgemental glance from Judith made Martha feel like a teenager again. It made her want to behave like one too; she pictured herself storming out of the ward, kicking the doors on her way past, putting her hands over her ears and shrieking, so she didn't have to listen to what her mother was saying.

'How's Patrick?' asked Judith suddenly. 'Have you spoken to him?'

'Yes, first thing this morning. He says he's sorry to hear what happened and sends you lots of love,' lied Martha. 'He'll try to get down to see you at some stage.'

'Oh, he mustn't bother,' said her mother. 'That poor boy. I don't want to be a burden to him. He's so busy and works so hard. I don't know how he does it.'

5

Martha only meant to be away for twenty minutes or so, but it was such a relief to be outside that she slung her bag over her shoulder and walked – not caring where she ended up. The fug of the hospital ward had done nothing to help the headache she'd been battling all morning, and it was good to be able to take in deep breaths of fresh air. She tried to call Simon but his phone went straight to voicemail. 'Hope you're okay?' she said into the silence of the recording. 'I'll try again later. Don't forget, Joe needs to be picked up from nursery by six, and there are clean pyjamas in the airing cupboard, the ones with Tigger on.'

She ended the call and could imagine the expression on Simon's face as he listened to it later; the way he'd sigh and tut, shaking his head in irritation.

'God, Martha, the world won't end if Joe wears the wrong colour socks,' he'd said to her the other day. Of course, she knew that, and Simon made no secret of the fact that he thought she was fussing about silly, unimportant details. But she wanted to be sure she was doing her best; it felt as if she'd done so much wrong already throughout her boy's short life, she needed to believe she was doing something right. Anyway, whatever Simon said, children needed routine in their lives, Joe more than most, so she had every right to make sure his dad was sticking to the tried and tested formulas. Not that he saw it like that.

She walked out of the hospital grounds and turned right, passing an industrial estate, then a couple of residential streets and a small park. At the far end was a row of shops and she queued in a café to get a coffee. There were no free tables, so she carried the styrofoam cup outside and walked back to the park, sitting on a bench just inside the gates. Shadows scurried along the grass in front of her, as high clouds scooted through the sky.

Now that she was away from the ward, she was calmer. Thinking about it, there was no reason why she shouldn't go back home tomorrow – the doctors could do nothing at the moment, except look after Judith while she regained her strength. So there wasn't a great deal Martha could do either, except sit beside the hospital bed and make small talk with her mother. Which pretty soon was going to start driving her mad.

She texted Claudia:

Mum is stable, so I'm hoping to be home soon, thank God! Miss my boys xx

Obviously, it was important for Judith to have some company while she was stuck in hospital, but it sounded as if it would be days or even weeks before the hip replacement could go ahead. Martha flushed with embarrassment as she remembered the consultant's arrogant retort to what she'd thought was a sensible question. Obviously, she wasn't worried about missing out on her social life, but since nothing was going to happen immediately, surely it made sense for her to go home, sort out any immediate work issues, have a proper discussion with Simon and plan how she was going to manage this? She would stay one more night, then drive back in time for the weekend. She sipped at her coffee, pleased with her own logic.

Martha had always been a planner. She loved making lists and scheduling tasks: she was the sort of person who needed to know exactly what was coming up and how it would fit in with every other aspect of her life. At school, she'd been one of the few who always got their homework in on time – not because she was a swot, or excessively academic, but because she couldn't bear to miss a deadline. As an adult she'd enjoyed planning holidays, then booking them months in advance to get a good deal, and she had never forgotten to pay a bill on time. At work, she glowed when she saw the words 'organised' and 'efficient' written in her annual review.

'You're such a control freak,' Simon had said to her, soon after they met. They were on their second or third date, sitting in a pub near his flat in Archway. 'I've never met anyone who's so organised. Are you going to take over my life as well? You might not find it quite as easy to control me.'

He had laughed as he said it, leaning across the table to grab her hand and pull her towards him for a kiss. She remembered feeling slightly hurt, then instantly mollified by the amusement in his voice, loving how the tanned skin at the side of his eyes crinkled as he smiled at her.

'You make it sound like a bad thing,' she had said. 'But it's good to be in control of your life, to know where you want to be.'

While she drank her coffee, she watched a woman pushing two little girls on the nearby swings, their hair flying behind them as they shrieked with delight at being pushed higher. Martha suddenly realised who the little girl was in that new photo on her mother's bookcase; it must be Gracie, Alice's daughter. How strange Judith had put it on display. Maybe she'd been given it by Alice and put it on show to avoid offending her.

As she finished the coffee, her phone began to ring: Clive.

'How are you doing?' he asked. Martha could picture him sitting in the chair in his windowless office, the wheels squeaking in protest as he leant back and stared up at the ceiling. She loved working for Clive; he was a good boss and a warm, generous human being, albeit one of the most reserved men she'd ever known. In all the years she'd worked in the accounts department alongside him, he'd never divulged more than a few scant details about his private life. He had a wife called Maureen, they spent their summer holidays in the Lake District, their grown-up daughter lived in the States, and he played cricket for a local village team. That was all she knew. Every now and then someone would ask what he'd done at the weekend, but he ducked and weaved and parried them off.

'Oh, just this and that,' he'd say.

'I'm fine, thanks, Clive,' she said now. 'Mum seems to be okay, but they can't operate until she's stronger. I don't know how long that will take, but I'm going to head home tomorrow, then come back here next week. Would that be okay? I'll come in as usual on Monday and we can look at what would work.'

'Not a problem,' he said. 'Janey can probably cover some of your projects if you give her some notice? But don't worry too much, we'll sort it all out.'

She threw the cup into a bin and walked back to the hospital, joining the stream of visitors making their way towards the entrance. As she stood waiting for the lift to go up to the ward, her phone pinged with a reply from Claudia:

Good! Don't forget you're coming to supper here on Saturday night – you'll need cheering up xx

Martha smiled to herself; she really did need that.

'Ah, there you are,' said Patrick, when she walked into the cubicle. He was lounging on a chair, tipping it onto its back legs, his feet crossed and resting up on the edge of Judith's bed. 'Thought you'd done a runner.'

Judith was sitting up in the bed, beaming through the oxygen mask. 'Look who's here!' she said. 'Isn't this a lovely surprise, Martha?'

'Yes, lovely. What are you doing here?'

When had she last seen him? It must have been Christmas: the annual, awkward gathering of two families with nothing in common, where Simon and Patrick drank enough beer to help them feel pleasantly disposed towards the world, and Martha and her sister-in-law, Helen, drank enough wine to help them feel pleasantly disposed towards each other.

'Well, that's a nice greeting,' he said. He'd had a haircut and looked smart in his suit, handsome. 'I'm here to visit my mother. Where did you get to? I've been here for nearly an hour. Poor Mum was looking all lost and lonely when I arrived.'

Judith giggled and put out her hand, resting it on Patrick's arm. 'You silly thing,' she said. 'I was fine!'

'I had to make some calls,' said Martha, immediately on the defensive. 'I rushed straight down here last night and didn't get the chance to sort things out at work.'

'Well, thank God for you, little sister,' said Patrick, swinging his legs off the bed and sitting forward. 'Aren't we lucky that you were able to ride in to the rescue.'

Judith was laughing, patting him on the arm.

'Anyway, I've got to go now, Mum,' he said. 'We're closing this major deal today and I really shouldn't have left the office – all hell's bound to have been let loose since I walked away. Can't trust the little people to see things through in my absence.'

'Oh, darling. Thank you so much for coming to see me,' said Judith, wheezing through the mask. 'I do appreciate it. I know how valuable your time is.'

'Martha will keep me posted,' said Patrick, leaning over to

give Judith a kiss. 'Take it easy and get lots of rest. Speak to you soon, Martha.'

As he headed towards the end of the bed, she followed. 'Wait a minute!' she hissed. 'I need to talk to you.'

They stood facing each other in the corridor, Patrick already digging his phone out of his pocket and scrolling through messages. 'What is it?' he said, his eyes on the screen in his hand. 'I only put an hour's change in the meter.'

'Why didn't you tell me you were coming down?'

'Only decided to do it at the last minute. Thought I'd pop in and surprise Mum. Why, what's the problem with that? I don't need to run my movements past you.'

'No, but you gave me the impression you couldn't make it.'

He looked up, frowning. 'So here I am, and it's a bloody bonus,' he said. 'What's your problem, Martha? Say what you want to say, I've got to go.'

She didn't know what she wanted to say. As usual, in the face of Patrick's indifference, she felt angry and resentful, but mostly just hurt. 'Don't you want to know what the doctors have said?' she asked. 'What's going to be happening with her?'

'I talked to the guy on duty when I came in,' he said. 'Basically, it sounds like fuck-all is going to happen in the short term, until she's stronger. So, if you'd told me that, I could have saved myself the hellish race down here and waited until the weekend.'

'But we need to talk about how we manage this!' she said, aware of the colour rising in her cheeks. 'I can't stay here for long, and I don't see why it should all fall to me anyway. I've got a job to do too – I can't just drop everything!'

'With all due respect, Martha,' he said, sliding his phone into his pocket. 'It's a lot easier for you to be here than it is for me. I've got a bloody department to run. People depend on me. If I'm not back in the office by four, this deal may not close. We're talking big money.'

'And I've got Joe to think about,' she said. 'Simon's doing everything at home, which isn't ideal. Joe probably doesn't understand where I've gone, and that's going to upset him. I ought to go home tomorrow, so why can't you come back then? This isn't fair.'

'Life isn't fair, Martha,' he said. 'Get over it. Anyway, this sort of stuff is much more up your street than mine. I can't brush my mother's hair or wipe her bottom. She'd hate it. She needs you to do that kind of stuff.'

Martha's mouth dropped open. 'God, Patrick. Even for you, that's vile.'

He shook his head at her. 'You're just trying to palm off some of your guilt onto me,' he said. 'But you're her daughter, you're the one who ought to be dealing with it. I'm happy to be involved, but I don't have time for the detail – don't bother phoning me in a panic to tell me her temperature has gone up, or her feet are swollen. I just want the bigger picture. When we know when they can operate, that's when we can start planning how to move this situation forward. Right, got to go.' He leant forward and pecked her on the cheek, his lips dry and cold against her flushed skin.

As she watched him turn and walk away through the double doors at the end of the corridor, she realised her head had started to thump again.

6

_____

Alice was walking up the path, slightly ahead of an older woman with dyed black hair and heavily made-up eyes. Martha smiled to cover up her irritation and stepped out through the front door, making it obvious she was on the point of leaving.

'Hi!' said Alice. 'I hoped I'd catch you.'

Martha had hoped she wouldn't, which is why she'd set an alarm this morning, and was going to the hospital earlier than yesterday.

'You remember my mother, don't you? Mum, this is Martha, Judith's daughter.'

Martha put out her hand, immediately regretting the formality.

'Don't think we've met,' said the woman. 'I'm Sharon. I've heard all about you, of course.'

'Likewise,' said Martha, although she couldn't remember Judith saying much about her. She resisted the temptation to add: *And having spent a couple of nights in this bungalow, I know you're a crap cleaner.*

Alice was unlike her mother in every way. She was tall and

slim to the point of skinny; her blonde hair was scraped back in a ponytail and she wore no make-up. Sharon was shorter and heavyset. You would never have picked them out in a crowd as being related.

'How's Judith?' asked Alice. 'I thought I might get the bus to the hospital to see her this afternoon.'

Martha tried to think of a reason why that wasn't a good idea, but couldn't come up with anything. Much as she hated to admit it, her mother would be happy to see this girl – probably happier than she'd be to see Martha. 'That would be kind,' she said. 'I'm planning to head home today. Mum's stable and they're not going to be able to operate for a while.'

'So, what's the plan with Nipper?' asked Alice. 'Shall I come in to feed him in the evenings as well, if you're not going to be here.' The dog had flown across the front step when he heard Alice's voice and was now on his hind legs, scrabbling up against her. 'Wait a minute, you,' she laughed. 'We'll go for a walk in a bit.'

Yet again, Martha felt wrong-footed: she'd forgotten the bloody dog. She'd had so much on her mind that it hadn't even occurred to her to ask whether Alice could fit in an extra visit each day. 'Actually,' she said. 'I thought I'd take him home with me.'

The two women stared at her.

'I'm going to the hospital now, then I was going to pop back here and pick him up.' As the words came out of her mouth, Martha couldn't believe she was saying them. 'I can't leave him here on his own, and it wouldn't be fair to ask you to do more. You've already been such a great help.'

'But, will he be all right with you?' asked Alice. 'I know you've got Joe and everything…'

'He'll be fine!' Martha cut in. 'It's not ideal, of course, but I can't see anything else I can do.'

What the hell was she saying? This was crazy. She was out at work for three days a week, and Joe was allergic to animal fur. Not only that, but Simon would probably file for divorce if she turned up with a yapping Jack Russell who would wee on the carpet, eat his shoelaces and scratch holes in the knees of his jeans.

'He doesn't know you,' said Sharon. 'He's quite sensitive; he won't take well to being somewhere new. Especially without Judith.'

Martha smiled tightly. 'Well, I'm sure he'll get used to me. I can't leave him here alone until the next time I'm back.'

'How about I take him?' said Alice. The dog was now running in circles on the front lawn, chasing his own stump of a tail. 'You wouldn't mind, would you, Mum? We could have him at ours for a while – he knows us all pretty well. It would be easier for me, to be honest, Martha. Because then I wouldn't have to come over here to fetch him and take him out.'

It was the perfect solution, and Martha's shoulders were already dropping with relief; she'd been struggling to picture the expression on Simon's face when she walked through the door with Nipper. But although this was ideal, it seemed wrong somehow – as if she wasn't being a dutiful daughter. This was her mother's dog, therefore with Judith out of action, he was Martha's responsibility.

'But have you got room?' She didn't care about the size of their house, but felt she ought to sound concerned. Maybe this wasn't such a good idea: not only would she feel indebted to Alice if she took the dog, it would also be yet another thing her mother could use to praise this young slip of a girl who was being so selfless and bloody marvellous.

'Don't worry about that,' said Alice. 'We haven't got a proper garden, just a yard at the back, but I can take him out more often. And Gracie would love it, I know she would.'

Sharon was nodding. 'That's true. She's mad about Nipper.'

'Okay, well thank you, Alice. That would be really helpful,' said Martha. 'I know Mum will be glad to hear you're looking after him.'

'That's settled then,' said Alice. 'When he's had his walk, we'll come back and pick up his bed and he can move in with us for a bit. You'd like that, Nipper, wouldn't you? Gracie will be so excited, she won't know what to do with herself!'

'It's definitely the best thing.' Sharon was nodding. 'Alice is so good with animals. I always told her she should become a vet, didn't I, love? She's good with people too, that's why Judith loved her so much.'

Alice was looking embarrassed. 'Mum! Don't be silly.'

'It's true!' said Sharon, turning back to Martha. 'I mean, I know Alice does a lot for your mother, in all kinds of ways. But it isn't just a working relationship. Judith has always been so fond of my girl. She loves her like a daughter, and she's told me as much in the past. I'm not ashamed to say, there are times when I feel a bit left out.' She threw her head back and laughed so loudly it made Martha jump.

'Mum, stop!' said Alice, her cheeks pink.

'Right, well I'll be back after the weekend,' Martha said. 'I'm not sure exactly when, but I'll sort something out.' She hoped the uncertainty in her voice wasn't too obvious. She had no idea how she was going to organise all this, or how quickly she'd be back. But right now, she just wanted to get away from these two women. Everything would feel more manageable once she was home again tonight, and could kick off her shoes, pour herself a glass of wine, then collapse onto the sofa with Joe and give him a proper cuddle.

As she drove away from the bungalow, she glanced in the rear-view mirror and saw Sharon and Alice walking in the other direction, Nipper bouncing between them, his tail wagging so much it looked as if his entire rear end was dancing backwards and forwards on the pavement.

When she got to the hospital, it took twenty minutes to find a parking space, then all the lifts in the main foyer were broken. Martha started to climb the stairs, stopping to get her breath back at each landing, appalled at her own lack of fitness. Once this was over, she would start eating sensibly and exercising. As she reached the third floor, her phone began to ring and her heart jolted into her throat as she saw Simon's name on the screen.

'Is everything all right?' she gasped. 'How's Joe?'

'He's fine, everything's fine.' Simon sounded pissed off. She decided to ignore it; asking him why would only cause a row.

'Listen, I'm heading home later,' she said, walking out of the stairwell and up to the doors of the ward. 'I've just got to the hospital, so I'll spend a few hours here, then drive back. I can't wait to see you both. You might have to pick up Joe again this afternoon, if that's okay? Just in case I get delayed.'

'Did you ring about that appointment?' he asked.

'What appointment?'

'The school!'

Shit. She hadn't. This was so unlike her: first she'd forgotten about Nipper, now this. She couldn't believe she was being so inefficient. The letter was crumpled at the bottom of her handbag and she'd been meaning to call yesterday.

'No, sorry. I'll do it now,' she said.

'For God's sake, Martha! This meeting is important. How could you forget? They'll give the place to someone else.'

'No, they won't. I'll call straight away and explain about Mum and tell them why we can't make it.'

Simon was huffing on the other end of the phone. 'I can't believe you forgot to do it,' he said. 'It's just one phone call. You're sitting around all day beside a hospital bed; surely you can find the time to do something that matters this much. I really don't understand you.'

'I'm not just sitting around,' she said. 'That's unfair–'

'We've waited so long to get to this stage,' he said. 'We can't afford to mess things up now. It's going to look really bad that you're only calling a few hours before we're due to go down there.'

'Listen, I'm going to get onto it right now!' said Martha. 'I'm sure it will be fine. I'll tell them I'm stuck at the hospital and ask to rearrange for next week. I meant to do it yesterday, but everything has been so strange.' She knew how lame that sounded. Simon would never understand how disconnected she'd felt for the last two days: how disconcerting it had been, to be dragged away from her usual existence to this strange limbo where the most familiar things were the beeping of machines, the soft padding of footsteps in the hospital corridor and the harsh wheezing as her mother gasped for air.

'It sounds to me,' he said, his voice cold, 'as if your priorities are all wrong, Martha. You told me Judith is stable, so surely your son's future should now be the main thing on your mind?'

Martha's chest felt tight, her body reeling from the injustice of his words. As she was buzzed onto the ward, she delved into her bag and pulled out the letter, emblazoned with the school's deep blue insignia across the top, the time of their appointment this afternoon in bold, halfway down. Simon was being a shit, and what he was saying was totally unfair; but on the other hand, she really shouldn't have forgotten to rearrange this.

7

From the moment she pushed open the front door, she could feel the tension draining from her body. It was such a relief to be back. The hallway was bright, evening sunlight streaming down the stairs from the tall window on the landing, and her heels rang out against the stripped wooden floors as she walked in and dumped her bag.

'I'm home!' she called.

There was a reassuring smell – a combination of furniture polish and pine disinfectant – and every surface looked shiny. It was Friday, so the cleaner would have been in earlier; not for the first time, Martha revelled in the fact that someone else had worked hard to make her home look and smell this good. It was an indulgence Simon insisted they couldn't justify but, whenever he moaned about the cost, she came up with reasons why it was essential.

'It saves us so much time,' she would say. 'Otherwise, we'd spend all weekend cleaning this place ourselves. Having someone else to do it means we can be with Joe, it frees us up to do things as a family.'

Although they rarely did anything as a family.

There was a pile of mail addressed to her on the hall table and she riffled quickly through the envelopes to check there was nothing important: her mobile bill, a bank statement, a postcard from her cousin, Lucy, who seemed to spend her life on holiday and was the only person Martha knew who still bought a stamp and stuck it onto a postcard. Most of her friends now used social media to spread the news of their exotic holidays: posting pictures of golden beaches or romantic candlelit dinners, choosing only the most flattering photos to show what an amazing time they were having. Martha had a Facebook page but hadn't posted anything on it for years. She could see the appeal though: it was the ideal way to gloss over the family arguments, delayed flights and unexpected thunderstorms, and instead big up the façade of perfect lives, loving relationships and beautiful kids.

'Simon? I'm back!' she called again, putting her head around the sitting room door. The room looked like it hadn't been touched since she left, which it probably hadn't. Simon didn't tend to sit in front of the outsized television in the evenings, even if there was a decent film on, or a programme she'd suggested they watch together. Instead, he sat up in the office, hunched over his laptop, ostensibly working but more often, she knew, trawling the internet or playing computer games. She had no idea what. He used to be addicted to *Grand Theft Auto*, but when she'd asked him about that a few months ago, he'd shaken his head and laughed, making her feel stupid for mentioning it.

'No one plays that any more,' he'd said.

There was a clatter from the kitchen, and she walked down the hallway into the big open-plan space. Joe was strapped into his chair and Simon was sitting at the table, a newspaper open in front of him. He was holding a bowl of food, but it didn't look as if much of it had been eaten. As Martha came in, he was tapping the spoon on the side of Joe's chair to get his attention.

'Come on, mate. Have some more of this.'

'Hi!' she said, her voice sounding overly loud in the echoing space. 'How are you both? Oh, I've missed my boys.'

She bent down beside Simon, kissing him on the cheek, then moved across to Joe, wrapping her arms around him, hugging him tightly to her.

'Hello, my lovely one,' she whispered. 'I'm sorry I had to go away.'

She could smell the lemon scent of shampoo in his hair, and his skin was soft against hers. He was fidgeting beneath her grasp and she pulled away slightly, lifting one hand to stroke his cheek, smiling at him as he strained past her to see the spoon Simon was waving in the air.

'Not as keen to see me as you are to eat your tea!' She laughed, standing back and watching as he opened his mouth for the spoon. The lack of a welcome always hurt, even though she should be used to it by now.

'You're late,' said Simon.

'Yes, sorry. The motorway was awful – two lanes closed on the M4 because of an accident. But I'm here now – and it's so good to be back!'

The kitchen was impressively tidy. Simon wasn't the sort of man who shut cupboard doors or wiped down surfaces, but he and Joe probably hadn't been home long enough to disturb the cleaner's perfection. It was unlikely Sharon had ever left Judith's bungalow looking and smelling this good.

The television was on in the corner of the room, garish cartoon characters streaking across the screen. Simon must have switched it on to keep Joe entertained while he was finding him some food, but no one was watching now, so Martha walked across and turned it off. She ran her hand along the granite worktop, watching the gold and copper speckles glitter under the overhead spotlights. This had been her greatest indulgence when they redid the kitchen; it had cost thousands. But it finished off the room beautifully, as she always pointed out when Simon brought up the subject of 'money we've wasted on this house'.

'It's like something out of *Grand Designs*,' Judith had said, shortly after they'd had the work done. And it was. This designer kitchen, with its sleek lines, subtle lighting and high-tech equipment was the sort of room Martha had always dreamt she'd own one day. The heart of her bustling household; a modern, stylish hub where her growing family would live, laugh and love.

'Shall we have a drink?' she said, going across to the fridge. 'I could do with a glass of wine. Or a gin? What do you feel like?'

Simon scraped back his chair and got up from the table. 'Nothing for me,' he said. 'I'm going out now you're back. The lads are having an extra drills session tonight – if I leave now, I'll catch the last half hour. Then we'll go to the pub.' He was already walking down the hallway, jiggling his car keys in his pocket. 'I'll probably be back late. Don't wait up for me.'

The front door slammed and she stood in the centre of the kitchen, listening to the silence echo throughout the house.

'Fine,' she whispered, to herself. 'Have fun then.'

It occurred to her that he didn't have his sports bag with him, but maybe it was still in the boot of his car from Wednesday, when he'd been forced to miss a vital match after she'd selfishly rushed off to Surrey to look after her injured mother.

What would Judith be doing now? The evening meal was served ridiculously early in hospital, so she would already have eaten. Visitors might be drifting into the ward, their arms full of books, magazines and bars of chocolate, going past the lonely elderly woman in the first cubicle and moving on to sit with their loved ones. Poor Judith. Martha had been so relieved to drive away from the hospital this afternoon, so pleased she wasn't going to have to spend another night tossing and turning in that single bed in the bungalow. Being able to come home had felt like such a release after the last couple of days. But now she was back here, the guilt at having left her mother on her own was eating away at her. It wouldn't be so bad if Simon was here too, if he'd stayed to open a bottle of wine and tell her what a good job she was doing, what a dutiful daughter she'd been over the last few days. She suddenly realised he hadn't even asked how his mother-in-law was. He hadn't asked how his wife was either.

Joe started to bang his hand against his chair, and she went over and put her arms around him again, needing to feel his warm body against hers. He yelped, then began to shriek, a wail so high-pitched that it went right through the side of her head. She held him more tightly but he was now rocking from side to side, turning his face away from hers. In the end it was easier to pull away and step back, letting the tantrum blow itself out.

8

———

'Hey, guys, great to see you!'

Adam slapped Simon on the shoulder and took the bottle of wine from him, before turning back to Martha and kissing her on the cheek. She started to move her head and his second kiss landed on the tip of her nose.

'Oh, sorry!' she said.

'Twice darling, we kiss twice in this house!' guffawed Adam, his breath ripe, his teeth already stained from red wine. He and Claudia must have started early, although Martha suspected she and Simon were more than fashionably late: it had taken longer than usual to get Joe settled this evening, and the agency had sent a new sitter, so she'd spent nearly twenty minutes walking her through the house, showing her where everything was, writing out emergency contact numbers.

'She's a trained nurse, for God's sake,' Simon had muttered when they finally left. 'She'll cope.'

'I know,' said Martha. 'I just wanted to make sure she had everything she might need, in an emergency.' They'd sat in the car in silence: Simon driving too fast, Martha clutching the handle of the passenger door and trying not to make it obvious she was glancing across at the speedometer. How did he manage to be so relaxed about everything to do with their son? Martha was the first to admit she could be overprotective, possibly unnecessarily anxious. But Simon was so far the other way, it sometimes seemed as if he hardly cared.

'Come in, come in!' boomed Adam. 'Sorry to hear about your mother, Martha. Hope she'll soon be on the mend. You know Sally and Mark, don't you? And this is Anna and her husband, Craig.'

Greetings were exchanged, formalities observed, as the eight adults in the room moved around each other, struck up conversations, accepted and started to drink glasses of expensive wine.

Martha didn't want to be here. She wanted to be curled up on the sofa at home, watching mindless rubbish on the television, safe in the knowledge that Joe was sleeping soundly nearby. She was still so tired after the trip to Surrey. She'd had two bad nights' sleep in the back bedroom of Judith's bungalow, then last night Simon had woken her at 1am when he rolled in from the pub, his breath beery and his hair stinking of cigarette smoke. He had fallen asleep beside her almost immediately, while Martha lay awake for what seemed like hours, listening to his deep belly snores and worrying about her mother.

In the darkness everything seemed so much more complicated. She would have to go back to Surrey; it was just a question of how long she could delay it. Nothing much would happen in the hospital over the weekend – there would be no consultants around to make any decisions – so she would go into work on Monday, run through everything with Clive, then drive back to Surrey that night. If she spent Tuesday at the hospital, maybe she could persuade Patrick to go down the next day, so she could come home again? He would have closed his incredibly important deal by then; surely he'd be able to take half a day out of the office to go and sit by his mother's bedside?

When Joe's insistent shouts woke her at dawn, her head was thumping and her guilt hadn't been eased by a few hours' disturbed sleep. She could have done without this dinner party tonight, but she'd told Claudia they'd be there and it would have been rude to back out.

'Food everyone!' Claudia was calling now, from the kitchen. 'Come and find a seat.'

They went to the table, exclaiming that something smelt delicious and admiring the extravagant flowers on the windowsill, holding out glasses to be refilled and discussing where to sit.

'Boy, girl, boy, girl!' bellowed Adam as he opened more wine, his cheeks flushed.

Martha found herself between Craig and Mark, both of whom were talking to the person on their other side. Mark was pleasant enough – they'd seen each other infrequently at similar dinner parties over the years – but this was the first time she'd met Craig, and he didn't seem particularly interested in speaking to her. She glanced across the table, trying to catch Simon's eye, but he was leaning towards Sally, deep in conversation.

Nine years ago, when they first started seeing each other, Martha had felt there was a kind of telepathy between her and Simon. They could be out for the evening with a crowd of friends, both distracted and chatting, but one would sense when the other was looking over. She would feel a prickling on the back of her neck and glance up to see Simon staring at her, grinning. The same happened in reverse; by concentrating hard enough on him, it was almost as if she had the power to make him turn around and look at her. But that didn't happen anymore; it hadn't for years. She realised she'd probably imagined it: they had just been in love and excited by the mere thought of each other, so they wanted to spend most of their time looking at each other – even when they were meant to be concentrating on someone else.

The main course was fish, with a beautifully rich dill sauce. Claudia was an excellent cook. The volume of conversation around the table had risen as more wine was poured. Martha had stopped drinking; she watched as Simon's glass was topped up yet again – there was no way he was going to be capable of driving them home.

'I hear Sammy got into St Edward's!' someone said to Mark. 'You must be so pleased.'

He sat back in his chair, nodding. Martha could actually see his chest puffing out with pride. 'Yup, big relief. He's a bright boy, but you never know with these grammar school tests.'

'We spent enough on bloody tutoring, though,' Sally piped up from the opposite side of the table. 'It would have been frustrating if he'd failed, after all that.'

'It's the only way to give them a good start in life though, isn't it?' said Adam. 'You've got to make sure your kids get the best education possible. They need to be able to stand head and shoulders above everyone else in this world, otherwise they won't have a chance.'

There were murmurings of agreement around the table. Simon's eyes were down, studying his wine glass, his fingers twisting the stem backwards and forwards.

'The twins are only six, but we're already thinking about where they'll go for secondary school,' said Anna. Martha hadn't met her before tonight, and wasn't warming to her. 'It sometimes feels as if your kids are at a huge disadvantage if they're just normal nowadays, doesn't it? I mean, if you're black or gay or disabled, you'll get a helping hand for whatever you do, you virtually get pushed to the front of the queue.'

There was a silence around the table. Martha saw Sally wince, and Claudia took an audible breath in.

'Oh sorry, that's not very PC, is it?' giggled Anna.

Adam got up from his chair and lunged forward to pick up a bottle of wine. 'Who needs a top-up?'

'There's more fish if anyone wants some?' said Claudia, also rising from the table.

Martha shook her head, smiling at her. 'It's fine,' she said, both of them knowing she wasn't talking about the food.

Anna was looking confused, mouthing *What?* at Mark. He must have kicked her under the table.

'The thing is, Anna,' Simon's face was flushed; Martha knew it wasn't just the wine, 'that's bollocks. You can't get a head start in life if you don't have anything going for you in the first place.'

Martha could sense the tension in the room. Everyone could sense it – except Anna.

'Well, you hear all these stories about people who come good, in spite of their backgrounds,' she carried on. 'I just think that if you can tell everyone you're transsexual, or you've only got one arm, that means you're put at the top of the list, because in today's society we have to make sure we're not discriminating. We have to be so right-on about everything. I mean, if you've only got one arm, you aren't going to be able to do a job as well as someone who isn't disabled. It stands to reason.'

A muscle was twitching underneath Simon's right eye, so small a movement, it would be imperceptible to anyone who didn't know him well. Martha wanted to reach across the table and grab his hand, squeeze it to reassure him that she understood how he was feeling. But, more importantly, to get his attention and make him look up at her, so she could beg him silently, with her eyes, not to make a scene. Not to react.

'Anna!' said Claudia, slightly too loudly. 'Pudding! What

would you like? We've got chocolate mousse or a pavlova. Or, if you'd rather, you can just wait and have some cheese.'

Sally had started talking as well, asking Simon about football, and Mark turned to Martha and complimented her bracelet. 'That's very pretty, where did you get it? Most unusual design.'

She ought to be grateful to them all for steering the conversation in a different direction, but she was so tired she wasn't sure she even cared. Maybe it would be a good thing if Simon did react; if he stood up and swept his fists across the table, sending glass and china smashing to the floor. For a second, she imagined doing it herself. Just for once it might be satisfying to break free from the restraints of politeness and behavioural norms, and let rip at this arrogant, thoughtless bunch of idiots who had no bloody idea how hard it was to live a life that was ever-so-slightly less than perfect. These so-called friends of theirs, with their expectations and ambitions, and the happy, successful futures they were already planning for their flawless children.

But Simon let himself be mollified by Sally, and Martha sat and smiled at Mark and twisted her bracelet around as she told him where she'd bought it. The conversation moved on, to reality television and property prices.

Two hours later, people started to get up from the table and make noises about going home. Martha pulled on her coat, grabbing Simon's arm to steady him as he stumbled against the kitchen door frame.

'Thanks,' she said to Adam. 'What a lovely evening.'

Claudia pulled her into a hug and whispered into her ear. 'Sorry about Anna. She had no idea. She's just a bit tactless, doesn't know when to stop wittering on.'

Martha pulled back and smiled. 'It's fine,' she said. 'Not a problem.' She wondered how well Claudia knew Anna, where the connection came from.

'How is Joe?' asked Claudia, quietly. 'Everything okay?'

The smile was now plastered onto Martha's face, her cheek muscles aching with the effort of holding it. 'Yes, he's fine,' she said. 'You know that school in Wiltshire I told you about months ago, the one run by a charitable trust? They've had our application for so long, we'd sort of given up hope. But now they've asked us to go for a meeting to discuss getting Joe in there. They've got lots of new ideas about sensory stimulation.'

Why was she saying all this? Her friend was nodding and trying to look interested, but Martha knew she wasn't. It was much easier for everyone – even Claudia – not to hear the details, not to have to get too involved in the cold, hard facts.

'Lovely,' said Claudia. 'Tell me all about it over a coffee!'

Martha and Simon didn't speak when they got into the car, or during the drive home. They didn't speak as they paid the sitter, then crept into Joe's bedroom to plant soft kisses on his forehead. They didn't speak as they got into bed and turned away from each other, pretending to fall asleep.

9

Her mobile rang as she was whisking up eggs, ready to pour them into the saucepan for scrambling. A wedge of butter was moving slowly around the bottom of the pan, softening and sizzling as it melted. They were late this morning; she'd got up with Joe at dawn as usual, but then fell asleep on the sofa having put him in front of CBeebies. What a crap parent. Nearly as bad as Simon, who was only now wandering into the kitchen in his pyjama bottoms, his hair flattened into his face, rubbing crusts of sleep from his eyes.

'Yes, hello?' It was *No Caller ID* again.

'Is that Martha Evans?'

It was strange how the next minute of her life seemed to pass so very slowly. She stood at the worktop, its gold speckles glittering in the sunshine, whisking the eggs in a measuring jug; the voice in her ear talking, explaining, as her left hand grasped the phone and her right hand pushed the fork round and round. She couldn't tear her eyes away from the jug, mesmerised as the yellow yolks lost their shape and fused with the clear albumen, becoming pale and stringy.

Even when the call ended, she carried on whisking, harder

and harder, the fork clattering against the edge of the jug with such force it jerked across the worktop.

'Martha?'

The eggs were ready; she could stop now. Except she couldn't.

'Martha! For God's sake – what's the matter?'

Suddenly Simon was beside her, his hand on top of hers, grabbing the fork, prising it from her fingers which were clawed around the handle. She looked up at him, saw the confusion on his face, heard Joe wail in the background somewhere. She could smell the butter burning in the pan, noticed a wisp of black smoke twisting up into the air.

'It's Mum,' she whispered. 'She's dead.'

She had no idea how long she cried for. The sobs seemed to start deep within her gut and thrust themselves up through her chest and into her throat: sobs that were so enormous, she wasn't even sure she could get them out of her body as she gasped for breath. It was exhausting; every joint was throbbing, every sinew stretched and pulsating. Simon held her tightly for a while, then gently moved her towards the kitchen table and sat her down.

He made her a cup of tea, cooked the eggs and began to feed them to Joe, asking questions, gently. 'Do they know what happened? Was it very sudden?'

'Her lungs collapsed,' she said. 'She couldn't stop coughing. It was because of the fall. There was fluid on her lungs and she couldn't breathe.' The sobs had stopped, but she was suddenly so tired, she could hardly sit up straight. She wanted to drop forward and put her arms on the table, resting her head on them and closing her eyes, pretending none of this was happening.

The doctor had said other things as well, but she couldn't remember now what they were. Something about trying to suction out the fluid. Something about resuscitation.

'What will they do?' asked Simon. 'I mean, did they say what happens now?'

Martha looked up at him, shaking her head. 'I don't know,' she said. She pictured her mother as she'd left her on Friday afternoon, lying on the high hospital bed in the little cubicle, wires and tubes connecting her to the bleeping machines that were supposed to keep her alive.

Why had she left? She should have spent another couple of nights in that single bed in the bungalow, then she would have been at the hospital this morning when things started to go wrong for Judith. If she'd been by her side, maybe she would have seen some warning signs? She might have raised the alarm earlier – even a few seconds could have made a difference. As it was, her mother must have found herself in sudden pain, coughing with a lack of oxygen, gasping as her weakened body gave up its fight to support her, panicking as the life ebbed out of her. Martha began to cry again, wiping at her eyes with the back of her hand. What kind of a bloody awful daughter was she, to have walked out of that hospital on Friday afternoon, when so much could still go wrong?

On the other side of the table, Joe was writhing in his chair, pushing away the last mouthful of Simon's hurriedly scrambled eggs. He began to rock from side to side, pulling against the straps that held him in place, his head drooping forwards, a moan turning into a high-pitched shriek.

'Okay, mate,' Simon was saying. 'Don't get yourself in a state, I'll get you out of there.'

They should have warned her. They should have told her how ill her mother was. Although, maybe they had, and she just hadn't listened? She remembered one of the young doctors who'd talked to her on the ward, before she left on Friday; the way he'd refused to be drawn about a timescale for the hip surgery. 'It may not be possible,' he'd said gently. 'Sometimes patients just aren't strong enough to go through it.' Martha should have asked what would happen then: what could be done to repair broken bones if a patient's body was too weak to take an anaesthetic. But she'd chosen not to hear what he was saying, not to ask any questions that would open up the kind of possibilities she didn't want to have to acknowledge. At the time she'd reassured herself that the overbearing consultant hadn't said anything like that, and he must know best; this young doctor clearly didn't know what he was talking about.

Simon had undone the straps and was lifting Joe out of the chair, the boy's bare feet dangling down and kicking his father's shins. He was getting so big now, Martha thought, watching the struggle. She could just about lift him on her own, but it wouldn't be long before he'd be too heavy. She watched Simon carry him over to the purple sofa in the corner of the room, set him down and put the iPad in his hands, pressing the screen until tinny sounds started to come from it and Joe's eyes were drawn to one of the many blocks of cartoons they'd loaded onto it.

The sofa was almost the same colour as the bruises which had been splashed across Judith's hands. Martha screwed her eyes shut to block out the memory of her mother's damaged body; guilt and grief were rumbling up against each other inside her, as if someone was stabbing her in the chest.

She got up from the table, pulling her dressing gown tightly around her.

'Where are you going?' asked Simon.

'I've got to get dressed,' she said. 'I need to go back there.'

'What?'

'To the hospital. I need to go back and see her. I must call Patrick as well – I don't know if he'll be able to come down, but I have to let him know.'

'Martha, don't be ridiculous.' Simon got up from the sofa

and moved towards her. 'For a start, you're in no state to drive at the moment. But anyway, what's the point? Sorry if this sounds blunt, but she's dead, you can't change anything. They won't expect you to go rushing back there now.'

She glared at him. 'But I have to! There will be things to arrange. I'll have to sign documents.'

'Surely that can wait? You won't need to do it straight away.'

'I don't know, Simon. I don't bloody well know!' She was shrieking now, her eyes blurry with tears. 'I haven't had a parent die unexpectedly in hospital before. I don't know what's supposed to happen. But I'm going back. You'll have to stay here and look after Joe.'

'Oh, brilliant!' he'd put his hands on his hips now, standing beside the table, glaring at her. 'I can't take more time off work, Martha! Last week was chaotic while you were away.'

'Well, I'm sorry about that!' she yelled. 'I'm sorry that my sick mother messed up your plans. How selfish of her!'

'That wasn't what I meant,' he shouted back. 'But there is no point in us going through all that again. You don't have to go to the hospital immediately. Why can't you phone them back and talk it all through? Anyway, what about Patrick? Why can't he do it?'

'Yes, good question,' she screamed. 'Why can't he? Where is my fucking brother when I need him? Get real, Simon, you know Patrick isn't going to be any help with this.'

There was a clatter from the other side of the room, and Martha looked past Simon to see that Joe had fallen on his side. The iPad had dropped from his lap and crashed onto the tiled floor. His face was pink and his eyes were rolling back in his head.

'Jesus,' she said.

They ran to the sofa together, gathering the boy in their arms, checking his airway, turning him on his side, holding his limbs tightly as they convulsed. Actions they had done so many times over the years that they were now automatic. As the twitching calmed and Joe slowly relaxed, his body becoming limp against her, Martha buried her face in his hair, whispering over and over, 'I'm sorry, I'm sorry, I'm sorry.'

10

They'd given her a plastic bag containing Judith's possessions. Back at the bungalow, Martha took out everything and put it on the kitchen table. As well as the clothes her mother had been wearing when she was rushed into hospital, there were the extra bits and pieces Martha had taken in for her – a couple of nighties, a washbag, a paperback she didn't think Judith had even opened. There was something left in the bottom of the bag, making a clinking sound, and she reached in and pulled out the gold chain her mother had worn around her neck for as long as she could remember. Martha threaded it through her fingers, watching as the links twisted backward and forward.

'We'll need to get onto everything else in the morning,' Patrick was saying. He had enveloped her in a hug when he arrived, but that seemed to be the extent of any outward signs of affection or grief. Instead, he was being clinical and efficient. As always. He had scanned the details on the documents the ward sister had given to Martha, then googled the number of a local funeral director, to ask for their mother's body to be collected from the hospital mortuary. It was a relief he had done that bit. Martha hadn't wanted to speak to anyone.

'It's a bugger they're referring it to the coroner,' he said. 'It's just a formality, but it may hold things up a bit. No idea how long you have to wait to get a funeral slot around here, but it would be good to get a date diarised as soon as possible.'

Martha was astounded by how calm he was. She didn't think there were any tears left inside her, but she was far from calm. Her stomach was churning, her head thumping, her mind jumping from one thing to another. Overriding everything else was the image of her mother lying on the hospital bed.

As she drove there, earlier, she'd been dreading seeing the body, but – strangely – it hadn't been as bad as she'd expected. When Martha was ushered into the side room, Judith just looked as if she was asleep: composed and peaceful. Her eyes were closed, her mouth was set in a line which could almost have been the start of a smile. Someone had brushed her hair and it was so much less wild than when Martha had first seen her, lying on a trolley down in A&E. They hadn't quite got the parting in the right place though; she wanted to reach out and flip one section of hair across to the other side, to make this person really look like her mother.

The nurse had told her she could stay as long as she wanted and fetched her a cup of tea. Perched on the edge of the chair beside the bed, Martha had slowly reached out her hand, resting her fingers on Judith's arm, which had been placed across her stomach. The skin was cool and clammy, as if damp, and it was so pale it looked grey, particularly on her face – her hollowed cheeks a stark contrast to those which had been pink and full of life, just forty-eight hours earlier.

'But it makes no sense,' Martha had said to the doctor on duty. 'How can she have died? She only had a fall!'

'It was bruising to her lungs,' the woman had explained,

gently. 'Pulmonary contusion. Blood vessels are damaged, which can cause a build-up of fluid in the lungs and lead to a lack of oxygen.'

Martha didn't really understand, but had nodded anyway.

When she finally left her mother's bedside and went to the hospital toilets to splash some water on her face, she hardly recognised herself in the mirror: her cheeks white with shock, streaked with black channels of mascara. She looked wild and terrifying. She had run the cold tap and scrubbed at the make-up, running her hands through her hair and pulling it into a ponytail. She couldn't look like a madwoman when she went back to the bungalow to meet Patrick. She'd called him from the car, when she was on the motorway, and he'd sounded distant, almost cold, as he pieced together what had happened through her sobs. How could he take this kind of news with such composure? Martha had wondered whether, when he'd finished the call, her brother had put his head in his hands and wept quietly for a while, as most normal sons would do on learning of the death of their mother. She hoped he had; she desperately wanted to know he'd displayed some glimmer of humanity. But seeing him now, she doubted it. This was the man who was keen to get the date of the funeral diarised.

'There are calls we'll need to make, letting people know,' Patrick was saying. 'But there's no point doing that until we've got a date. Otherwise, we'll end up having to speak to everyone twice.'

He had pulled his phone out of his pocket and was tapping away at the screen. 'I'll make a list of what we need to do and send it through to you, then we can be sure we're both on top of everything. Even if the coroner requests a post-mortem, it shouldn't take too long. I can't see the report coming back with anything that will hold us up too much.'

How did he know all this? Martha had watched dozens of

hospital dramas but still wasn't really sure what would happen now.

'But if we speak to the funeral director again in the morning, we can probably pencil in a date,' he was saying. 'I'm presuming we'll have it near here? She's probably got friends who'll want to come along, old biddies from the WI and all that. We'll have to make sure we put on a decent spread – I bet the oldies enjoy a wake. For some of them it's probably a social highlight.'

Martha couldn't take any more. 'Jesus, how can you be so callous?' she said. 'You're treating this like another work project. Your mother has died, Patrick. *Our* mother has died. You're acting like you don't care.'

He glanced up from his phone and shook his head at her. 'Why are you giving me a hard time? Of course I care. But the bottom line is there's nothing we can do to change the situation. We have to work with it and be practical.'

There was a knock at the front door, and Martha was starting to get up from the sofa when she heard a key being put in the lock and the door opening.

'Hello?'

Nipper came bounding along the hallway and into the sitting room, yapping and leaping up at Martha, his sharp claws scratching her legs.

'Nipper! Come back here!' Then Alice was standing in the doorway. 'Hi! I'm sorry, hope you don't mind me coming in? We were out for a walk and I saw the cars parked outside, so I knew you were back. I thought I'd pop in to see how you were all doing. Nipper get down!'

Patrick was looking confused, and Martha realised she hadn't told him about the arrangement with the dog. 'Alice,' she said, pushing the dog down onto the floor. 'How are you? This is my brother, Patrick. Alice is Mum's dog walker.'

'Nice to meet you!' the girl smiled. 'How's Judith doing?'

There was an awkward silence, which Martha knew she had to fill. She should move forward, guide Alice to the sofa, sit beside her and gently explain what had happened. But her mouth was dry, her head fuzzy; she didn't know which words to choose, and it was as if she'd forgotten how to make her arms and legs work.

'I'm afraid she's dead,' said Patrick. 'She died early this morning, it was a problem with her lungs.'

Alice's smile faded and her mouth fell open, before she put up both hands to cover it. 'Oh my God!' she whispered.

Martha finally came to her senses and moved towards her, putting her arm around the girl's shoulders and pulling her into an awkward hug. 'Alice, I'm so sorry,' she said. 'It's horrible news to have to pass on. I know how fond you are of Mum. Were,' she corrected herself. 'How fond you were of her.'

She could feel the girl's shoulder bones poking through the material of her jumper, her body trembling.

Alice pulled away from her. 'But she was fine!' she said. 'She was fit and healthy before she had that fall. There was nothing wrong with her lungs!'

'I know,' said Martha. 'It's hard to understand. I wasn't expecting her to die.' It sounded so trite, but she didn't know what else to say.

'Sorry to be the bearer of bad news,' said Patrick, sounding anything but sorry. 'Martha and I are both here so we can start sorting out the logistics. Obviously, we've got quite a lot to do now. What's happening with the dog? Is it staying with you?'

Alice stared at him, clearly not taking in what he was saying. Nipper was sniffing at Patrick's shoe and he moved his foot slightly, nudging him away.

'Is the dog staying with you?' Patrick repeated. Martha could hear the impatience in his voice.

Alice nodded. 'I said I'd take care of him, when Judith went into hospital.' She turned back to Martha. 'I just don't understand how it can have happened so suddenly. I was going to visit her tomorrow night, after work. You told me she was okay. That's why you were going home again.'

Martha immediately felt the weight of her own guilt being thrown back at her. 'She was!' she said. 'She seemed to be. There was a problem with her lungs, but I don't really understand why it happened, Alice. They're referring it to the coroner, so we'll get a report.'

The girl's cheeks were streaked with tears and she looked young and vulnerable. 'This is so awful,' she said. 'I can't believe it.'

Martha could sense Patrick shifting from one foot to the other, impatient to get back to whatever important items he'd been adding to the list he was tapping into his phone.

'Listen,' she said. 'Would you be able to hang on to Nipper for a bit longer? Patrick and I have got a lot to sort out and, to be honest, I don't think we've even got our heads around what's happened yet.' *Or I haven't*, she wanted to add. *Patrick seems to have got the measure of it.* 'It would be a huge weight off my mind to know you're looking after Nipper for the time being.'

Alice nodded, wiping away tears with the tips of her fingers. 'Of course,' she said. 'He's no trouble.' The dog had wandered over to her and was sniffing at her trainers. 'Poor Nipper, you're going to miss her, aren't you?'

'Right, well that's good then,' said Patrick. 'Thanks for popping by Annie, and we'll be in touch.'

'Alice,' said Martha.

'Yes, absolutely,' said Patrick. He'd put out his arms and started moving towards the door of the sitting room, as if shepherding the girl out. Alice took the hint and began to back away.

'I'm so sorry,' she said to Martha, her voice wobbling. 'Your mother was such a wonderful woman.'

Martha could only nod. She wondered if she ought to put her arms around her again, but it was all too awkward. 'Thank you, Alice,' she whispered.

11

Martha had made mugs of tea, and they were sitting, side by side, in the uncomfortable upright chairs in the sitting room. Patrick had just finished making his list and texted it to her. 'I'm up against it at work for the next few days,' he said. 'So, you're going to have to do most of this. Talk to the funeral director first, obviously, then find out more about the coroner's report.'

Her phone pinged as the text came in, and she looked at it and nodded. Usually, she would be the one taking charge of a situation, issuing orders and delegating tasks. But she never seemed to behave normally when Patrick was around. For as long as she could remember, her older brother had been able to make her feel she wasn't doing anything well enough: that her efforts were pointless and her presence insignificant. It had always been easier to let him take charge, than to try and assert her right to have a say.

Now he'd finished compiling his list of tasks for her, he appeared to be skimming through the top stories on the BBC News website. She gripped the arms of the chair and forced herself to breathe deeply. She wanted to lean over and grab the phone from his fingers, hurl it against the wall. What was going on in his head? He really didn't seem to care that his mother had just died. He'd been so rude to Alice, as well; not just uninterested in her feelings, but almost irritated she'd been in the bungalow at all. He reminded Martha of the consultant on the intensive care ward, who'd made her feel two inches tall. He and Patrick would get along like a house on fire.

But however angry she was, she couldn't afford to fall out with him. There was a funeral to organise, a house to sell, a lifetime's possessions and personal belongings to deal with. She wasn't kidding herself she'd get much practical support from Patrick, but she certainly didn't want to have the emotional responsibility of doing it all on her own.

'She'll have made a will,' he was saying now. 'Don't suppose there'll be anything untoward in it, but we ought to see if she's put a copy somewhere.'

'Don't you usually leave your will with the solicitor?' said Martha. 'That's what Simon and I have done.'

'Probably,' said Patrick. 'If we can't find anything here, we'll have to arrange a meeting. We also need to think about the house. It's a good time to sell right now, summer coming up, the garden looking its best. If we get onto a couple of agents in the next few days, I reckon we should be able to put it on the market fairly soon. We'll have to get rid of some of this stuff though, make it look less like an old lady's pad.'

Martha supposed he was right but, even though she'd never particularly liked this cluttered, dark bungalow, she felt obliged to defend it. 'It's not to your taste, but it's probably going to be bought by another elderly person,' she said. 'It's that kind of property.'

'That's no reason why we shouldn't market it more widely,'

said Patrick. 'It won't take long to clear some of this rubbish. All that bloody glass, for a start.'

He pointed to a cabinet against the wall, where matching sets of crystal tableware stood in strict formation. There were glasses for every occasion: sherry, champagne, beer, wine, port. The same cabinet had been given pride of place in the large sitting room in their old house, and Martha remembered her mother polishing the glasses, twisting a yellow duster around the sparkling stems before replacing them on the shelves.

'Don't touch those,' Judith used to say. 'They were a wedding present. Too special for everyday use.'

So, they never got used at all.

The rows of glasses were now bleary, dust clinging to the rims like dandruff. They clearly hadn't been a priority for Sharon.

'Let's go and see if there's some paperwork anywhere,' said Patrick, getting up from the chair. 'I'll go through that desk in the hallway; you try the bedroom.'

As Martha walked into Judith's room, her heart felt as if it was thrusting its way up her throat. It was hard to believe her mother would never come back in here, never again sit at the dressing table and brush her hair with the mother-of-pearl backed hairbrush. Everything was just as Judith had left it, a jumper and skirt thrown over the chair, a pair of slippers at angles on the floor near the window. The bed had been made and a set of reading glasses were on the bedside table, next to a half-drunk glass of water.

Martha sat down at the dressing table. Some necklaces were hanging over the edge of the mirror and several china pots held other items of jewellery. She picked up a pretty diamond ring: she vaguely remembered her parents buying this decades ago, on a trip to Canada. She tried to slip it on, but could only squeeze it onto the little finger of her left hand.

Outside in the hallway, she could hear Patrick opening and closing drawers in the small bureau, exclaiming every now and then at something he'd found. 'For God's sake, she kept all her bloody bus tickets! There must be dozens of the things in here, for trips into town. What was the point in that?'

She opened the drawers in the dressing table: one was full of underwear, tan-coloured tights rolled up beside neatly folded sets of pants and bras which had probably once been white, but were now faded, like paper left too long in the sun. The next drawer contained make-up and half empty tubs of moisturiser and hand cream. The bottom drawer was where she found what she was looking for: cardboard folders full of insurance documents and old utility bills, transparent wallets containing bank statements. There was a bundle of Airmail letters held together with an elastic band. Martha recognised her own teenage scrawl and remembered writing these weekly letters home while she was on a six-month backpacking trip around South-East Asia, more years ago now than she cared to remember. She was touched Judith had kept them.

She started to peel the band away from the letters, intrigued to see what her nineteen-year-old-self had written in them. But then she noticed a folded sheet of paper lying in the bottom of the drawer. It was pale blue, with a Basildon Bond watermark embossed across the centre of the page. The thick paper crackled slightly as she opened it.

'God, can you believe this,' Patrick was saying, out in the hall. 'There's a receipt in here for some books she bought in Woolworths. That closed down years ago!'

Martha gasped as she read the words on the sheet of pale blue paper. She didn't understand. She made herself go back up to the top and read it all again, more slowly, trying to take in every word.

'Patrick,' she said, but it came out as a whisper.

It was definitely her mother's writing: her familiar loose script, slanting slightly to the right, with large loops under the Gs and Ys. It was her signature at the bottom as well.

'Patrick!' she said, louder this time. 'You need to come and look at this.'

She passed back the note as he came and stood behind her. She watched his reflection in the dressing table mirror; incomprehension spreading across his face, as it must have done across hers.

'You're joking,' he said. 'You're bloody joking.' He looked up and their eyes met in the mirror.

Martha turned to face him. 'Can you believe it?'

He moved sideways and sank onto the end of their mother's neatly made bed. For the first time since Martha had seen him at the hospital, four days ago, he looked shocked. He stared down at the piece of paper in his hand and his brow furrowed as he read it again. When he looked back up at her, there was hurt as well as bewilderment in his face.

'Why would she do this to us?' he said.

She reached out and took back the note, reading it again. At the top, Judith had written and underlined the word *Codicil* and underneath had put her full name and address. Further down the page were three lines: *I wish to add a codicil to my existing Last Will & Testament, leaving my house in Willow Road to Alice Gordon. The remainder of my estate is to be shared between my children, Patrick Cook and Martha Evans.* At the bottom of the page, Judith had signed her name and put the date.

'This is that bloody girl, isn't it?' Patrick said. 'The one who was here earlier. The dog walker.'

Martha nodded. 'I don't know her surname, but it must be.'

The codicil was dated six months earlier, just before

Christmas. Martha tried to remember what had been happening back then, whether Judith had given any indication about this. She couldn't think of anything, but that wasn't surprising – she hadn't known she needed to be looking out for signs that her mother was on the point of making such a huge decision.

'But she doesn't even know this girl!' Patrick was saying. The colour had returned to his cheeks now, and the pain in his face had turned to anger. 'She's been walking the dog for, how long – a few months?'

'A couple of years,' said Martha.

'Well, that's not very long. So, this virtual stranger comes in to take the bloody dog out and all of a sudden our mother has changed her will and left her everything.'

'Well, not everything,' said Martha, realising she had no idea how much 'the remainder of my estate' might be. Judith had made a small profit on the sale of the old house, once she'd bought the bungalow, and had been advised to invest it, but there was no guarantee any of that was left. Maybe the bungalow *was* everything she had?

'This is crazy,' Patrick was muttering. 'Just crazy.' He got up and started to pace up and down the bedroom. 'What was she thinking? Okay, leave the girl a bit of money, that's one thing. But the whole fucking house?'

'Maybe she...' Martha started. But she didn't know what else to say. She had no idea why Judith had done this.

'Where's my phone?' Patrick went out to the hallway and came back holding his mobile, swiping at the screen. 'We have to see if we can do something about this. She can't be allowed to get away with it.'

Martha needed some air. She went through to the kitchen and opened the back door, stepping out onto the patio and breathing in deeply as the sunshine warmed her face. A pair of birds were fighting in the branches of an old apple tree at the end of the garden, one swooping down towards the other, wings beating, beaks clattering. She leant back against the outside wall of the bungalow, warmth from the bricks seeping through the soft cotton of her shirt. Even though she'd never liked this place, never felt at home here, she was reeling from what they'd just discovered. It wasn't about the house itself; it was the intention behind those handwritten lines. Their mother had made a deliberate decision to leave her most valuable asset to someone they knew nothing about.

'Alice is such a lovely girl,' she heard Judith saying. 'She's got a real spark about her.'

Patrick stepped out onto the patio. 'Listen,' he said. 'I've been checking this out. You can't just make a codicil to a will. You have to have it properly witnessed.' He was waving the piece of paper in the air. 'This isn't witnessed. Mum signed it, but she didn't do it in front of someone else. It's null and void.'

Martha stared at him. 'So that means...'

'That means we can get rid of it,' he said.

'Of course, we can't! Mum wrote this, it must have been what she wanted. How can we just ignore it?'

'Easily. It's worthless, Martha. It means nothing at all and isn't legally binding, because she didn't do it in the right way. So, that means we don't have to accept it. We don't even have to tell anyone about it.' He leant towards her, and she could see pinpricks of perspiration across his forehead. 'We can forget about it and pretend we never found it.'

'But that's wrong!' Martha said. 'She wanted to leave the house to Alice, so if we destroy this, we're going against her wishes.'

Patrick nodded. 'Too bloody right we are. Don't get all moralistic about it. You need the money from the sale of this place just as much as I do. I've got school fees to pay for the kids, a big mortgage. I'm sure you're the same. Plus, you've got all those extra bills for Joe, the medical stuff.'

Martha's heart was beating so fast, she could hardly breathe.

'Anyway,' said Patrick. 'Who's to say she really knew what she was doing? No mother in her right mind would do this to her children – unless she'd fallen out with them, which wasn't the case. We both had a perfectly good relationship with our mother; she loved us. Or I thought she did! Maybe she was losing her marbles? It happens when old people spend too much time on their own.'

They stood, side by side, on the patio. The two birds were back again, sparring in the apple tree: their fluttering wings sounded like someone flicking through the pages of a book. Watching them, Martha felt slightly dizzy.

'You know I'm right,' said Patrick.

She shook her head. 'I don't know what to think,' she said. 'I just... I'm shocked, Patrick. That she did this.'

'Can you imagine what Dad would have thought?' said her brother. 'He would have been appalled. It's total madness. He wouldn't have wanted her to leave this place to a complete stranger.' He turned and went back inside the house. 'Come on,' he called over his shoulder. He started pulling open kitchen cupboards, then drawers, rummaging through their contents.

'Aha!' he said, dragging out a box of matches. 'Here we go.'

'What are you doing?' Martha whispered.

'I'm going to burn it,' he said.

'No way – you can't. What's the matter with you, Patrick?'

He was shaking his head as he looked at her. 'You really don't get this, do you, Martha? If we do nothing about this, a girl we don't even know gets to inherit what's rightfully ours. Does that seem fair to you?'

Martha couldn't speak. No, of course she didn't want that,

and it didn't seem fair. But she couldn't stand by and watch him destroy the note, either. 'We can't,' she said, flatly.

'Get real. No one will ever know, and it just saves us having to sort out a big problem. Can you imagine what people will say when they hear about this? They won't believe it any more than we do, at first. Then they'll start to wonder what was going on in Mum's head, and they'll start to ask why she wanted to leave everything to that girl, rather than to us. They'll wonder what kind of children we were, to make our own mother hate us that much.'

'She didn't hate us,' said Martha, feeling her lip start to quiver, knowing she wasn't going to be able to stop the tears welling up in her eyes. 'She really didn't.'

'That's what it feels like,' said Patrick.

'Anyway, what does it matter what other people think? This isn't about anyone else, it's just about us. Our family.'

'Which that girl,' said Patrick, 'is not a part of.' He slid open the box of matches. 'We need to get rid of this.' Pulling out a match, he scraped it along the edge of the box, the kitchen filling with the sulphurous smell of burning as a flame crackled into life.

'No!' said Martha, reaching out and pushing the match from his fingers. It had gone out before it landed on the floor, but she stepped on it anyway, grinding her shoe into the lino. 'Not like this, Patrick. It's not right.'

'Well, you do it however you want then,' he said. 'Rip it to shreds, chuck it in the bin. I don't care. We just need it gone.'

He turned and walked out of the kitchen into the hall, grabbing his coat from the row of hooks by the front door. 'I've got to go,' he said. 'Helen will be wanting to know where I am. I haven't got any more time to waste on this bloody thing, so I'm leaving it to you to deal with it. Just make sure you get rid of it properly.'

Martha had followed him out and was hugging her arms around her chest, aware that her cheeks were now wet with tears.

Patrick shook his head at her, a smile playing on his lips. 'Cheer up, little sister,' he said. 'There's no point getting upset about this. In the circumstances, it's the only thing we can do.'

12

Once Patrick's silver Audi had purred out of sight, Martha wandered through the bungalow again, feeling her mother's presence in every room. Her heart was racing and she couldn't keep up with her jumbled thoughts. There was too much she didn't understand; too much that hurt. Instead, she concentrated on reinstating order in the house, washing up the mugs and plates they'd used earlier, folding Judith's clothes in the bedroom and putting them away. The strangest things brought her to tears again: the row of perfectly ironed blouses hanging in the wardrobe, the sight of her mother's toothbrush standing to attention in a glass in the bathroom.

Each time she cried, it seemed to take her longer to recover. Her bones ached, as if she was coming down with a virus; her eyes were itchy, her head thumped, her hand trembled as she wiped the kitchen table. She realised it must be shock; things were bound to get easier as the days went by. But right now, it was all so raw.

The sheet of pale blue notepaper was still lying on the worktop, where Patrick had left it. Martha stopped to stare at it each time she went past, her eyes following the familiar lines of her mother's handwriting. What the hell had been going through Judith's mind when she wrote this?

The hurt she was feeling right now was about so much more than money, but that was the thing she couldn't stop thinking about. She and Simon weren't badly off – by many people's standards they had a pretty decent quality of life – but an extra few hundred thousand pounds wasn't to be sneered at. Martha had little sympathy for Patrick's struggle to pay extortionate school fees: it was his choice to privately educate his precious children. But she and Simon had always needed to find the money to pay whatever it took to look after Joe – the high fees for a nursery with special needs facilities, the specialist care they had to put in place if they ever wanted to do things normal couples took for granted, like going for a meal with friends on a Saturday night. On top of that was the cost of the equipment Joe needed, from his adapted wheelchair to the stairlift they'd soon have to install now he was getting too heavy for her to carry upstairs. They had never resented paying for any of it, but there was no element of choice.

Judith had known all this, and had always been sympathetic. So why had she decided to give away part of her daughter's inheritance? It seemed cruel. Martha sat in one of the upright chairs for a long time, staring through the windows as the sky turned dark outside and the street lamps flickered into life along the road. She was too exhausted to get up and close the curtains. She remembered feeling a little like this ten years ago, after her father died. But back then, in those first few awful hours, there had been Judith to care for. They had kept each other going, almost taking it in turns to be strong, while the other went to pieces. Now it was just her.

But she had to get up and get herself away from here. She was desperate to be back in her own home. There was no way she could face another night in the small bedroom of this bungalow, and she didn't need to be here to start contacting people and planning the funeral. With an effort she dragged herself to her feet and began to gather her mother's files and folders. She locked the back door and shut the windows, before carrying everything out to the car. There was just one more thing. She walked into the kitchen and picked up the piece of paper, folding it in half, then in half again, before stuffing it into the pocket of her coat.

After she started the engine, she picked up her phone and sent a text.

What about Alice? What shall we tell her?

A reply pinged in from Patrick immediately:

There's nothing to tell.

If she did what he wanted, and destroyed the codicil, he was right, there was no point in saying anything. To anyone. As she drove away from the bungalow, the sheet of paper felt like a brick in her pocket.

The journey down the motorway was quick; there was hardly any traffic on the roads so late on a Sunday. She usually listened to the radio or an audiobook, but tonight craved silence: so much was already going on inside her head, there was no room in there for anything else.

It was just after midnight when she got home. She pulled up outside the house and stared up at the dark windows. She'd called to tell Simon she was on her way back; he could at least have left some lights on. She had expected him to be relieved, because he wouldn't have to take any more time off work; she'd hoped he might even sound pleased she was coming home. But he'd been distracted, Joe screaming in the background, the sound of the microwave beeping insistently.

'Okay, see you later,' he'd said.

They always used to say 'safe drive' when one of them was travelling anywhere. They always used to end phone calls with 'love you'. Martha wasn't sure when they'd stopped doing that; she just knew it no longer felt natural.

After shutting the front door quietly, she crept upstairs and went into Joe's room. He was sleeping on his side, his arm firmly around Fluff, his mouth slightly open as his chest juddered with each breath. She knelt beside the bed and leant forward to kiss him, her lips barely touching his forehead – just enough for her to feel the warmth of his skin and smell the rich scent of the coconut oil they always put into his bathwater.

The boy whimpered and wriggled slightly and Martha held her breath until he lay still again; Joe angry and confused at being woken from a deep sleep wasn't something she needed right now.

She was biased – of course she was – but he was a good-looking little boy, with a mop of thick brown hair that refused to be tamed unless it had been recently cut, high cheekbones and perfect rosebud lips. He had blue eyes, like her, but otherwise was every inch Simon's son. People who had heard about his condition were often surprised when they met him for the first time.

'He looks so normal!' said a young work experience girl at the nursery, when Martha first started taking him there. The girl had immediately blushed and apologised, aware she should have known better. But Martha had smiled at her; she liked hearing this. Her son had issues, but he didn't look so different to any other little boy, and it was reassuring when people pointed that out. There were photos of Joe everywhere in this house: reproduced on outsized canvases on the walls, in frames along the bookshelves, pinned to the noticeboard in the kitchen, stuck onto the front of the fridge with little magnets. It was excessive, but she didn't care. She needed to remind everyone how beautiful her child was; show whoever came into this house that they were a normal, happy family.

Except that 'normal' and 'happy' were two words she could never use in connection with this life.

She went downstairs and poured herself a glass of wine from the bottle Simon had left standing open on the worktop. It was far too late for wine – she'd regret it in the morning – but she needed to feel the gentle warmth spread through her as she sipped, craving the sense of well-being it would bring.

Simon had left the kitchen in a mess, as usual, and she began closing cupboard doors, putting away packets of food and stacking dirty plates into the dishwasher. She usually resented this, but tonight it was strangely therapeutic. Possibly because tomorrow's agenda would consist of making phone calls to tell more people that her mother had died. Then there was the funeral. She'd never had to do anything like this before and didn't know where to start. Judith had single-handedly arranged their father's funeral. Martha was sorry now that she hadn't offered more support, but her mother had insisted she was happy to do it by herself.

'I need to keep busy,' she'd said. 'I want to deal with this. It's not a chore; it's part of the grieving process.'

So, Martha had stepped back and let her rattle ahead with it all, impressed by Judith's resilience. When she sat between Patrick and her mother in the front pew of the church, three weeks later, she'd been taken aback by the overly religious nature of the service. She had never known either of her parents to step inside a church, yet Judith had chosen a reading from the Old Testament and the vicar gave a gracious, personal eulogy – as if he'd actually known the deceased.

Was that the sort of funeral her mother would have wanted for herself? Martha had no idea and felt totally unprepared. They'd never had a conversation about this; there had been no need.

'Do you think we ought to do something religious?' she'd asked Patrick earlier.

He'd shrugged. 'Up to you. I don't care either way. Don't suppose it matters.'

Martha would think about all this in the morning. Right now, the wine had worked its magic, the kitchen had been restored to a reasonable state and her aching body was longing to slide under the duvet upstairs. The image of Judith's face, grey against the hospital pillow, was still playing at the edge of her mind, but it wasn't quite as insistent. Martha realised she was already calmer, prepared to cope with whatever the next few days threw at her.

She walked across the kitchen and put her glass into the dishwasher. There was a shopping list on the worktop – she'd started writing it first thing this morning, little realising what the day held in store. *Carrots, potatoes, salad, mince, jam.* It was as if she'd written those five, ordinary words a lifetime ago.

13

Her phone had been pinging all morning: replies to the string of texts she'd sent, copying and pasting the carefully phrased message to let friends know about her mother. Reading the sympathetic words was making Martha feel loved and supported; the outpourings of tenderness reassuring her that she would make it through this – that life would get better.

Now here was Claudia at the door, carrying a bunch of irises and opening her arms to fold her into a hug. 'I'm so sorry,' she whispered in Martha's ear. 'It's just awful. I know what you're going through.'

They went into the kitchen and Claudia perched on one of the high stools at the breakfast bar. 'You poor thing,' she said. 'The worst bit is breaking the news to everyone. I remember how hard that was, when my dad died.'

To Martha's relief, she didn't cry when she started to explain what had happened. There was the occasional wobble in her voice, her eyes were prickly and itchy, but the tears held off. It was incredible how quickly the rawness of grief was replaced by something else, still so sore, but somehow more manageable.

'It sounds like it was quick, at the end. Hopefully she didn't suffer?' said Claudia.

'I guess so, although she must have known what was happening, when she was struggling to breathe. I don't know, because I wasn't there. That's the hardest part.' Martha didn't want to dwell on this; she couldn't bear to think about her mother, frightened and alone in the last few minutes of her life.

'It was the same with my dad,' said Claudia. 'I felt dreadful because I wasn't with him when he died. But you mustn't let yourself think like that, because there was nothing you could have done.'

Martha wasn't sure that was true. If she'd stayed at the hospital and been by Judith's side when the crisis began, might her mother have stood more of a chance? She couldn't help wondering whether there'd been warning signs she'd missed. But, if anything, Judith had seemed stronger and more positive in the hours before Martha left on Friday afternoon. The two of them had done a cryptic crossword together, with Judith eventually getting one of the answers they'd been struggling with since they started.

'Unstable!' she'd wheezed, through her oxygen mask. '*The French one* – that's un – *makes it home for the horse* – stable!'

She hadn't seemed that ill. She wasn't breathing with ease, but she hadn't looked or sounded like someone who was about to die. Martha still found it unbelievable that one careless tumble outside the local post office could cause so much damage.

'This is the worst time, right now,' continued Claudia. 'For the first few weeks after we lost Dad, I was distraught. I could think about nothing else for a long time. Grief is so overwhelming, it's impossible to carry on as normal.'

Martha nodded. Listening to Claudia's gentle sympathy, she felt like a fraud. She was distressed, still shocked at the realisation that there was a gap in her life without Judith, but there was something else tormenting her as well. Packed away amongst the grief and worry about practicalities – phone calls to the hospital about the coroner's report, to the funeral director about dates, to the solicitor and the bank and the estate agent – there was guilt.

She had texted Patrick when she woke up this morning:

I can't do this x

When the reply came back, several hours later, it was the expected kick in the gut.

Pull yourself together, Martha. That girl doesn't deserve our inheritance.

Maybe he was right. But it didn't feel as if this was about who deserved what.

After Simon had left for work this morning and she'd delivered Joe to nursery, Martha had pulled the note from her coat pocket and sat at the breakfast bar, staring down at it. It would be easy to destroy this. She imagined finding another box of matches and setting fire to the edges, watching them blacken and catch light, throwing the smouldering scraps of paper into the sink, mashing the pulpy bits of burnt paper down the plughole with her fingers. But she couldn't bring herself to do it. What would Judith have said if she'd overheard their conversation yesterday? She would have been appalled. She wouldn't have believed her children were capable of something so callous; would never have imagined the lengths they'd go to in order to make sure her wishes weren't carried out.

Martha wanted to be able to blame Patrick, to throw the responsibility for all of this onto his shoulders: they were broad enough. But that would be wrong; he was the one who'd suggested destroying the codicil but, although she'd stopped him burning it straight away, she hadn't stood up to him. She hadn't insisted they must honour their mother's wishes. And now she'd let him put all that responsibility back onto her.

There were times when she wondered how on earth they were related. As a child, all she'd ever wanted was to be just like the older brother she adored, and the four-year age difference had never been an issue, until Patrick was sent away to boarding school at thirteen. Their father had gone to the same school: an old-fashioned place with high standards of discipline and excellent exam results. There was chapel every morning, outdoor sports in all weathers, probably corporal punishment – although that was never spoken about. Martha still remembered turning around and staring back through the rear window, as they drove away after dropping Patrick there for the first time, seeing him grow smaller in the distance, dwarfed by the imposing, grey building.

When he came home for the holidays, he already seemed different, more self-contained. Although he was kind to Martha and allowed her to crawl into his bed and listen to his stories about the other boys, that Christmas was the last time he let her get so close. From then on, he grew taller and more aloof each time she saw him.

At the end of the following summer, the day before Patrick was due to be taken back to school, Martha had heard noises coming from his room. She opened it to see him curled up in a foetal position on the floor, his foot kicking against the carpet, his face screwed up and scarlet, wet with tears, his mouth open as if screaming, although no sound was coming out. She had darted across to him, terrified he was hurt. But the boy had pushed her away then thrown himself on top of her, holding her arm behind her back so tightly that she shrieked in pain, making her swear never to tell anyone what she'd seen.

The kettle boiled and Martha made Claudia a cup of coffee, stirring the teaspoon round for longer than was necessary. She wished she hadn't sent that text to Patrick now; it was foolish to expect the grown-up version of that angry boy to share any of the guilt and misery she was going through.

'Seriously though, you need to be kind to yourself,' Claudia was saying. 'You've gone through a trauma. I'm sure Simon's being amazingly supportive, but don't forget to look after yourself.'

The words came out of Martha's mouth before she could stop them. 'Something happened when Patrick and I were at Mum's,' she heard herself saying. 'We found this piece of paper. She'd changed her will.'

Claudia was looking at her, waiting for her to go on. *Stop*, Martha told herself, *don't say any more*. But the burden of this horrendous secret was so great. If she were able to share some of it, maybe the whole thing wouldn't seem as awful.

'She added a codicil to her will.' Martha stared down at the worktop, rubbing at a mark on the surface. 'It said she wanted to leave her house to this girl who walks the dog. I think there might be a bit of money in savings accounts as well, but the house is the main thing. She didn't want to leave it to me and Patrick.'

Claudia's mouth had dropped open. 'Jesus!' she said. 'How do you feel about that?'

Martha shrugged. 'Hurt. Upset. But mostly just confused. Patrick was angry.'

'I'm not surprised,' said Claudia. 'That's awful. Why would she do that?'

'I don't know. I guess she thought this girl, Alice, needed it more than we did. After we found the piece of paper, Patrick looked some stuff up on the internet and said what she'd done wasn't legal. He thinks we should destroy it.'

The silence stretched between them, and understanding dawned on Claudia's face. 'So, if you do that, it means no one else will know about it; you and Patrick will just inherit everything, as you would have done before?'

Martha nodded. She didn't feel relieved at having shared this secret; she felt sick. Why hadn't she kept her stupid mouth shut? Now the words had been spoken out loud, it all seemed even worse. Talking about it had made it real. When the knowledge of what they'd found and the conversation they'd had were safely tucked away inside her head, she'd almost been able to pretend none of it had happened.

Claudia was staring at her. 'Wow,' she said.

Martha looked back down at the worktop. She was still rubbing at the mark, and now started scraping at it with her fingernail; it must be some of the pasta sauce Simon had cooked for Joe last night.

'Do you know,' Claudia said, 'I totally understand why you'd want to do that. I think I'd do the same. In fact, I know I would. This is your inheritance; it's nothing to do with that girl.'

Martha's shoulders sagged in relief. She hadn't realised she'd been holding her breath, waiting for Claudia to speak.

'I don't know why your mum made that decision, but it wasn't fair,' Claudia was saying. 'You've done so much for her; you've been such a good daughter.'

'But even so, we can't destroy it,' said Martha, hoping she knew what Claudia was going to say.

'You have no choice! It wouldn't be right if that house were given to a total stranger. Did your mum leave you a letter or anything else, explaining why she'd done it?'

Martha shook her head.

'Well, you have every right to protect what's yours,' said

Claudia. 'It's such an extraordinary thing for her to have done, especially without telling you. You have to get rid of that note. Property prices in Surrey are astronomical. We must be talking serious money here.'

Martha shrugged; she really had no idea.

'How did your mum think you were going to react to discovering something like that? Any child would do the same.'

'I still feel awful,' said Martha. 'Patrick doesn't seem to care, but I've been feeling so guilty about the whole thing.'

'Well, don't,' said Claudia, hopping off the stool and walking around the edge of the breakfast bar. She put out her arms and drew Martha into another hug. 'You've got plenty of other things to worry about right now. Forget about this and put it behind you.'

'Thank you for saying all that,' Martha clung tightly to her friend. 'It means a lot. Please don't tell anyone about this, will you? Not even Adam?'

'Don't worry,' said Claudia. 'I won't tell another soul.'

14

———

Janey was speaking to her husband. Martha could tell it was her husband, because Janey was hunched over the phone, whispering and gesticulating with her free hand, anger radiating from every pore. They frequently had these sorts of conversations.

'That is absolutely not fair!' she hissed. Then muttered something else that Martha couldn't catch. 'Bollocks!' she said suddenly, then lowered her voice again. 'I never said that and you know I didn't.'

Martha didn't want to listen in, but it was hard to avoid it. Janey's desk was four feet away from her own and although their chairs were both turned towards the window they were still in each other's line of vision. Janey's marriage had been in crisis for the entire time she'd worked here, and Martha had long ago given up worrying about it. In the first few weeks, she had frequently looked on with horror as Janey slammed down the phone, tears flooding her cheeks. She would run after her into the ladies' toilet at the end of the corridor and lean against a basin holding out fresh supplies of loo roll as Janey wailed and remonstrated about Rob's irrational behaviour, his selfish pigheadedness and his total inability to show her any of the attention she needed. But a few hours later the trauma would be forgotten, and the next day Janey would arrive at work chatting about the film she and Rob had seen the night before or the meal they'd cooked together, or their plans for a summer holiday in Mauritius.

It hadn't taken Martha long to work out that Janey's marriage was one of those relationships which thrived on conflict. She learnt to ignore the heated phone conversations and sudden tearful exits from the office. It was a relief; as much as anything, coping with someone else's emotional turmoil was too draining. Martha had enough of her own crap to deal with – she didn't need to set aside sympathy for anyone else's disintegrating life.

Janey slammed the phone down now and sighed deeply.

Martha didn't react.

Janey blew her nose and sniffed loudly.

'Who wants a tea?' Martha called out, pushing back her chair and looking round the office.

Having lined up empty cups in the little kitchenette next door, she threw teabags into them with more force than was necessary. Janey's selfishness was unbelievable. *She* was the one whose mother had just died. *She* was the one whose bloody marriage was in crisis. Not that anyone else knew that; for once, Martha wished she was the sort of person who was able to share whatever was going on in her life. Everyone had been very kind when she came back into work yesterday, but after asking a few obligatory questions and making sympathetic noises about the shock of it all and the challenges of organising a funeral, they had drifted back to their desks and office life had carried on as before.

Martha knew they were taking their lead from her: she was giving the impression she was coping well. Unlike Janey, she had never been outwardly needy, so her colleagues presumed she was just getting on with it and dealing with the loss of her mother with dignity and self-control. It was the habitual tough outer shell thing: the capable persona Martha had worked so hard to establish over the years. And now it was pride that was stopping her from stepping out from behind that pretence and letting anyone know how much she was hurting.

Clive had been kind. 'You don't have to be back in here yet, you know,' he'd said, when she got to work. 'You're entitled to compassionate leave.'

'I know.' She'd smiled at him although, as usual, he was looking at a point over her shoulder, not meeting her eye. 'But to be honest, I'd rather be here. It helps to keep busy. There will be a lot to sort out in Surrey, so I may need to change some of my days around in the next couple of weeks.'

Clive had nodded and turned to walk back to his office. 'Just ask,' he said, over his shoulder. 'If you need some time off.'

What a lovely man. However many times Martha tried to thank Clive for being so understanding, it would never ease the guilt she constantly lived with, about letting him down, not pulling her weight in the office. She had worked here for eight years, so was already part of the team when she got pregnant. But Clive had been unfailingly supportive after Joe's birth. As someone who closely guarded his own privacy, he never sought to invade hers, but let her know that he valued her as an employee, and the job would always be there for her. She had lost count of the number of occasions he'd cut her some slack – from the numerous times she'd had to leave the office early to collect Joe, to the last-minute crises when she'd been called away to rush her son to A&E. He was a kind, sympathetic boss and, without his support, she doubted she would have been able to continue working after Joe was born.

As the kettle boiled, Martha's phone started to ring. Alice's name came up on the screen.

'Hi!' Martha said, her voice bright. She suddenly realised she hadn't thought about Alice in the last couple of days. The girl had been so upset when she heard the news about Judith, but Patrick had made sure they shooed her out of the bungalow in a matter of minutes, giving her no chance to ask them any questions. It must have been such a shock. Martha bit the inside of her lip: she really ought to have called her yesterday, or at least sent a text. 'How are you?' she asked now. 'I'm sorry everything was so rushed on Sunday.'

'I'm okay,' said the girl. 'What about you?'

'Fine,' said Martha, nodding although Alice couldn't see her. 'I'm fine.' As she spoke, she suddenly realised there was a lump in her throat and her eyes were filling with tears. She wasn't fine at all.

'I just wanted to give you a call, to say that Nipper's doing well,' said Alice. 'I was worried he'd be missing Judith, but we're keeping him busy and taking him out several times a day. Gracie and Mum are walking him when I'm at work.'

Martha closed her eyes. Damn: she'd been so wrapped up in everything else she hadn't thought about the dog either. It had been such a relief when Alice offered to have him, but she should have been the one to call and ask for an update. Wrong-footed again.

'Thank you,' she said, trying to keep the tremor out of her voice. 'That's very good of you, Alice.'

'Also, I popped into the bungalow earlier, just to check on the post,' the girl carried on. 'I didn't know if you were planning on coming back down here at any stage. There wasn't anything urgent there, just some circulars, but if something important arrives, I can forward it to you.'

'Yes, that would be useful, thanks. I'll text you my address.'

Now Martha could feel irritation prickling in her scalp. She ought to feel grateful, of course: Alice was helping her out in ways she hadn't even thought about. But it seemed intrusive. If only she'd thought to ask her to check on the bungalow – then it would still have been a favour carried out, but Martha would have been the one in control of the situation. Right now, it felt like Alice was running this relationship; she knew it really didn't matter and she should be grateful for any help she could get, but it was strangely annoying.

'Mum says she's happy to carry on cleaning the bungalow, if you want her to?' the girl was saying now. 'She goes once a week, for a couple of hours, but she can do a bit less if you'd like?'

'No, that's fine,' said Martha. 'Let's just carry on with that for now, if she doesn't mind. I hadn't thought about it, to be honest with you, Alice. But it's probably a good idea.'

Don't push me! she wanted to scream. *I can't make these decisions at the moment.*

'I just wondered...' the girl hesitated. 'Whether you'd made any plans – you know, about a funeral? It's just that we – me and Mum – we'd very much like to be there. I know you might want to keep it to friends and family, but we were both so fond of Judith. If you don't mind, we'd really like to come. I'm sorry, I know you've got a lot to do, so I don't want to hassle you. But I hadn't heard anything, so...'

'Alice, of course you must come!' It hadn't occurred to her that the girl would wait to be invited. 'I haven't organised a date yet, because we need to get the coroner's report back. But as soon as I know what's happening, I'll be in touch, I promise.'

'Thank you, I'd appreciate that. This is all such a shock, Martha. You know how I felt about Judith, she was such a lovely woman and so kind. I still can't believe she's gone, to be honest. It doesn't seem real.'

'I know, I feel the same.'

'Please let me know if you need me to do anything at all,' continued Alice. 'It must be hard for you, living so far away. But I can keep an eye on the bungalow or run any errands that need doing. I used to spend so much time at Judith's, it seems odd not to be doing that any more. She was such a good friend to me.'

As she stood stirring milk into the row of mugs, Martha tried to quell the resentment rising in her stomach. She was being ridiculous – and paranoid: Alice wasn't deliberately stepping on her toes or taking over. She was just kind and thoughtful; she'd loved Judith and was now just trying to do what she could to help out during a traumatic time. Martha ought to be grateful.

But it was still bloody irritating.

15

'The wheels on the bus go round and round, round and round! Come on, everyone, you can do better than this! Louder!'

Suky was staring straight at her. Martha forced a smile and sang, her hands clasping Joe's and making circular motions with them as he lay heavily against her. His bony little bottom was digging into the top of her thigh and she tried to shift herself without making him slide off.

'What's next?' Suky was saying. 'How about "I'm a Little Teapot"? We all know the words to that. Right, off we go...'

Martha bent her left arm towards her waist in the shape of a handle and gently tipped Joe to the right, dutifully pouring him out. During these sessions, she often wondered if anyone else here hated Wednesday mornings as much as she did. It never looked like it. The other parents were smiling, singing loudly in a disharmonious medley, grasping their children tightly as they mimed actions and moved small limbs in time to the music. They all looked like they were having a good time. Mind you, she was doing the same: an outsider coming into this room wouldn't notice anything different about Joe's mummy; she wasn't obviously letting the side down. So, either she was the only callous cynic who was wondering why she bothered to come here every week, or they were all accomplished actors, doing a fantastic job of pretending to enjoy themselves.

'We've got time for a few more!' called Suky. 'Any requests?'

The speech and language woman at the nursery had recommended music therapy. 'It's a marvellous stimulus and really helps develop communication and social interaction,' she'd told Martha. 'And it will be fun for you too!'

These weekly groups weren't fun: Martha felt duty-bound to take Joe to them, because it was the sort of thing a good mother would do for her disabled son. But she hated every minute. It wouldn't be so bad if Joe seemed to get anything useful from these sessions, but Martha couldn't kid herself that was the case. They'd been coming here for four months, and her son, floppy and heavy on her lap, showed no more signs of understanding what was going on now than he had done at their first session. The whole thing made her feel even more of a failure.

Today it was harder than usual to pretend to be enjoying herself. She wanted to stand up and yell, 'My mother died on Sunday!' Partly to shock them, partly to get their sympathy. Mainly because it felt so strange to be following her normal routine when something so momentous had happened in her life. But there was no point; even after all these months, she didn't know any of these other parents well enough to share that sort of news.

'How about "Row your Boat"?' called out a woman in a bright pink jumper. Martha knew her daughter was called Chloe, but couldn't remember the woman's name, even though she was sure she'd introduced herself, ages ago. There were nods of approval and one of the children, a little girl with Down's syndrome, started to clap enthusiastically. The grown-ups laughed and gamely embarked on the next song, pushing their children backwards and forwards on their knees, pretending to row a boat through choppy waters.

She felt something bang against her foot, and turned to find that the man sitting beside her was trying to get up. 'Excuse me,' he whispered. 'We need the bathroom!' His son was younger than Joe, possibly three, and looked up at her through a pair of thick, round glasses, grinning. 'Poo!' he said.

Martha hadn't seen them at the group before. She grinned back at him. 'I know,' she said. 'I can smell it!'

The dad snorted with laughter. 'Sorry,' he whispered. 'It might be a false alarm, this boy farts for England. But I can't risk it.'

Martha laughed and shifted sideways to let him shuffle out between their chairs, before continuing to row her boat with Joe.

'Poo!' the boy was yelling, as his dad carried him towards the doors at the back of the hall. 'Poo! Poo! Poo!'

Twenty minutes later, as they packed up at the end of the session, the man leant across to her. 'I'm Dan,' he said. 'And this stinky boy is Johnny.'

'Hello stinky Johnny,' said Martha. The child screamed with laughter, throwing back his head and kicking his legs as his father strapped him into a buggy. 'I'm Martha and this is Joe. First time here?' she asked, as she hoisted Joe onto one hip and pulled his wheelchair towards her.

'Yup,' said Dan. 'Not sure we're going to shine. Neither of us can sing, can we, Johnny?'

'I wouldn't worry about that,' said Martha. 'I don't think any of us have voices to write home about. I mime the words most of the time.'

Suky bustled up with a sheet of paper. 'Great to see you, Dan,' she said. 'Glad you both could make it. I just need you to sign some forms for me.'

Martha smiled at the man and gave a small wave as she

started to push Joe towards the door, and Johnny waved both arms back at her. 'Bye!' he yelled.

The other adults were strapping their children into buggies and wheelchairs and pushing them down the front ramp; Martha said goodbye to familiar faces, feeling like a fraud. These heroic mothers and fathers smiled and chatted and laughed. She tried to do the same, but felt hollow and inadequate alongside them. She invariably drove away from these sessions filled with a dejection that lasted for the rest of the day. She adored her gorgeous little boy and was fiercely protective of him and determined to do what was best for him. But Wednesday mornings were a reminder that things were never going to get any better.

Joe fell asleep in the back of the car on the way home, so Martha left him in there, with the door open, while she made a cup of coffee and took it out into the front garden, sitting on the grass in the sunshine while she checked the news on her phone and replied to a couple of texts she'd not seen earlier.

There was a missed call from a landline she didn't recognise, but she thought it might be her friend, Nancy. As she scrolled through her contacts, to check Nancy's office number, another name flashed up before her. Her heart billowed inside her chest. How many times had she tapped on this icon, *Mum*, and put the phone to her ear, listening as it rang at the other end and waiting for her mother to speak into the empty space.

Judith had always sounded slightly breathless – even if she hadn't run to answer the phone – the intonation rising slightly at the end of 'Hello?' then, when she heard it was Martha, warmth would flood through her voice: 'Darling, how lovely to hear from you!'

Staring down at the name and number on the screen of her phone, Martha wondered if her mother had been like that with other people. It had never occurred to her before, because she'd presumed that warmth was special: just for her daughter. But maybe she'd greeted Alice in the same way?

She found herself pressing the number and putting the phone to her ear. Judith's mobile didn't ring at the other end – Martha knew it wouldn't; it was out of charge, sitting on the worktop in the kitchen of the bungalow in Surrey. But the answerphone clicked in immediately and she breathed in sharply as she heard her mother's familiar voice: *Hello, this is Judith's phone. I can't take your call at the moment, but please leave a message and I'll get right back to you!*

There was a long beep, then an echoey silence. Martha shut her eyes and listened to the sound of her own breathing.

16

'What I must emphasise is that it's not just a case of finding out whether Greenways is right for Joe. It's important that he is right for us, too.'

The principal was an attractive woman in her fifties, with beautifully cut hair and immaculate make-up. The hands clasped in front of her on the desk looked as if they'd been professionally – and recently – manicured, and Martha twisted her own fingers out of sight in her lap, embarrassed by nails that were bitten to the quick.

'That's why we would like him to come and spend a day with us, before we decide whether it's appropriate to offer him a place.'

Martha nodded, and Simon shifted in the seat beside her. 'That would be fine,' she said. 'We can bring him whenever you like.'

She wasn't sure how easy that would be: it had taken them nearly two hours to get here in early morning traffic. But they could think about the logistics later. Right now, she was just glad they'd been able to rearrange their missed appointment so quickly, and was amazed by what they'd seen: this place was extraordinary.

During their hour-long tour of the facilities, there had been so much that was positive and inspiring, from the bright classrooms where teachers worked one to one with the pupils, to the modern art suite and vast soft-play area. They had also been introduced to Betsy, the therapy dog. 'Medical research has shown that therapy dogs can reduce anxiety, fatigue and depression,' explained the principal. 'They also provide great emotional support for all the children, especially those with poor verbal communication.'

In the fitness suite, Martha and Simon had seen a boy being helped to do exercises on an area of matting, then they watched two physios in a therapy pool, supporting a young girl. Floating on her back, she was kicking her legs and screaming with delight as the water lapped against her. 'She suffered an extensive intracranial haemorrhage six months ago,' explained the principal. 'The consultant told her parents it was unlikely she would regain any speech or movement.'

Upstairs, they had walked along softly carpeted corridors, where individual bedrooms were painted in primary colours and daylight flooded in through large windows. Past the open doors they could see teddies on pillows, framed photos of laughing families on side tables. It was warm and welcoming, and felt safe.

'How many of the children are weekly boarders?' Simon had asked.

'Eleven at the moment,' said the principal. 'We have space for one more.'

Martha couldn't imagine not holding Joe in her arms as he went to sleep in his own bed every night. She couldn't bear the thought of someone else giving him a bath, getting him into his pyjamas, lifting him gently under a duvet and waiting beside him while he settled down for the night. But if he came here, there would be no other option: it was too far for him to travel every day. It also made sense for him to live at Greenways during the week, because it would mean he'd receive extra therapy sessions.

'This works best as a 24/7 programme,' the principal had explained.

Half an hour later, they were back in the car, pulling out of the long drive onto the main road and heading for home.

'I can't believe this might be happening at last,' Simon was saying. 'How old was Joe when we first heard about this place – three? It's been such a slow process. But if we can get him in now, it will have been worth the wait.'

Martha nodded, staring out of the side window at the chequered fields streaming away from her towards the horizon. He was right, they had been waiting so long for this. They'd first heard about Greenways when it was featured in a television documentary. They'd watched, in stunned silence, as the programme showed the school and its staff at work, while independent experts extolled its methods and marvelled at its successes.

'That's what Joe needs,' Simon had said, turning to her as the credits rolled, his face bright with hope. 'Just think what they could do for him.'

She'd agreed, of course she had, and she'd made supportive noises while he made phone calls, requested brochures and spent evenings searching the internet for more background. But when they were told the school was full, with an oversubscribed waiting list, she'd felt a jolt of relief. Her little boy was only three years old. He wasn't ready for this place yet – or anywhere else. He was fine at nursery. She was coping well at home.

'I've put his name down,' Simon told her one evening. 'They

say it could be ages before he gets the chance of a place, but we've still got to try.'

'Definitely.' She nodded.

Then, just under two years later, they'd got a phone call from the principal. Joe's name was at the top of the waiting list and there was a place available. They could come and have a look round, if they were still interested.

'I told her we're more than interested!' Simon had grinned, as he put down the phone. 'They're going to send a letter of confirmation. This could be perfect, Martha. He can't stay on at nursery for much longer; it's the ideal time to move him.'

She had forced a smile and put the date in her diary. Simon was right, it was an incredible opportunity for Joe.

'I just...' she said. 'I hate that he has to go anywhere. I wish I could look after him myself; I'm his mother, I should be taking care of him.'

Simon had looked at her and sighed. 'We've talked about this so many times,' he said, not even trying to keep the frustration out of his voice. 'It's too much of a challenge, and it's only going to be harder as he grows up and gets bigger and heavier.'

That had been a month ago. Now here they were, driving away from this phenomenal school, having been as impressed as they'd anticipated by everything about it.

'It would be so hard,' she said. 'To only see him at weekends.'

'Yes, but think about everything he'd be getting from the place,' said Simon. 'It's amazing. The standard of care is incredible – even better than we'd imagined. Look at what they've achieved with that little girl who had the brain haemorrhage.'

Martha nodded, biting at her thumbnail, ripping the skin down the side, the sharp tang of blood on her tongue. He was right: if there was the slightest chance this school could help Joe, they had to make sure he came here. For years, healthcare professionals had shaken their heads and lowered their eyes. They had apologised and sympathised, while telling Martha and Simon not to have any expectations when it came to their little boy and his future. But today they had spoken to a group of special needs teachers and therapists who were enthusiastic and inspiring, and seemed to be suggesting anything was possible.

'We have the most advanced equipment in the country,' the principal had told them, as they stood in the doorway of the sensory stimulation suite. 'We get results here which astound parents who have been told their child will never smile, never laugh, never talk.'

It was just what both of them had been desperate to hear.

'If they offer him the place, we've got to take it,' Simon was saying now. 'I know it's a lot of money, but it would be worth every penny.'

He was accelerating past a lorry on a section of single carriageway. Up ahead, Martha could see a car approaching on the same side of the road. She tightened her grip on the door handle and closed her eyes, only relaxing once Simon had swerved back into his own lane, the other car's horn fading into the distance.

'We can afford it, but it will be really useful to have money from your mum's estate,' he was saying. 'I know you'll have to wait for probate, which may take a few months. But if Joe gets in, he'll be there for years.'

When they first looked into the possibility of Joe going to Greenways, Martha had been shocked by the fees. But there had never been any question that they would pay whatever it took. They were lucky: she and Simon both earned decent salaries, they didn't live an extravagant lifestyle and there were no other children to factor into their financial equations. But even so, the inheritance she would get from Judith would be a bonus.

Which was another reason why she ought to destroy that piece of paper.

She hadn't told Simon about the codicil. The morning after she got back from Surrey, he'd been short tempered and distant, rushing out of the house earlier than usual, saying there was an IT crisis at work – someone had hacked into their systems. Then, later that morning she had confided in Claudia, which had been such a relief. Simon had been so busy for the next couple of days, she didn't see much of him. Obviously, she would tell him. She definitely would. But it would be sensible to wait until he was in a better mood, or until they were sitting down with a glass of wine in the evening, relaxing and catching up on each other's news. But more days went by, and that never seemed to happen. Now she didn't know how on earth she would bring up the subject, because too long had passed. He would want to know why she'd kept it from him – and she didn't really know the answer to that. It was best to forget the whole thing. He need never know.

It was early afternoon by the time Simon dropped her at home, and she spent the next couple of hours on the phone, making funeral arrangements, calling Judith's banks and pension provider, cancelling her insurance policies, requesting forms needed to close down other aspects of her existence. With each phone call, it was becoming easier. She realised she was reeling off a rehearsed speech, pausing at certain places to wait for the sympathy and good wishes. They hadn't found Judith's will in the bungalow so one of the calls Martha made was to her mother's solicitor, who confirmed a copy was lodged there. An appointment had been arranged for her and Patrick to go to a formal reading. Even as she ended that call and wrote the details in her diary, she was already dreading it. The sheet of pale blue paper was still folded into a thick square in her coat pocket and the whole thing felt so wrong.

By the time Simon came back from work, just after 7pm, she'd collected Joe from nursery, fed him and was lifting him out of his chair, ready to carry him upstairs to the bath. The boy was tired, draped over her like a rag doll, his limbs heavy, his weight dragging on the small of her back. She moved towards the hallway, hoping Simon would offer to help, but he was standing on the other side of the kitchen, opening a cupboard door and searching for something to eat.

'The hospital called and the coroner's report is back,' she said, pausing by the open door, swaying gently to rock Joe and keep him calm. 'It was acute respiratory failure, because of the bruising to the lungs.'

Simon turned and looked at her, nodding. 'Well, that's what you thought, isn't it?'

'Yes, but good to have it confirmed, I guess.' Was it good? She had no idea. If nothing else, it meant they could move forward. 'I got on well this afternoon, with organising the funeral,' she went on. 'I picked a crematorium and booked a date, two weeks tomorrow.'

'Where?' asked Simon, ripping open a packet of biscuits.

'About half an hour from Mum's. The crematorium in Aldershot. We've got a slot at midday. Simon – don't fill up with biscuits! I've made a chilli; we can have it as soon as I've got Joe sorted... I've also been in touch with a place called The Hamilton Hotel, about hiring a room for the wake afterwards.'

'The timing isn't hugely convenient, is it?' he said. There were biscuit crumbs on the side of his mouth. 'The wake will probably go on all afternoon but we can't stay down overnight, because of Joe, so who's going to pick him up from nursery?'

'I thought we could take him with us,' said Martha. Joe was beginning to wriggle in her arms now, bored with being held.

Simon stared at her. 'Are you crazy?'

'He'll be okay,' she said. 'We can take his wheelchair and the iPad; he'll be happy to watch that during the service.'

'For God's sake, Martha!' Simon slammed the cupboard door shut. 'That's totally impractical. You'll be busy the whole time, talking to people, so that means I'll be left looking after Joe. Which is fine – I don't mind. But it's hard enough keeping him quiet here, at home. Do you honestly think he'll be happy to sit in the car for hours, then be carted into a crematorium and on to some posh hotel after that? He'll get overtired and work himself up into a state.'

'He can sleep in the car, on the way there,' said Martha. Joe was now moaning and kicking at her knee. He was slipping down in her arms, so she hoisted him up again, trying to balance him against one hip.

'Being around all those strange people is also going to upset him,' said Simon. He leant back against the worktop and folded his arms in front of his chest. 'It's the most ridiculous thing I've ever heard. Just book a carer to come in and look after him for the day. Call that agency we used the other week.'

'But it feels wrong not to have him there!' said Martha. She could feel tears welling up. 'She was his grandmother, Simon. He ought to be at her funeral.'

'Stop kidding yourself.' He was shaking his head at her now, sighing as he turned to stare out of the kitchen window. 'He didn't have a clue who she was, Martha, and he never would have done. He doesn't even know who we are.'

17

The hardest time was always first thing in the morning. As Joe's plaintive cries infiltrated her dreams and gradually dragged her away from them, Martha would open her eyes and find herself staring at the far wall of the bedroom, or at the ceiling, or at her bedside table. But wherever she looked, she saw her mother. Sometimes she saw Judith sitting in her garden, laughing; sometimes she was opening the front door of the bungalow, a smile spreading across her face; sometimes she was glancing over the top of her reading glasses, pen in hand, sharing a clue from a crossword. But, most often, she was lying on her back – still and grey – in the hospital bed, her hands folded across her chest, her cheeks hollowed, the parting in her hair just slightly off from where it ought to be.

The knowledge of what had happened would then hit Martha again. While sleep allowed her mind to block it out temporarily, each new morning she had to reaccustom herself to the fact of her mother's death. It was getting easier: the sharp stab of grief had now turned into a dull ache. But it would be a long time before it went away completely – if it ever did.

You need to be kind to yourself, she remembered Claudia

saying. That was true, and she'd read enough articles about bereavement to know she had to face up to the grief, not bury it away and pretend it wasn't happening. She was also sure it would help to talk about it, and last night had tried to start a conversation with Simon.

'Do you remember the first time you met her?' she'd asked, as she served up the fish pie, steaming hot from the oven.

'Who?' he said, not looking up from the open newspaper on the breakfast bar.

'Mum, of course! Do you remember that Sunday, when we drove down to have lunch with her for the first time?'

'Yes, of course,' said Simon. 'Why wouldn't I remember it?'

'No reason,' she said, as she put the plate in front of him. 'I was just thinking about it, that's all.' She wanted him to nod and remember it with her. To smile, as he thought back to how nervous they'd both been, to reminisce about how he'd politely ploughed his way through a plateful of roast lamb, which he hated, as she sat across the table, mortified she'd forgotten to mention that to Judith. She didn't care if he claimed not to remember much about that first visit; she was just desperate for him to exchange a few words with her. But he pulled the plate towards him and began to stab the pieces of fish with his fork.

On the drive down to Surrey, that Sunday nine years ago, Simon had pulled into a garage around the corner from Judith's bungalow, planting a kiss on Martha's cheek before running in to buy a bunch of flowers. Through the plate glass window, she could see him fumbling with the change at the counter before dropping it, then crouching down and reaching out for coins as they rolled across the floor, ricocheting off other customers' feet. He was clearly apologising as he ducked in and out, then a woman bent down to help and they banged foreheads. Martha had laughed out loud as she watched, her heart swollen with love for this funny, handsome man. She was so lucky to have him.

They had both been ridiculously nervous about that first meeting with Judith. They'd been together for two months and the relationship still felt exciting and slightly illicit. Part of Martha wanted to delay any formal family introductions and keep this gorgeous man to herself. But she had already been invited to Simon's parents for an awkward, stilted Sunday lunch, and it seemed only fair that she reciprocate.

Judith had opened the door with the usual wide smile on her face and had been warm and welcoming. She'd guessed how important this visit was, even though Martha had tried to play it down. They had discussed politics, climate change and television documentaries. Simon had talked about his work; Judith had told him stories about Martha's childhood that made her cringe: 'Mum, stop!' she'd said, burying her blushing face in her hands. 'I'm sure I never did that.'

Over lunch there was much reminiscing about the years they'd spent in the former family home, and how different their lives had been in the old days. Simon had encouraged it; he couldn't hear enough about Martha's life before him. At one point, Judith had told a story about Martha's father, something about a bonfire he'd lit in the garden, which had roared out of control and set fire to a neighbour's apple tree. 'They were furious!' she said. 'They threatened to report us to the council, take us to court. All over a few burnt apples!' Then, her voice suddenly softer and lower, she said, 'I miss him so much. Every single day it's agony being here without him.'

Martha had been shocked by the rawness of her mother's words, the brutality of the pain which still lay behind them. By then, her mother had been widowed for a year, and Martha had presumed her life was almost back on an even keel. It wasn't as if she and Judith had never discussed her father's death; they talked about little else for a long time, and thought about little else for even longer. But, as the weeks and months went by, there were fewer of those conversations, and Judith seemed resilient in her grief – always most concerned about how her children were coping with the loss of their father. 'Losing a parent is cruel,' she used to say. 'Even when you're a grown-up.'

'The loneliness must be awful,' Simon had said, later that Sunday evening, as they lay next to each other in the cramped bedroom of his shared flat. 'When you lose the person you've spent most of your adult life with.'

Martha had nodded, burrowing her face into his chest, wrapping her arms more tightly around him. But she couldn't really imagine it. With a busy social life, a gang of close friends, and now this exciting new relationship, loneliness wasn't something she'd been able to fully comprehend. When it happened to her years later, after Joe's birth, the circumstances were so different that she never compared her own situation with what her mother had gone through.

But the loneliness she was experiencing now was worse than that. Because now, not only had she lost her mother, but it also seemed as if she didn't even have Simon. The love and mutual respect between them hadn't dimmed during the first few months of Joe's life. Their baby had been so longed for and the whole process so exciting, that even the trauma of the birth and the increasingly bad news they were given by specialists during the weeks afterwards, couldn't dent their optimism. They knew their future no longer looked as golden, but, at first, they worked hard to make everything right again. They were a team; they would deal with this together.

Martha wasn't sure when that began to change, but by the time Joe turned one, the lustre was wearing off everything: her marriage, her child, their future. She and Simon were both exhausted and resentful that this had happened to them, and took out their frustration on each other. She didn't really know how he was feeling, but guessed that, like her, he was fighting a growing sense of terror at what might lie ahead, combined with fury and bitterness at the gradual realisation that their lives weren't going to pan out in the way they'd expected.

Now Joe was nearly five, and she had no idea how they'd got to this point: when they'd reached the stage where she and Simon had stopped pulling together and had begun, instead, to rip their own marriage apart. He bent his head over his fish pie, chasing the last pieces around the plate with a fork, still with one eye on a story he was reading in the newspaper open on the breakfast bar in front of him. It seemed like she would have to face this latest crisis on her own.

18

It was strange being here again. The bungalow smelt musty and dust was already collecting on the surfaces. Despite what Alice had said, it looked like Sharon had decided there was no point continuing to clean an empty house. Or maybe she was just doing the bare minimum, thinking no one would be there to check up on her.

Martha knew it was petty, but in a way she was glad she'd turned up without warning today: at least she now had a proper idea about what the woman was – and wasn't – doing. On the other hand, with estate agents due to visit in half an hour, it was disappointing the bungalow didn't look its best. Martha should have called Alice to tell her she'd be back – how stupid not to think about that. But there were so many things she was supposed to be doing: the lists – neatly typed up on her laptop as well as scribbled on numerous scraps of paper – seemed endless and insurmountable.

This time last week, she'd had no idea what lay ahead. It had been a warm Saturday afternoon and she had been in the garden at home with Joe, while Simon mowed the grass down at the far end. Joe had been stretched out on his back on a picnic blanket and Martha had picked leggy dandelions, tickling her boy's cheeks with the soft downy heads, before blowing hard enough to release the parachute-like seeds into the air, stroking his face as he watched them float above his head. That evening she and Simon had gone to Claudia and Adam's for that rather awkward dinner party. It hadn't been the greatest night out, but it had still been such a relief to be doing something normal.

Incredible how so much had changed in such a short space of time.

And now here she was, back at the bungalow already, waiting to find out how much money they might make on it. It was all so bloody mercenary. Martha hadn't even thought about getting the place valued yet, but – again – Patrick had taken matters out of her hands. He'd texted:

Two estate agents are visiting on Saturday. Midday and 2pm, so you'll have time to get down there.

She'd sworn out loud as she read the text. Even for Patrick, this was unbelievable. She texted back:

Why can't you go?

She'd stared at the blank phone screen for a couple of minutes, but he didn't reply. This was crazy: he lived so much closer than she did, and she had childcare to sort out, whereas he could presumably rely on Helen to deal with the children. Martha had wondered if she might hear from her sister-in-law after the harrowing events of the last few days, but it was no surprise when she didn't. The two of them had never been close, and Patrick hardly visited his own mother, so there was no reason why his wife should feel obliged to get involved.

Fed up with waiting for a reply to her text, Martha had tried to call. 'Patrick,' she said, as his voice asked her to leave a message. 'How dare you arrange this without asking me! It's such a long way for me to go, and didn't it occur to you that I may have plans? I don't know what Simon's doing on Saturday, he might not be able to look after Joe. Honestly, this is really unfair!'

Two hours later, another text pinged in.

In Paris until Sunday.

She had thrown her phone onto the purple sofa and screamed into the vast, echoing space of her kitchen.

But, of course, Martha did what Patrick had presumed she would do, and made all the necessary arrangements so she could come back down to Surrey today. She filled the kettle and, while it boiled, went around throwing open windows and flicking through the post Alice had left piled neatly on the hall table. The girl was right, there was nothing important amongst it. Martha threw away the circulars and put the rest in her bag. In Judith's bedroom, she stood in front of the open wardrobe, looking at the rows of clothes hanging from the rail, the pairs of shoes neatly lined up on the shelves below. What was she supposed to do with all this stuff? Most of it could go to a charity shop, but some items were so old or worn, it seemed insulting to expect anyone else would want them. She knelt down and pulled out an ancient pair of black court shoes, the leather tough and unyielding, moulded to the shape of Judith's feet. They were her mother's favourite shoes, the only ones she ever seemed to wear when she went out. She had worn them to Martha's graduation, more than twenty years ago, even though she'd bought herself a pair that went with her blue outfit.

'These are comfortable,' she'd said, when Martha asked

what had happened to the new ones. 'I don't care if they don't look as smart, my feet will thank me for it later.'

Martha sat down on the edge of the bed. There was a book on the bedside table, with a pair of reading glasses balanced on top of it: *The Testaments* by Margaret Atwood. Martha had read that herself last year; why had they never spoken about books they'd enjoyed? She felt a pang, as if she'd swallowed a stone and the sharp edges were digging into her stomach. There was so much she was going to miss about her mother, so many things they would never now get the chance to share.

As she picked up the paperback, a bookmark which had been between the pages fell onto the floor. Leaning down to pick it up, she saw it was home-made: a piece of white card with a ribbon threaded through a hole in the bottom and, above it, a child's drawing of some kind of animal. There were words written across the card as well, the characters spiky and uneven: *Nippa's Granny buks.*

Martha had no idea what this was. She turned the bookmark over and saw more writing: *lov Gracie xx*

Alice's little girl must have made this. She looked at the drawing again – if you were being generous, you could possibly guess it was a dog, although it only had three legs.

She slid the bookmark back between the pages and put the paperback on the bedside table. Judith must have known Gracie very well. Why hadn't this occurred to Martha before? How stupid of her. Obviously, if her mother saw a lot of Alice, then she would know her daughter. But thinking about the girl being here, in this house, caused a strange pulling sensation in Martha's gut. She pictured the child running down the hall and perching beside Judith in the upright armchairs in the sitting room, swinging her legs and showing her the bookmark she'd made for her. She imagined Judith clapping her hands together and exclaiming with joy as she looked at the drawing of what was presumably meant to be Nipper.

Martha stood up suddenly, marching out of the room and slamming the door shut behind her. It had all been so bloody cosy: Alice and her daughter spending time with Judith, taking care of her dog, giving her the sort of handmade presents she would never have received from her own grandson. She went into the sitting room and picked up the photo of Judith with the little girl on her lap. Gracie; of course this was Gracie. Now that she looked more closely, she could see it had been taken here, in the back garden. There was a pounding in her ears. It really was a lovely picture: Judith looked so happy and the little blonde girl was gorgeous.

Martha walked into the kitchen and pulled open the back door, her breath coming in shallow rasps. Without letting herself stop to think, she raised her arm and threw the photo frame onto the patio, the glass shattering as it hit the stone. Sunlight glinted off the photo as it lay amongst the broken pieces of wooden frame.

'You all right over there?'

Martha jumped and looked across to where she could just see eyes and a thatch of grey hair above the top of the fence. It was Judith's neighbour; Martha couldn't remember what his name was, he'd only moved in a couple of months ago. 'Yes! Fine, thank you. I just dropped something,' she said. 'Sorry to disturb you.'

She knelt down and began gathering the bits of frame together and picking up the larger shards of glass. It felt like someone was banging on her skull with drumsticks. She lifted up the lid of the nearby dustbin and threw everything inside, then went back into the kitchen and poured herself a glass of water, standing at the sink while she drank it, aware her hand was trembling.

Patrick was right. Claudia too. None of this was fair. Whatever their mother had been thinking, her actions weren't moral or justifiable.

The sheet of pale blue paper was still in Martha's coat pocket, folded into a small square, slightly worn at the edges where she'd run her fingers across it endless times. Now she pulled it out and walked into the bathroom, lifting up the toilet seat and beginning to rip the paper into shreds, smaller and smaller as they fell out of her hands and floated around in the bowl. She pushed down the handle, once, twice, three times, until all the evidence was gone and the bowl was empty. Then she slammed down the lid, sat on it, put her head in her hands and wept.

At exactly midday, there was a loud knock on the front door. 'Jeff Daniels from Moretons,' said the man, stretching out his hand. 'Sorry for your loss.' He didn't sound particularly sorry. What a stupid phrase anyway; her mother wasn't lost. That made it sound as if Judith had absent-mindedly taken the wrong turning when she wandered out of a shopping centre. Martha told herself to stop being oversensitive; it didn't matter, the man was just being polite. She smiled tightly as she shook his hand, and opened her mouth to continue the conversation, but he had already walked past her into the bungalow.

As she showed him through the rooms, Martha straightened bed covers and plumped cushions, chatting to fill the silence, pointing out features she thought might appeal. 'I've always loved the view of the garden from here,' she said, as they walked into the kitchen. 'And the patio's a good size.' She could hear the desperation in her own voice. The bungalow looked even less appealing now a disinterested stranger was peering into its dark corners and noting down its unimpressive specifications.

'Quite a bit of updating needed in the kitchen and bathroom,' said Jeff Daniels, eventually. 'Might have to reflect that in the asking price.'

Martha nodded.

'Could also do with replacing some or all of these.' He ran a finger down the edge of a windowpane, where the seal was grey with mould and peeling away from the frame.

'I know there's some work to be done,' said Martha. 'But we thought there would be a demand for this sort of place. It's quite a popular road?'

The agent sniffed and shook his head, as he produced a tissue and wiped the dirt from the tip of his finger. 'There's never a shortage of properties like this,' he said. 'The turnover's too regular. That's what happens in an area where you've got a predominantly elderly population. They die or get moved into homes. I took on a bungalow just like this two days ago, and we already have a couple of others on our books.'

Martha stood at the front door and watched him striding down the street, his highly polished shoes clicking loudly against the pavement. He was on his phone, throwing back his head and laughing loudly, gesticulating with his free hand as he talked. Martha wanted to run after him, grab his sleeve and spin him back around so that he could see the fury in her face.

'This was somebody's life!' she imagined shrieking at him. 'Somebody's home! It's not just a bloody commodity.'

Although, sadly, that's exactly what it was. That was the reason Patrick had lined up the viewings, and it was why she'd been so keen to show off the bungalow at its best as the agent made his disdainful appraisal. She and Patrick needed to get a good price for it; Jeff Daniels wanted to earn as much commission as possible for the sale. There was no point in pretending anything else mattered.

19

She woke with a start, her heart pounding as her eyes adjusted to the darkness and she made out the outlines of the furniture on the other side of the room, the shadows thrown by the thin strip of light beneath the bedroom door. She must have had a nightmare, but could remember no details; there was just a vague sense of unease lurking at the edges of her mind about something she'd been about to see or do.

Then a wail came from along the hall: Joe. That's what had woken her. She threw back the duvet and grabbed her dressing gown, pulling it around herself as she tiptoed out of the bedroom and pulled the door closed behind her. Simon hated being woken in the night; he was useless and bad tempered if she ever needed his help with Joe, and the next day he would be bristling with resentment about his interrupted sleep.

'We both work, Simon,' she sometimes said. 'Why is it always me who gets up?'

'You're better at it,' he would say. 'You can cope with less sleep.'

They both knew that was rubbish. They both also knew she would always be the one to go and comfort their son in the night. She sometimes lay listening to Joe cry for half a minute or so, waiting to see if Simon would stir. He never did. Either he was a very deep sleeper or he was expert at bluffing it out: lying there motionless for as long as it took for her to drag herself out of bed.

Joe was on his side, kicking at the safety rail along the edge of his bed. She leant over to stroke his face but there were no tears, and the smell of urine stung her nostrils.

'God, Joe, not again.' She sighed. He wore nappies at night but they often leaked.

She hauled the boy out, changed his pyjamas and put a new sheet on the mattress, before settling him back into bed and stroking his cheek gently, watching enviously as he slipped back into sleep almost immediately. How she'd love to be able to switch off so easily.

She was now wide awake; that was the trouble with these disturbed nights, it was impossible to stop her mind from racing out of control. In the darkness, even normal fears and anxieties were magnified and, if there was something specific worrying her, everything about it would seem ten times worse in the lonely hours before dawn. There was always grief, which bubbled up with no warning when she was at her lowest ebb, knocking her sideways as it bombarded her with memories of her mother. She tried not to cry too much during the day, but gave into it at night, shutting herself in the spare room so Simon wouldn't hear, sobbing into a pillow until she was so drained, she could barely lift her head off the sodden pillowcase.

But right now, there was something even worse: regret at what she'd done to her mother's carefully handwritten note. She'd been so angry and upset when she'd realised how important Alice and Gracie had been to Judith, but if that piece of paper hadn't been in her coat pocket, maybe she would have calmed down and started to think rationally. Ripping it up and flushing it away had made her feel better for no more than a few seconds. Immediately afterwards, she was horrified at what she'd done.

She went downstairs now, switching on all the lights to banish the shadows. It was 4.30am – not worth going back to bed. Joe would be awake again in an hour. She filled the kettle and spooned hot chocolate powder into a mug. She mentally ran over what was planned for the next few days. She wasn't working today, so was meeting Claudia and her kids in the park, then tomorrow Joe was booked in for his taster day at Greenways and Clive had said she could have the day off to take him. Because of that, she'd decided to drive on to Surrey and had booked an appointment with Judith's solicitor, to read the will. Her stomach clenched at the thought of it. She and Patrick had arranged via text to meet beforehand, so she had no idea what he was thinking. But she was panicking about it. Standing in a queue at the supermarket, a couple of days ago, it had suddenly occurred to her that the solicitor might have a copy of her mother's handwritten codicil. A proper copy, signed, witnessed and legal.

She'd been so shocked at the thought, that she'd not heard the cheerful 'Good afternoon!' from the girl sitting behind the checkout. She hadn't put down her basket or unloaded the handful of items in there. She'd just stood, open-mouthed, looking through the plate glass window into the car park but not seeing anything in it, paralysed with horror.

'Are you all right?' The man behind had tapped her on the arm.

'Excuse me, can you put your items on the belt?' asked the girl.

Martha had stared at her, idiotically, before frantically unloading the milk, cheese and broccoli from her basket and fishing a ten-pound note out of her bag to pay for it.

Outside, walking towards her car, she'd felt sick. Of course, her mother would have done this whole thing properly. Why hadn't she and Patrick thought about this? The note she'd left in her dressing table drawer had just been a practice, something she'd scribbled for herself to get the wording right. At some stage after that she would have gone to see her solicitor and had the codicil officially added to her will.

If that was the case, it didn't matter what she'd done. Alice would get the house anyway.

Martha was desperate to speak to Patrick, to find out if the same thought had occurred to him. But every time she called, his mobile went to answerphone, and she didn't want to leave a message. What if someone else picked it up? Helen or one of the children? What she'd done was so appalling, Martha couldn't bear the thought of other people knowing about it. If only she hadn't told Claudia. She was a good friend and had been incredibly supportive, but she wished she'd kept her mouth shut.

20
_____

Sometimes Martha found it hard to like Barney – even though he was a sweet little boy, cheeky but funny with it, and polite when he needed to be. It wasn't Barney himself who made her so angry – just what he stood for.

They watched as he ran across to the slide and started to haul himself up the steep ladder; he turned and waved at them when he got to the top, before launching himself down the other side, screaming in delight, his yellow T-shirt picked up by the wind and billowing towards his chin.

'Be careful!' called Claudia. But she didn't sound worried. She didn't need to be. Her normal, happy, healthy five-year-old was just doing what almost every other child his age would do.

'I'm going to go again!' he yelled as he scrambled off the bottom of the slide. 'Watch me, Mummy!'

'I'm watching!' called Claudia.

Martha turned away and fiddled with the arm of Joe's chair. It didn't need adjusting, but she loosened a screw underneath anyway, so that she could tighten it again.

Claudia had put Megan on the picnic blanket, but the

toddler was crawling towards the edge, pulling at the grass with her chubby fist and scattering blades across the blanket.

'So, were you happy with the valuations?' asked Claudia, opening a packet of biscuits and passing one to Martha. 'Come on, tell me how much you're going to get for it? I bet property is worth a small fortune in that part of Surrey, commuter belt and all that.'

'Probably not as much as you'd think,' said Martha. 'The agents only gave me a ballpark figure, we're waiting to get official letters from them.'

'Three quarters of a million at least, I'd reckon,' said Claudia. 'I know it's only a bungalow but there's usually potential for extending. A friend of mine lives near Caterham and she made a killing when she moved a couple of years ago.'

Martha swallowed down her irritation. It was no one else's business how much the agents had suggested they might get for the bungalow. She had always hated talking about money, but Claudia was the opposite. She had no qualms discussing how much Adam earned, what they'd paid for their house and their cars, how much she'd spent on the designer outfits in which she dressed Barney and Megan, and she expected reciprocation from her friends.

'Did you destroy that piece of paper?' Claudia carried on.

Martha nodded miserably.

'Good. It would have been awful if that girl got the house instead of you – it's a massive amount of money to miss out on. I just can't imagine how I'd deal with something like that. I'd be so angry.'

'You won't tell anyone, will you?' said Martha, hearing the desperation in her own voice. 'I feel like a real shit for doing that.'

'No, of course not!' said Claudia. 'You did the right thing.'

'I think I've just about got everything sorted for the funeral,' said Martha, desperate to change the subject. 'The order of service is being printed; I've called everyone I can think of to tell them the details. I went through Mum's address book, but there may be other friends she knew locally who weren't in there. It's hard living so far away: I'm realising now that I didn't know much about her life.'

'Can you ask that dog walking girl? She must know more about what your mother did – the people she used to see?'

'Yes, I will do,' said Martha.

She had no intention of discussing this with Alice. The girl probably did know a great deal about Judith's routines and her group of local friends. She had been in and out of the bungalow every day for the last two years and, although she'd initially just been someone who was paid to do a job, that had clearly changed. *We'd been planning a trip out to the cinema at the end of the week*, Martha heard her saying. *Judith was so looking forward to it.*

'I'm sure she'll have been telling people about the funeral anyway,' she said. 'Word will have got around.'

Was it just pride that was stopping her from asking for Alice's help? Only one thing mattered – that as many of her mother's friends as possible were at her funeral; it wasn't important how they'd heard about it, or whether the invitation had come from Martha herself. But still, she couldn't bring herself to discuss this with Alice. It would be another favour, yet another reason for her to feel indebted to that young girl.

'What will you do with Joe, when you're at the funeral?' Claudia asked. She leant across in front of Martha and ran her hand up Joe's arm. 'Hey gorgeous! How are you doing?'

Martha wanted to smack her hand away.

'I would offer to have him, you know I would,' Claudia carried on, leaning back again. 'But it's the logistics. I can get the wheelchair in the back of my car, but I'd need another seat for

Joe if I was going to pick him up from nursery. Plus, I'd need his kitchen chair. I'm not sure how he'd react to being at our house anyway.'

He wouldn't care, thought Martha. *He wouldn't know where the hell he was. So long as he gets fed when he's hungry and a sippy cup of water when he's thirsty, and a change of clothes when he wets himself.*

'Don't worry,' she said. 'I've booked a carer to come in and we'll just keep him at home that day. It seems easier. But thank you.'

It wasn't the first time Claudia had offered to look after Joe; to be fair, she always made the right noises when it came to helping out. But they both knew it wasn't practical. Looking after Joe was hard work and Claudia had her hands full with her own two. That was probably, thought Martha cynically, why her friend was so willing to offer help: she was well aware Martha would never be able to take her up on it.

'Adam's got a promotion at work,' Claudia was saying now. 'It came totally out of the blue. He had an appraisal last month and knew it went well, but they've given him the whole south-west region to run now.'

'Great,' said Martha. 'Good for him.'

'It's a lot more money and he's going to have an additional team working under him. Hopefully it won't mean longer hours, but we're going to see how things pan out...'

Martha couldn't be bothered to listen. Claudia didn't really need an audience anyway. On the picnic blanket in front of them, Megan was singing to herself, tracing the checked pattern with her finger. She was such a pretty little thing and, as she looked up and grinned, Martha smiled back at her. It was so much easier with Megan than Barney. Megan hadn't started at school, Megan wasn't learning to read and write, Megan wasn't going on playdates with new friends and learning to ride a bicycle and having swimming lessons and doing all the things Joe ought to have been doing by now.

When she was younger, Martha had always thought she'd have at least two children, maybe even three. She'd imagined herself as the mother of a little girl, not because she wanted a baby to dress in pink or spoil with dolls, it was more to do with the relationship they'd have in the future. She would bring up her girl to be independent and confident, though not cocky. They would be mother and daughter first and foremost, but as the years went by, she was sure they would also end up as best friends.

It was probably idealised nonsense: Martha had had a good relationship with her own mother, but they'd never been as close as that. But it didn't stop her expecting she'd produce a different sort of daughter. Except she'd never had the chance. In the months after Joe's birth, as the extent of his disability became ever more obvious, she and Simon stopped talking about the future, and having a second baby was never discussed. They were physically exhausted and emotionally drained by the endless battery of tests and scans and appointments. Referrals to different specialists raised their hopes temporarily, only for them to get dashed again when yet another consultant explained there was little that could be done. They had been given an official diagnosis of sorts when Joe was eighteen months – cerebral palsy and epilepsy as a result of trauma during birth – but even then, they were warned it was more complicated than that. The lack of oxygen had caused brain damage that was too extensive and wide-ranging to be contained in one easy explanation.

'He'll never be able to walk or talk,' one neurosurgeon had told them bluntly. 'He will never know you, or be aware of his surroundings.'

'But he smiles at me sometimes,' Martha had whispered. 'When he wakes up and sees me in the morning.'

The man had shaken his head, but his voice had softened. 'He's not reacting to you,' he said. 'It's the stimulus of light, when he opens his eyes.'

In her lowest moments, when the weight of it all seemed too much to bear, Martha wondered whether this was some kind of punishment. She didn't deserve another child. Not only would she and Simon be unable to cope, but what if it went wrong again? What if they brought a little brother or sister into the world for this poor son of theirs, but she produced a second imperfect child? She knew she wasn't being rational, and could never voice her fears to Simon. But that didn't matter, because he never mentioned them having another baby either.

By mid-afternoon, Barney was bored of the park and Megan had fallen asleep in her pushchair. They began to pack up, putting the remains of the picnic lunch back into Tupperware boxes, picking up stray shoes, shaking out the blanket and rolling it up. Joe was watching cartoons on the iPad, his eyes flicking backwards and forwards as the brightly coloured figures streaked across the screen. Martha didn't bother to turn it off, he would only start to shriek if she did, and she couldn't face the judgemental stares she'd get from other parents in the park.

'Well, it's been great to see you,' said Claudia. 'Good luck with the solicitor's appointment – let's go out for a glass of wine that evening so you can tell me all about it?'

'Okay, I'll call you,' said Martha, leaning down to hug Barney then kiss the top of Megan's head. 'Take care, you lovely lot!'

She began to push Joe's wheelchair towards the wide gate at the edge of the park. She could hear Barney's chatter growing fainter as they walked away in the other direction. After a few seconds, she looked over her shoulder and saw they'd reached the railings along the far side: Barney was clutching the handle of the buggy, taking giant moon steps across the grass. She could hear the tinkle of his giggling, interspersed with the louder, lower sound of Claudia's own laughter.

The first time she'd heard that infectious deep belly laugh, she and Claudia had been lying side by side on their backs, practising relaxation techniques in their second antenatal class. Most of the other women there had husbands in tow, but that evening Simon was away for work and Martha couldn't now remember where Adam had been. Told to partner each other for the session, the two women had spent most of the time giggling and making fun of the overly intense NCT instructor, and Martha found herself immediately warming to this loud, funny woman whose bump was extending upwards beside hers. As they spilled out onto the pavement after the class, Claudia had suggested going to the pub around the corner. Nursing glasses of orange juice, they discovered their due dates were just a fortnight apart, so they were going to be on maternity leave at the same time.

Over the next few weeks, they compared birthing plans, shopped for baby clothes and stocked up on nappies and nipple pads. They sat in cafés, their hands on their burgeoning bellies, and planned how they'd meet up once the babies were born, take them to the park and sign up for newborn swimming sessions. There was talk of sharing childcare – maybe they could find a nanny to look after both children once they went back to work? These two unborn babies would grow up to be such close friends. They would go to toddler groups together, then playgroups, they might even share birthday parties. They would be in the same school year and would both go to the little primary in the next village.

After Joe was born, it had taken Martha a long time to accept that none of that planned future would now be possible. She still had Claudia as a friend, but the foundations of their relationship had shifted seismically. She wasn't sure Claudia ever realised quite how much.

The three of them had now gone out of the gate on the far side of the park, but Martha could still hear Barney's high-pitched voice travelling back to her on the wind. She turned around and leant forward over the top of the wheelchair, putting out her hand to stroke the side of Joe's face. 'Okay, let's get home now,' she said. 'We'll go to see Daddy and make you some tea.'

Joe didn't turn his head away from the colourful cartoon figures streaking across the screen of the iPad.

21

The solicitor was a strange looking little man: late fifties, with wisps of thin, grey hair splayed out from a centre parting, his watery eyes magnified behind a pair of round glasses which slid down his nose whenever he looked at his desk.

'We don't do many of these readings any more,' he said, flicking through a pile of papers. 'Most of our clients take copies of their wills.'

'Well, we couldn't find one,' said Patrick. He was slumped back in his chair, one leg carelessly crossed over the other, the foot in the air tapping in time to a rhythm none of them could hear.

'But some of our older clients do prefer to keep all their documents here, in our safe,' the man continued, pushing his glasses back up his nose. 'The sense of security is reassuring for that generation.'

'Is this going to take long?' said Patrick, looking at his watch. 'I've got to get back to the office.'

Martha wanted to smack him. He'd been in a foul mood when she picked him up from the station.

'Such a bloody waste of time,' he'd muttered as he got into the passenger side and reached for the seat belt. 'I don't know why they couldn't just tell us what was in the will over the phone. It's all going to be pretty basic. They'll probably charge us for this visit as well – even though they're not doing any work. God, I hate solicitors.'

'Patrick,' she said, turning to face him. 'Are you not worried about this?'

He looked confused. 'No. Why should I be?'

'What if Mum went to the solicitor to officially change her will?'

Surprise flickered across his face. He obviously hadn't thought about this possibility at all. 'Why would she have done that? She'd left the note; she clearly thought that was enough.' But there was uncertainty in his voice.

Martha herself had thought about little else. She'd slept badly last night, tossing and turning and imagining them sitting in an office being told that their mother had left her house to Alice. If it happened, she would have to act surprised, shocked – like she had been when they'd found the note. It wouldn't be hard; she was still reeling from it. But what then? How would they deal with that news? She'd felt physically sick this morning, unable to face eating any breakfast, so her stomach was now growling with hunger.

'Come on,' Patrick had said. 'Have you got the address? Let's hope it's quick – I have so much I need to be doing right now.'

She could never work out whether he repeatedly emphasised his own importance for her sake, or for his own. She didn't care where else he needed to be, or how many millions he was missing out on earning. But his indispensability was something Patrick felt the need to remind her of, every time they saw each other.

Martha had nowhere else she needed to be – although she

wanted to point out that the round trip to Surrey would take her even longer than usual today, since she'd gone via Greenways to deliver Joe. The timing had worked perfectly, and she hadn't minded the extra driving time. It was a relief to be on her own, even though her head was so full of what lay ahead.

Simon had been in a foul mood again earlier. She had expected him to be pleased when she told him she'd arranged to combine Joe's taster day with this solicitor's appointment, because it meant he wouldn't have to finish work early or factor Joe into his day, but he'd just grunted and nodded. She knew better than to expect gratitude, but it would have been nice to get a response that was a little less antagonistic. It seemed they could hardly speak to each other at the moment, without one or other of them storming out of the room.

'So, what we have here,' the solicitor was saying. 'Is the last will and testament of Mrs Judith Ann Cook, of Willow Road.'

Martha's heart was racing and she made herself take deep slow breaths, in and out. She focused on a framed certificate behind the solicitor's head. *Henry James Adams – Qualified to practise under the regulations of The Law Society of England and Wales.*

Patrick uncrossed his legs, then immediately crossed them again, the other way. Martha willed him not to interrupt.

'You are both named as executors by your mother, so it is your duty to make sure that her wishes are carried out in accordance with her will.'

Patrick sighed loudly and leant even further back in his chair, uncrossing his legs yet again and stretching them out along the floor in front of him so that the tips of his highly polished shoes were nearly touching the solicitor's desk.

'In this document, Mrs Cook states that she wishes to bequeath all her assets to her children, Patrick James Cook and

Martha Clare Evans.' He glanced up at them both over the top of his spectacles. 'Those assets include her property in Willow Road, and her savings and investments. She also wishes her daughter, Martha, to have all her jewellery and her son, Patrick, to have his father's collection of pewter tankards.'

Patrick snorted and put his face in his hands. Martha blushed as the solicitor looked back up at them again. How could Patrick be so rude? She kicked his ankle and glared at him, as he raised his eyes to the ceiling.

'Jesus!' he whispered. 'As if I'd really want that old crap.'

'There is also a small bequest of £500 to the RSPCA Animal Rescue Centre in Godstone,' said the solicitor.

'That's where she got Nipper,' Martha said. 'Her dog.'

'As I said, you are both named as executors, which is perfectly normal, even though you are also beneficiaries.' The solicitor put the piece of paper down on the desk in front of him.

'Well, that's great.' Patrick was standing up and adjusting the sleeves on his jacket. 'Many thanks, we appreciate your time.'

'Is that all?' said Martha, her voice slightly husky.

The man peered at her over the top of his glasses. 'That's the extent of the will itself, but I can obviously answer any questions you may have, in connection with how you go about fulfilling your mother's wishes.'

'No, no, that's fine. We're all good,' said Patrick, buttoning up his jacket.

She stood up, feeling she ought to apologise for his rudeness, but at the same time she was equally desperate to get out of this stifling room. 'So, there's nothing else in there that we need to know about?' she asked. Patrick was glaring at her from the door.

'No, Mrs Evans. You will now need to apply for a grant of probate to carry out your mother's wishes. You can do that yourselves or we can do it for you. I can give you a list of our charges, if you'd like.'

'That's fine, thank you,' said Patrick. 'Come on, Martha. Let's get out of here.'

22

'What was that all about?' he said, as they walked to the car. He was striding ahead, Martha running to catch up with him. 'God, you were almost begging him to tell you there was something else he hadn't mentioned.'

'I just couldn't believe it,' panted Martha. 'I'd been so worried we were going to find out Mum had told someone else about that codicil. I thought he might have a copy.'

'Well, he didn't, so that's the end of it,' said Patrick. 'And a bloody good thing too. I need whatever we can get from the sale of that house. We'll lose a couple of hundred thousand in death duties anyway, possibly more if she's got savings, so it's not as if we'll just walk away with whatever the place is worth. You have no idea how much I have to pay out each year in school fees, plus there's the extra tuition and the transport. It's bloody thousands each term. I earn a decent whack, but that doesn't mean I'm not glad to get some help towards it.'

Martha started the engine and pulled out of the car park. She didn't say anything; she didn't think he wanted her opinion.

'Helen was livid when I told her about Mum's note and the fact that the house might have gone to that girl,' he went on.

'She's planning for us to go to Antigua before the kids go back to school in the autumn. There's a spa resort on the south-east coast, which she's taken a bit of a fancy to.'

'Wow, lucky you,' muttered Martha. 'I'm sure you'd have been able to afford to do that anyway.'

'Well probably, but that's not the point,' said Patrick, missing the sarcasm. 'It's a question of what's right. This is our inheritance.'

Now that they were away from the solicitor's office, Martha was feeling even worse than before. She'd been running on adrenalin all morning and, although relief had flooded through her when she realised Judith hadn't officially changed her will, her head was now thumping and she desperately needed to eat something.

'I still can't understand what she must have been thinking,' Patrick was saying. 'I mean, how did she imagine we would react to her leaving her house to that girl? The whole thing is crazy.'

A few minutes later, as she watched him walk away from the car towards the station, already putting his mobile to his ear, Martha wished she could share his sense of righteousness. But it was easier for him to be like that: he had no guilt to deal with because he'd made sure she was the one who'd destroyed the handwritten codicil.

She didn't even make it as far as the motorway before she started to cry. Pulling over into the car park beside a children's playground, she sat staring through the windscreen at the fencing in front of her, the weathered grain of the wood swirling and blurring as the tears rolled down her cheeks.

The whole mess should be over now, but how was she ever going to be able to put it behind her? Why had her mother done this? She'd clearly grown very fond of Alice, but what had turned this from an arrangement about walking the dog into such a firm friendship that she wanted to give the girl her home?

On paper the two women were an unlikely match, even if you didn't count the fifty-year age difference.

Judith had been a secondary school teacher all her life and was bright and articulate; brought up in the home counties, she had been well-spoken, with old-fashioned attitudes towards modern society which sometimes made Martha cringe with embarrassment.

Alice came from a broken home and had left school at sixteen, falling pregnant shortly afterwards. She had no qualifications and no prospects. She must have reminded Judith of some of the girls she'd taught over the years at the secondary school where she'd been head of history for two decades – the handful who refused to work hard to secure their own futures, preferring instead to run wild and drop out. Judith always held up these girls as bad examples when Martha moaned about school or threw a teenage hissy fit about homework. 'You've got so much potential!' she would say. 'Don't throw everything away at this stage in your life. You'll never be able to make it up later on.'

But that was exactly what Alice had done, so surely it would have frustrated and irritated Judith? This girl was the antithesis of everything she had encouraged her own daughter to be. Yet, despite their differences, the two women had become good friends.

Right now, Martha was finding it hard to feel anything for Alice, apart from jealousy. But, in spite of herself, she could see what her mother had liked about the girl: she was friendly and open, and seemed to have a good sense of humour. She was also a hard worker and had clearly loved both Nipper and his mistress. Martha remembered the girl's shock at hearing the news; her tear-streaked face as she left the bungalow.

She suddenly felt as if she might be sick. She got out of the car and walked towards the entrance to the playground, taking deep breaths and wiping the tears off her face with her sleeve. On the other side of the low fence, a young man was pushing a toddler on a swing, the child squealing with delight as she flew backwards and forwards.

This wasn't really about Alice, though, was it? The girl was involved, but none of it was her fault. Judith was the one who had chosen a course of action which she must have known would hurt her children, even though it seemed so completely out of character. Martha knew her mother had loved her. She'd loved Joe as well. The fact that they lived a hundred miles apart, meant she didn't get to see her grandson as often as she would have liked, but that was only – Martha always reassured herself – because it was such hard work. Last summer she had taken Joe to Surrey for the day and the three of them had sat in the garden; Judith had made lunch and they had taken it in turns to try to feed the little boy, who'd been fractious and tired.

'Come on, darling,' her mother had said, putting a spoon up to his mouth. 'Just a little bit more.' He'd grunted and turned his head away, clamping shut his lips. As he began to wail, Martha had suggested they give up and let him drink milk from the sippy cup he'd had since he was a baby. She didn't want a scene.

'Sometimes it's easier to give in!' she'd said brightly, fishing in her bag for the cup and putting it up to Joe's mouth. She had noticed the cloud of doubt crossing Judith's face, the slight disapproval in her mother's voice when she started to take the lunch things back into the house. 'Well, if you're sure? You know him best.'

She had prickled at that. Yes, she did know her son best. She could read his moods and anticipate how he was going to react in almost every situation. She could pick up on changes in the way he was sitting, or how he was holding his head, and predict what that might mean. She knew how to look after Joe better than anyone else in the world. Better even than Simon. She'd ignored the implicit criticism in Judith's voice that day because, actually, how could anyone else understand what it meant to dedicate your life to caring for a severely disabled child? No one – even her own mother – had the right to suggest Martha wasn't doing the very best she could.

'How could you be so bloody cruel?' Martha screamed now, into the playground.

The man with the toddler turned and stared at her. He looked terrified.

'I'm not talking to you!' Martha yelled. 'I'm talking to my dead mother!'

The man grabbed the chain of the swing and pulled it to a halt, taking his protesting child by the arm and moving away towards the far side of the play area.

'I hate you!' Martha screamed into the air.

But she didn't. Of course she didn't. Her mother had been one of the three people she loved most in the world. 'I'm sorry,' she whispered. 'I just don't understand.'

The man was now hoisting his toddler up onto a roundabout, still casting nervous glances back at Martha. As she turned and walked towards her car, she realised there was now no need to mention any of this to Simon. The codicil had been destroyed and she was going to inherit her share of her mother's estate, which they could put towards the cost of sending Joe to Greenways, if he was offered a place.

Thinking about Joe made her heart jolt; she'd been so wrapped up in what was going on today, her son hadn't even crossed her mind for the last couple of hours. *Please let the taster session be going well.*

As she stood beside her car, Martha noticed a scrape along the front wing; she was certain that hadn't been there before. Someone must have parked too close while they were in the solicitor's office. Damn, this was all she needed right now. Back in the car, she blew her nose and pulled back her hair into a messy ponytail. None of this was helping: screaming in a children's playground wasn't going to make her feel any better.

She despised herself for it, but couldn't stop thinking about the money. Judith had known it cost a lot for Martha and Simon to look after Joe and had always been sympathetic. When Joe was two, she'd been staying with them for the weekend, and Martha had been looking online at options for his first wheelchair, telling her mother about the different specifications, and the modifications they'd have to request to suit Joe's needs.

'Let me pay for this,' Judith had said. 'I would have loved to buy him a little bike, when he was old enough for one of those. So, if I can't do that, why don't you let me buy the wheelchair?'

Looking back now, Martha could see how kindly the offer was meant. But at the time, she'd taken offence. She didn't hear the words themselves, more the disappointment that lay beneath them: Judith knew her grandson would never be able to do all the things other children took for granted.

'Thank you, but it's fine,' she'd snapped. 'We can manage.' They could; but that wasn't the point. She should have seen Judith's offer for what it was, and accepted it graciously. She should have allowed her mother to find an almost imperceptible chink in her own emotional armour, and gently push her way through it.

It hadn't really occurred to her before, quite how much her relationship with Judith had changed over the last few years: a distance had grown between them, but it had stretched itself out so slowly that Martha hadn't been aware of it. On her thirtieth birthday, she and her mother had met in London and spent the morning wandering around the shops, followed by a boozy lunch in a bistro on the South Bank. Afterwards, she had walked Judith to Waterloo, their arms linked, both weighed down by shopping bags, laughing about the stuffy woman who'd served them in Hobbs. Three years ago, on her fortieth birthday, neither of them had suggested doing anything similar. Judith had sent a card with a generous cheque inside, and left a message on Martha's mobile, saying she hoped she'd have a lovely day.

When had they become so formal with each other, afraid of saying or doing the wrong thing? Martha had no idea, but she suspected it was mostly her fault. Since having Joe, she knew she'd become less tolerant of her own mother. Surely the opposite should have been the case: when she became a mother herself, it ought to have brought them closer? Maybe it would have done, if Joe had been healthy and if Martha had had the chance to be the sort of parent she'd longed to be. Maybe, maybe, maybe. It was pointless wishing for a different past – or wishing she'd handled the past in a different way. But she felt like such a failure.

The man and his daughter were now leaving the playground, the little girl pulling on his hand and jumping up and down as they walked towards the gate. He stopped and turned to speak to her. It looked like he was getting cross with her. Martha wanted to wind down the window and shout across: tell him how lucky he was to have a child who pulled and jumped and misbehaved. But she'd done enough shouting for one day.

She started the engine, but still didn't have the energy to start driving. Her body ached; she couldn't remember feeling this drained since she was pregnant, when it had sometimes been an effort to keep her eyes open in the middle of the day.

Judith must have believed both her children were doing so well for themselves that they didn't need her help. Patrick certainly took every opportunity to brag about his job, his earning power and his hefty bonus. Martha wasn't guilty of doing this; she'd never been the sort of person to boast. But maybe this wasn't just about money. It had always been a matter of pride that she didn't tell Judith, or anyone else, how much they were struggling emotionally and how hard it was just to deal with the relentless daily grind.

She didn't care about keeping up appearances; it was the pity that was so hard to bear. If Judith or any of Martha's friends knew she was struggling to deal with the less than perfect lot life had dealt her, it would have been yet another item they could add to the list of 'reasons to feel sorry for Martha'. She'd had enough of other people's pity when Joe was born; in the intervening five years, life had been about getting on and dealing with all the shit — sending out the message that she was fine and didn't need anyone to feel sorry for her.

Maybe she should have let down her guard every now and then – at least to her own mother – and admitted how bloody awful her life was. Admitted she was only human.

23

Claudia came back to the table with a bottle of wine in one hand, two glasses in the other.

'I said I only wanted one small glass!' said Martha, moving her bag onto the floor. 'I really can't be late back; I've hardly seen Simon recently.'

'Forget Simon,' said Claudia. 'You need a night out. And you need a proper drink.' She set the glasses down and sloshed wine into them. 'Right, here you go. Happy days!'

Martha picked up a glass and clinked it against her friend's. 'Happy days,' she echoed. The wine was great: dry and perfectly chilled. The first mouthful slid down her throat and she could feel the tension ebbing away as the alcohol trickled through her body. She'd been drinking too much recently, but life had been so stressful. She felt guilty every time she opened the fridge and reached in for another bottle. But she would then remind herself that nothing was normal right now. Her mother had died: she was going through a traumatic experience, and the occasional glass of wine wouldn't do her any harm. In fact, possibly the opposite – if drinking wine made life more bearable, surely it was a good thing? It's amazing how easy it is to lie to yourself about things like that.

'So how did it go with the solicitor?'

'It was fine, better than I'd expected,' said Martha. 'I was really worried about it. I'd convinced myself that Mum would have gone to see him to make that codicil official. I was so nervous, sitting there waiting for him to announce she was leaving the bungalow to Alice.'

She desperately needed to share this with someone. Simon should have been the one she confided in, but he was hardly around at the moment – the IT problems at work had been solved but there was an ongoing impact on everything else: clients were furious, projects had been delayed, Simon and his colleagues were up against it. When she did see him in the evenings, he was moody and short with her and took himself up to the office as soon as they'd eaten. In such a charged atmosphere, it hadn't been possible to find the right time to tell him about any of this. But she kept picturing herself back in the solicitor's office, Patrick's body rigid in the chair beside her, the solicitor's yellowing fingernails grasped around the sheet of paper.

'But he didn't?'

'No, it was all fine. That handwritten note was all there was.'

'How did you destroy it? You never told me the nitty-gritty,' said Claudia, leaning forward, her eyes wide with anticipation.

'Does it really matter?' asked Martha. Claudia wasn't the right person to be talking to about all this; she seemed to be enjoying it too much, turning the whole thing into a spectacle. She took another mouthful of wine.

'Yes, of course it does!' said Claudia, slopping more wine into their glasses. 'You had to make sure you did it properly, so go on – tell me! Did you burn it?'

'No,' said Martha, miserably. 'I ripped it up and flushed it down the loo.'

'Okay, well that's sensible,' said Claudia, nodding. 'Your mum obviously didn't know her note wasn't legal, otherwise she would have done it properly. I wonder if she was intending to do that? You know, go to see her solicitor at some stage and get him to change the will.'

'I have no idea what she was thinking,' shrugged Martha, 'it's irrelevant really. The bottom line is that she wanted to leave her bungalow to Alice, but Patrick and I have stopped that happening.'

'But you had to!' exclaimed Claudia. 'It's your house. The whole thing would have been appallingly unfair.'

'Well, there you go. It's done.' Martha really didn't want to talk about this anymore.

'So, when is it going on the market?'

'What?'

'The house, of course!' Claudia took a long sip of her wine. 'The sooner you get it listed the better. It's a good time of year to sell property, the garden's probably looking good and the weather's getting better.'

She was beginning to sound like Patrick.

'We aren't going to do anything straight away,' said Martha. 'We can't sell right now anyway.'

Claudia had picked up the bottle and was already topping up their glasses again, even though the levels had hardly gone down. 'Why can't you sell now?'

'There's so much to organise. We need to apply for probate and then I'll have to start sorting through all Mum's things.'

They sat in silence for a few seconds, staring at their glasses. Martha was suddenly aware of other conversations around them in the pub: the couple at the next table discussing their children, a group of men behind them talking about football. Had anyone else overheard what she'd been telling Claudia? Guilt stabbed at her again. But surely, what she and Patrick had done could never be used against them? The only people who would have cared were Alice – who didn't know about it – and Judith, who would never have any idea that her wishes wouldn't be carried out.

'Who is this girl?' asked Claudia, eventually. 'I mean, why did your mother like her so much?'

Martha shrugged. 'She's nice enough, but I don't understand how they came to be so close. It doesn't really matter now though, so there's no point me trying to work it out.'

Another lie. Alice, and her strange friendship with Judith, was constantly at the forefront of her mind. She was able to think about little else, and she always came to the same conclusion. Whatever it was that had drawn the two women together, it was more powerful than her own relationship with her mother. Judith hadn't just left her home to any dearly beloved friend – someone of her own age, whom she'd known for decades. She had left it to someone much younger than her – a woman she had probably started to look on as a surrogate daughter. So, it followed that the person who was the weakest link in this chain was Martha, Judith's own daughter, who presumably hadn't made the grade.

Claudia tipped the rest of the wine into their glasses. Martha was shocked to see they'd already worked their way through the bottle.

'Hey, Martha?'

She looked up, but for a second didn't recognise the man standing beside their table.

'It's Dan, from music therapy?'

'Oh yes! Sorry, I was miles away. How are you?'

'Great,' he nodded. 'It's my night of freedom. My parents

have Johnny for one night a week, to give me a break. I'm out with some friends.' He indicated a couple of men sitting round a table at the far end of the bar.

'Oh, that's good. I only came out for a quick glass of wine, but it stretched into a proper evening!' She looked across at Claudia, who was raising her eyebrows at her. 'This is my friend, Claudia.'

'Pleased to meet you,' said Dan, before turning back to Martha. 'We missed you at the session yesterday. I think we're going to be regulars there – Johnny really loves it.'

'Oh, that's good. Sorry, Joe and I couldn't make it; I had a solicitor's appointment...' She paused, suddenly realising she didn't want to say anything else about where she'd been. It would mean telling this virtual stranger that her mother had just died, injecting a whole new element into their relationship, which would involve explanations and sympathetic responses.

'Anyway, I don't want to interrupt your evening,' said Dan. 'I just saw you here and thought I'd say hello. Maybe see you next week?'

'Yes, that would be great,' smiled Martha. 'See you then.'

'Well, *bye* Dan!' whispered Claudia, as he walked away. 'Wow, who the hell is that?'

'Oh, he's just one of the parents from that music session I take Joe to,' said Martha. 'Stop staring, Claudia! You're so embarrassing.'

'How well do you know him?'

'Not well at all. I spoke to him for the first time, last week. He's got a very cute little boy, called Johnny.'

'He looks,' said Claudia, 'like someone it would be worth getting to know better. He's gorgeous, and he seems to be quite taken with you too.'

Martha looked across to the other side of the bar, where Dan had rejoined his two friends. He was clearly telling them where he'd met her, and both men turned, openly curious. Dan caught her eye, and grinned. She smiled back and, to her surprise, felt her stomach do a small flip.

'Don't be silly,' she said to Claudia. 'He's just being friendly.'

24

'Right, I've had them both in and I think we'll be better off going with Moretons,' said Patrick. 'Commission rates are the same, but they're a bigger outfit and have a slightly higher spend on advertising.'

Martha was loading the dishwasher, trying to work out how to fit a couple of large water glasses into the already packed tray.

'Hang on a minute,' she said. 'Slow down! I have no idea what you're talking about?' It was unusual for Patrick to call – he usually sent her one-line texts.

'For God's sake, Martha. Listen!' He sighed. 'I had the agents' valuations through for the bungalow earlier this week. Should have got onto it sooner, but I'm really up against it at the moment. I know we can't agree a sale until we've got probate, but it would be good to get things moving. They can take photographs, get the details ready.'

She slammed the dishwasher door shut. 'Do we need to push this through so quickly? It feels a bit obscene, Patrick, to be honest. We haven't even had the funeral yet and...'

'What's the point in hanging around?' he said. 'We need to get that house sold.'

'I suppose so.'

'No suppose about it. Once it's on the market they'll be able to handle all the viewings, obviously. But we'll need to get the place sorted first. All those bloody awful ornaments will have to go, plus the clutter in the kitchen, clothes, personal stuff.'

'What are you saying, Patrick? Are you expecting me to go down and sort everything out?'

'Well, I haven't got the time to do it,' he said, sounding astounded she'd even suggested it. 'I've got far too much on at work. The other thing is, I think we need to be very careful with that dog walking girl.'

'How do you mean, careful?'

'Watch what you say to her. There's a chance our bloody deranged mother may have told her what she'd done. We have no idea, because she didn't think it was important enough to tell her own children what she was planning to do.'

'Don't be ridiculous, Mum wasn't deranged,' said Martha. 'Quite the opposite!'

'Whatever. The fact is, she may well have had discussions with that girl about the whole thing. Maybe she didn't tell her exactly what she was planning, but I bet she hinted she was going to leave her something in her will. People rarely do things like this for purely altruistic reasons – they want gratitude; love and respect in return for the big favour they're doing someone.'

'But if Alice knew Mum was going to leave her something, why hasn't she shown any interest in hearing about it?' asked Martha.

'Oh, Martha,' sighed Patrick, 'you are so naïve. This girl has been scheming to get her hands on that bungalow. She's not stupid, she'll hang back and wait for us to go and talk to her about it, so she doesn't arouse suspicion. She knows there's no urgency, because it always takes weeks to sort out the formalities when someone dies.'

'Patrick, this is ridiculous,' she said. 'I don't think she had any idea what Mum was thinking of doing.'

'I'm just saying, be careful,' he said. 'Not everyone is as trusting or honest as you, Martha. We need to think about how we deal with this, if she demands to know what Mum left her in the will.'

After he'd rung off, Martha stood staring out into the garden, listening to the dishwasher motor hum gently as water poured into the machine.

It was hard to believe Alice knew anything about the will. Admittedly Martha had only met her on a handful of occasions, but she didn't agree with Patrick's assumption that the girl was hard-nosed and manipulative, and had persuaded Judith to sign away her house. It was the sort of thing that only happened in TV dramas; anyway, their mother hadn't been at all gullible. For the first time it occurred to her that Judith might have looked on Alice as some sort of project.

She could do so much with her life, she heard her mother saying, as she lay in the hospital bed. *I'm always telling her she needs to go back to college, get herself some qualifications.*

Maybe this was what it was all about? Judith had grown to love this young woman, who had so far not managed to do an awful lot with her life. She had wanted to give her some kind of kick-start. In which case, she had been trying to help Alice, not hold back Martha and Patrick.

But the bottom line was, with no explanation or warning, she had intended to disinherit her own children, and she must have known that would leave them confused and wounded. Or Martha would have been left feeling like that. Patrick would just have been furious. This hard edge to her brother's voice was nothing new – it had always been there, along with the arrogance and overbearing self-confidence. It had always made her feel uncomfortable, but now it was starting to scare her. It was ironic as well, she thought, that he'd told her she needed to be careful, because not everyone was as honest as she was. Honest was the very last thing Martha felt right now.

25

'When do you think we'll hear from them?' asked Simon. 'It sounds like he did fine on the taster day, so I can't understand why it's taking them so long to get back to us.'

Every time he mentioned Greenways, Martha's stomach lurched. It would be fantastic for Joe if they offered him a place, but the prospect of living here in this big empty house without her boy was making her feel physically sick. Every morning she woke to the sound of him calling out; every morning she wandered into his bedroom, rubbing the sleep from her eyes, dragging on her dressing gown; every morning she lifted him out of his bed and carried him downstairs to the kitchen. What would her life be like if she didn't need to do any of those things? She couldn't imagine it. She didn't want to.

'If they do give him a place, we'll need to sit down and sort out the finances as soon as possible,' Simon was saying. 'I know the basic fees are on the website, but I bet there will be extras on top of that. They'll probably want some kind of deposit to secure the place as well.'

Martha shrugged. She wanted to cry. How could he be so bloody cheerful at the prospect of their son going away?

'If they accept him, the timing will be great,' Simon said. 'I know it's been awful, about your mum, but the money you'll get from her estate will be really useful at the moment. Do you know how long probate is going to take? Has Patrick talked about doing it himself or are you going to use a solicitor?'

Martha shook her head; she didn't trust herself to speak. Part of her was so angry, she wanted to reach out and smack him across the face: she'd never hit anyone in her life, but his callousness was beyond hurtful. Her mother had died, but all he could think about was getting his hands on her money. She stared at him, wondering whether she even knew this man any more. How had they got to this stage? The Simon she'd met nine years ago had been thoughtful and sensitive – much more so than any of her previous boyfriends. She had loved that about him, but also teased him for it. 'You're too kind,' she'd said, after he gave a friend £400 to pay off gambling debts. 'You're a soft touch. People will take advantage.'

'Let them,' he'd said, leaning in to kiss her lightly on the tip of her nose. 'My friends and family matter to me. You can't go through life being hard-nosed and not helping anyone.'

Yet here was this same man, asking how long she thought it would be before they could get access to whatever his mother-in-law had squirrelled away in the bank.

Martha dropped her eyes to the table in front of her and used one thumbnail to pick at a loose flake of skin at the edge of the other. A bead of blood appeared as she ripped at the skin, swelling until it was heavy enough to trickle down the edge of her thumb.

'Jesus, Martha, that's disgusting. Stop it!' said Simon.

She shoved her hands down into her lap and looked back up at him. She so desperately wanted some support from this man. Why couldn't he understand the pressure she'd been under?

'You have no idea how hard all this has been,' she said, glaring at him.

It was crazy she hadn't told him what had been going on. But their whole relationship was crazy at the moment. They were still hardly speaking and an angry part of her had been glad to keep him out of the loop. In the last couple of weeks, her life had changed dramatically, but he'd been offhand, curt and distant. She knew things had been difficult at work – didn't she know it, that was all he seemed interested in talking about – but his behaviour had been cruel. She had needed Simon, but he hadn't been there for her.

'Of course I know how hard it's been!' he said. 'Losing a parent is dreadful. Don't make me out to be an insensitive monster.'

'It's not just that,' snapped Martha. 'God, if that was the only thing I'd had to deal with, it would be a breeze. There have been other problems.'

'What problems?' he said. 'What do you mean?'

They were sitting in the kitchen, the breakfast bar a physical barrier between them; the emotional barrier invisible, but so much more insurmountable.

'We found something at Mum's,' she said. She couldn't look at him, instead she stared back down at her hands, where the blood which had bubbled out from beside the thumbnail, was now smeared across the skin. 'She wrote a note, adding a codicil to her will leaving her house to Alice.'

There was silence; she looked up and saw incomprehension on his face. 'Who the hell's Alice?'

'The dog walker!'

He clearly still didn't understand.

'She's a girl who's been coming in to walk Nipper for the last year or so,' she said. *You would know that,* she was tempted to add, *if you ever listened to anything I said.* 'They'd obviously grown very close. So, Mum decided to leave her the bungalow.'

'Jesus, that's appalling!' Simon looked as shocked as he sounded. 'That place should go to you and Patrick, as her children. Did you know about this beforehand?'

Martha shook her head.

'So, when did you find out?'

'The day she died, when I met Patrick there. We found a note.'

'But...' he was now looking confused. 'Can she do that? Didn't you go to the solicitors? What happened there?'

'The solicitor just had her original will,' said Martha. 'In which she'd left everything to me and Patrick.'

He stared at her across the breakfast bar.

'We destroyed the note,' whispered Martha. She knew she should have started the sentence with 'I' not 'We'.

'My God,' said Simon. 'So, no one else knows about this, except you and Patrick?'

She nodded.

'Which means the original will stands?'

She nodded again. 'It's awful isn't it, what we've done? I know it's terrible, Simon. I know we should have respected her wishes and shown the note to the solicitor. Patrick said it wasn't a legal document because it hadn't been witnessed, but morally we should have disclosed it and done what Mum wanted.'

Simon got up and walked across to the big sliding glass doors leading onto the garden. He stood looking out, his arms crossed in front of him.

'If we'd done that,' Martha said, 'Alice would have inherited the house and we would have got Mum's savings and investments, which don't amount to much. Patrick says we would be the ones liable for Inheritance Tax, not Alice, so we would have ended up getting virtually nothing.'

'Why didn't you tell me about all this?' he turned towards her.

She glared back at him. 'I would have done, if you'd shown the slightest interest in what was happening. In case you haven't noticed, Simon, I've been having a really shitty time, with Mum being in hospital, then dying so suddenly. It's been so stressful and, and... shocking. I wanted to keep everything stable here for Joe, but I was rushing backwards and forwards...'

She'd been bottling up this anger and frustration for weeks: but now she'd started speaking, she could hardly keep up with the words as they came out of her mouth.

'And you've done fuck-all to help. Yes, I know you've taken time off work to collect Joe and you've been here with him on your own when I was in Surrey. Big bloody deal. That's your job; you're his father. But you've hardly spoken to me, or asked how I am. You haven't been interested in the funeral or any of the arrangements I've been making. I texted to ask what you thought about that reading, the other day. You didn't reply. You haven't even given me a bloody hug.'

Her voice broke on the last word, and she put her face into her hands and started to cry.

She felt his arm go around her and angrily shook it off, lifting her head from her hands and pulling herself round to face him. 'Stop it,' she yelled. 'Don't try to pretend you care.'

'Martha!'

'No! Get away from me! I hate you, Simon.'

She'd never said anything like that in her life. To anyone. She was shocked at the venom coming out of her mouth. It wasn't true, of course she didn't hate him. But he had been making everything so difficult, and the confusion and anger and hurt flooding through her were overwhelming. And now she'd said the words, she didn't know how to take them back again.

He put out his hands again and grabbed her shoulders.

'Martha, listen to me. I'm sorry, okay? I'm really sorry. I know I've been a shit. I've just had so much on at work recently and you've seemed quite distant.'

He was doing it again: throwing it all back at her. It was *her* fault because she'd been distant! She broke away, beating at his arms with her hands, not caring that she was lashing out like an animal; she wanted to batter and bruise his skin, not just to punish him but to leave physical evidence of her own misery. But when he grabbed her for the third time, she was suddenly dog-tired, as if there was no more fight left in her. She allowed herself to be pulled into his arms and laid her head against his shoulder, feeling the tears soak into the material of his shirt, her breath coming in jags as she cried. The smell of him was so familiar. Not just the fabric conditioner she always used or the shampoo they shared, but the underlying scent of his skin, the very essence of him.

'I'm sorry,' he said again, his voice echoing as she leant against his chest. 'I know I haven't been here for you.'

She kept her eyes closed, giving in to the sobs that were still shaking her body. After they'd been standing together for another minute, he pulled away slightly and she allowed herself to be led across to the sofa. Sinking into it, she dragged her sleeve across her eyes, wiping away the tears. Simon sat down next to her, his hand on her knee.

'You should have told me,' he said, more gently this time. 'This is such a big deal, Martha.'

She shrugged. She had no idea why she hadn't told him. Irrespective of how well or badly they'd been getting along, he had a right to know.

'I can't understand why she'd do this to you,' he carried on. 'It's not fair. Did she ever give you any hint that she was thinking about this?'

'Never.'

'You must have been so shocked.'

She nodded, but she couldn't remember that so much now, as the guilt. The heaviness in the pit of her stomach that she'd done something immoral to stop the worst happening and preserve her own self-interest.

'I mean, it's not as if you had a bad relationship with Judith,' Simon was now saying. 'You've always been really close – much closer than I ever was to my parents. The two of you got on so well. She was really supportive about Joe.'

She wanted him to stop talking. Her head was thumping and her eyes were itchy; she rubbed the palms of her hands into them.

'It's not just unfair; it's cruel,' Simon said. 'I don't know what was going on inside her head, but I can't understand why she'd do something like this to her own daughter. What's so special about this girl anyway?'

'Nothing. Everything. I don't know,' said Martha. 'I don't know why she tried to leave the house to Alice. I have no idea what my mother was thinking when she did this. I just know that it won't now happen, but I have to live with that.'

Simon nodded. 'I guess so.'

He had taken his hand off her knee and now sat back on the sofa. She looked at the place where his hand had been, willing him to put it back again, to throw his arm around her shoulder and pull her towards him. She needed him to say something to make her feel better about what she'd done. He didn't move. She turned to look at him as he stared out into the garden. He was shaking his head slowly from side to side, disbelief etched across his face.

'What a nightmare,' he muttered.

26

Martha stared at the phone screen, her mouth suddenly dry, her heart pounding. The ringtone sounded horribly loud in the otherwise quiet office. Her finger was trembling so much, that the call had stopped before she managed to hit the button to reject it.

She took a deep breath and put the phone back on her desk, but it started ringing again almost immediately.

'Aren't you going to answer that?' asked Janey.

'No,' said Martha.

'Might be someone important?'

'I know who it is,' she said.

'Ooh, intriguing. Who are you trying to avoid then?' Janey's laugh scraped across the four feet between them. 'Have you had a row with Simon?'

'Shut up, Janey, for fuck's sake,' said Martha, before she could stop herself.

She heard a sharp intake of breath from across the desk, but didn't look at Janey as she grabbed the ringing phone and ran down the corridor.

'Hello?' she said, pushing open the door to the ladies' toilets.

'Hi, Martha. It's Alice. I'm sorry to bother you.'

Martha was breathless; she wasn't sure if it was because she'd been running or because her heart was racing so hard, she could hear blood thundering in her ears. 'Alice!' she said, trying to sound surprised, as she locked herself into a cubicle.

There was a silence on the other end.

Martha shut her eyes and willed herself to calm down. This was ridiculous. 'I'm so sorry I haven't called you...' she started. 'I've been meaning to but it has been so busy here, what with organising the funeral and everything.'

'Oh, of course!' said Alice. 'I didn't expect you to call. I'm sorry to bother you.'

She sounded muted, almost distracted. Martha could hear noises in the background, the clanking of what might be plates or cutlery. Alice must be on a lunch break. Where did she work again? Martha couldn't remember, although Judith had probably told her.

'So, have you been okay?' That wasn't what she wanted to ask at all. *Do you know about all this?* she wanted to say. *Did my mother tell you she wanted to leave you her home?*

'I'm fine,' said Alice. 'How are you doing?'

'I'm okay. Well, as much as I can be. Is Nipper all right? I hope he's not been missing Mum too much.'

'He's great. Gracie loves having him with us, she plays with him and takes him out in the afternoons with me. He's getting a lot of attention. He's also having fun chewing the legs of the kitchen table, it's driving Mum mad!'

'Oh no, I'm sorry about that.' Martha was so glad she hadn't been forced to take the dog back home with her; God knows what damage he would have done to their furniture – and, if Nipper was constantly this destructive, Simon would have been even more foul-tempered than he was already. When Judith first brought the dog home from the rescue centre, he had chewed the skirting boards, leaving long splinters of wood sticking out from the white paintwork. Martha remembered exclaiming at the damage, but Judith hadn't seemed to mind.

'I'm just worried he'll cut his mouth,' she'd said. 'He'll grow out of it, he's still only a puppy!'

Three years on, it didn't sound as if Nipper had got past the chewing stage.

Someone came through the door to the toilets and went into the cubicle next to Martha. She squeezed her eyes shut and held her breath, feeling like a voyeur as she listened to whoever it was peeing into the silence.

'Nipper's the reason I'm calling, actually,' Alice was saying. 'I wanted to talk to you about this in person, but I wasn't sure when you'd be next coming down to sort through Judith's things.'

There was a rustling from the next-door cubicle, then the cistern clanked loudly as a rush of water swept down the toilet bowl. Martha didn't want to have to say anything. It would be weird if she suddenly started up in mid-conversation, having been silent all this time. Whoever was next door, opened the cubicle door, walked across the tiled floor and turned on the tap above the sink.

Luckily, Alice was still speaking. 'The thing is, this is a bit embarrassing. But I wondered if you'd be able to give me some money towards the cost of Nipper's food? I'm happy to have him living with us – we really love it, all of us. It's just that the food Judith used to buy for him is quite expensive; it costs about £15 a week. But I don't want to change his diet and try him on something cheaper.'

At last, the mystery woman finished washing her hands and the door to the outside corridor squeaked as she went back into the office. Martha's shoulders sagged in relief, and she realised she'd been holding her breath.

'I know you've had a lot to deal with, so I didn't want to bother you,' Alice was saying.

'Oh, Alice, I'm sorry!' Martha was mortified: she should have thought about this. 'Of course, we should be paying for that, and we should also be paying you to look after him for us. I can't believe I didn't think to talk to you about this. I'll send you a cheque to cover the food for a few weeks, with some extra on top for taking care of him. Or you can give me your bank account details, that's probably easier. Hang on, I haven't got a pen on me – can you text them to me?'

'Yes, of course,' said the girl. 'Sorry again.'

'Don't apologise, I'm the one who should have offered this. But it's all been a bit... well, you know.'

'Yeah,' said Alice. 'I really do. I know it's very hard, but I'm sure you're doing a great job, Martha. Judith would have been proud of you – she loved you all so much.'

Martha's relief at having been able to speak to the girl evaporated in a second. *Don't you dare tell me that my mother loved me!* she wanted to scream. *She wouldn't have done this if she'd really loved me!* The temptation to say the words out loud was almost overwhelming.

'Thanks,' she said, and hit the button to end the call.

She let herself out of the cubicle and went to the basin, splashing cold water on her face before drying it with a paper towel and taking deep breaths, staring at her reflection in the mirror. Now she had to go back to her desk and apologise to Janey.

'He's been in a bad mood all morning, but I'm not really sure what the problem is – am I, little man?'

Dan was sitting on the wall outside the hall, rocking Johnny in his lap. The boy had his thumb in his mouth and his eyes were closed, but his heels were kicking sharply against Dan's legs. They'd only managed to sit through half the music therapy session before Johnny's ear-piercing wails forced Dan to take him out.

Martha pushed Joe's wheelchair further along and sat on the wall beside them.

'I guess children are no different to adults, they have good days and bad days, and sometimes have no idea why they're feeling grumpy,' she said.

Dan smiled. 'True. I was in a really bad mood on Monday. I'd had a decent night's sleep, but I was out of sorts from the moment we got up. I felt like going around kicking doors and yelling at strangers.'

Martha laughed, partly in surprise: his honesty was refreshing. She often had days like that, but would never have admitted it to anyone. She wasn't sure why – probably because she didn't want to give the impression she wasn't coping. Maybe also because she was afraid of being judged. But right now, she wasn't judging Dan for what he'd just said; she understood exactly how he was feeling, and his frankness was endearing. 'That's such a good way of putting it,' she said. 'I know what you mean about kicking doors. Sometimes I want to throw my mug of tea at the wall.'

'Stand in the street and scream at the sky,' said Dan.

'Punch a hole in the wall,' she said.

'Listen to us.' He laughed. 'What appalling parents. We shouldn't be allowed out on our own, let alone left in charge of small children.'

The car park was nearly empty now and Suky came out of the hall and locked up.

'You two still here? How's Johnny?' She walked across to them. 'You missed some lovely singing. We did a new song this morning, "Five Little Speckled Frogs". I'm sure you'll enjoy that one next week.'

They watched as she walked across to her car and reversed out into the road, waving at them enthusiastically through the window.

'I'm already thinking we might murder "Five Little Speckled Frogs",' said Dan, shifting Johnny's weight on his lap. 'Come on then, sunshine, let's get you home for some lunch.'

'How was your drink last week?' asked Martha, suddenly reluctant to let him go. 'That's great you get to have a regular night out with your friends.'

'Yes, it's a lifeline sometimes,' said Dan. 'Good to have adult company.'

'Do you always go to the same pub?' Why had she asked that? What a stupid question; she felt herself blushing with embarrassment, but he didn't seem to notice.

'Mostly. It's handy for all of us. How about you? Do you often get to escape?'

'Every now and then,' she said. 'But Simon works long hours and he's out a lot in the evenings. At football, and with friends.'

Why had she mentioned Simon? It had come out automatically, but she wished it hadn't. Part of her wanted Dan to think she was looking after Joe on her own; a fellow single parent, struggling with the demands of a child who needed so much more intense and exhausting care than other children his age. But she was being ridiculous. There was no point pretending things were different: she was married, Joe had a father – albeit one who wasn't particularly hands-on at the moment.

Dan had strapped Johnny into his buggy. 'Right, we'll be off then. Great to see you, Martha.'

'You too, have a good week.' He smiled at her and she felt her heart do that silly little flip again. How old was he? Possibly a little younger than she was, late thirties. She couldn't stop thinking about him as she lifted Joe out of his wheelchair and strapped him into his car seat. She was still thinking about him as she drove through town and sat in traffic for nearly ten minutes, waiting to get past roadworks. By the time she parked outside the house, she had conjured up an entire relationship with this man she hardly knew. She imagined them going for walks with their boys, then chatting over a pizza – just the two of them in a local restaurant. She imagined sitting across from him in the pub where they'd seen each other last week, her asking about his life, him asking about hers. She pictured their hands resting on the table, the tips of their fingers almost close enough to reach out and touch.

She sat for a few seconds, listening to the engine tick as it cooled down. How pointless to let herself daydream about Dan. It was harmless fun, but none of it was real life and never would be. It didn't cheer her up, it just made her unhappy, and she didn't need that at the moment – Simon was doing a good enough job of making her feel bad. He had hardly said a word to her or Joe before he left for work this morning. He'd been in a foul mood all week, and she guessed it was due to the ongoing impact of the IT crisis. She ought to have been more sympathetic about all that, but she was tired too, and it didn't feel as if Simon was pulling his weight. Last night it had been his turn to bath Joe, but he'd been on his laptop in the kitchen, and didn't lift his eyes from the screen when she asked how long he'd be.

'I have no idea, Martha. I've got things I need to see to. I can't just drop everything because it's bath time.'

She had stood glaring at him, hands on her hips, but he'd ignored her. In the end, she had carried Joe upstairs herself, struggling on the last few steps as his toes knocked against her shins. She had laid him on the bathroom floor and began to peel off his T-shirt while water thundered into the bath beside them. Simon was being so selfish, so bloody lazy! She'd always done more than her fair share of the childcare, but things had got worse recently. Now she had to nag him to do the smallest thing, and he'd sigh and shake his head and reluctantly drag himself away from whatever he was engrossed in.

As she pulled Joe's arm from his T-shirt, he wriggled away from her and lashed out, catching her on the chin.

'Ow! That hurt!' Martha had sat back on her haunches, putting her hand to her face and realising his stubby little nails had drawn blood. Suddenly her eyes were itchy with tears and her face was screwing itself up in self-pity as she looked down at the red streak across her fingertip. She'd slumped back against the bath and wept, the sound of the running water covering her sobs as Joe lay beside her on his back, staring up at the ceiling. She couldn't tell whether his eyes were focusing on the trail of little silver stars she'd stuck up there for him to look at.

Today, with the sun shining and music therapy ticked off the list for another week, she told herself she must be more positive. It wasn't going to help any of them if she wallowed in self-pity; nor would it do any good if she started imagining herself living a different kind of life with a man she hardly knew. She must stop thinking about Dan. She must also stop giving Simon a hard time: he *was* working long hours and the stress was immense. She only worked three days a week, so it was fair that the bulk of the childcare and domestic drudgery fell on her shoulders. Plus, if she was being brutally honest, she was better at all of that.

Joe was now letting out a low whine that would soon turn into a howl. Martha grabbed her bag and opened the car door.

'Okay, lovely boy,' she said. 'Let's get you inside.'

28

The vicar's breath was rancid. Martha had to stop herself from physically recoiling as he stuck out his hand and leant towards her.

'So lovely to meet you at last,' he fumed. 'Although obviously the circumstances are far from ideal.'

She smiled and took his hand; the fingers were warm and limp, it was like squeezing a fistful of raw sausages.

'Is there anything you'd like to run through with me, before we start?' he asked.

'No, I think we're all ready,' she said. The entire service had been arranged via phone and email, which had made her feel guilty at the time. But now she was glad she hadn't made a special trip to Surrey, to get knocked for six by this man's appalling halitosis. She'd been dreading today, unable to sleep at night as she worried about the logistics. It was horrible to be here, but also a relief that the whole thing was finally underway.

The crematorium was beginning to fill up and Martha stood beside Patrick, outside the main entrance, smiling politely at people she didn't know, exclaiming every now and then as a familiar face appeared in front of her. Judith's goddaughter came, with a teenage girl who looked so like her, it was no surprise when she was introduced as her daughter. Then Martha's cousin, Lucy, arrived with her husband and Martha was startled at the emotion that overwhelmed her, as they hugged for the first time since her own wedding.

'You haven't changed,' said Lucy. 'You look wonderful. But isn't it sad that nowadays we only ever see each other at funerals?'

'I know,' said Martha. 'After this is over, we must get together for a proper catch-up.'

They would never do that, but it felt like the right thing to say.

As she turned around, she saw Alice and Sharon walking towards her.

'Hi!' she said, too brightly. 'Thanks for coming.'

Alice looked thinner than ever, clutching a black cardigan around her chest, her hair scraped back into the usual ponytail. There was something different about her today though, and Martha realised she was wearing make-up: black slicks at the edges of her eyes, mascara coating her lashes. It made her look older, yet strangely vulnerable.

'Nice to see you,' said Sharon. 'How are you holding up?' Her head was tilted to one side, in a way that was presumably meant to suggest sympathy, but which just made Martha irritated. Each time she met Sharon, she disliked her more.

'We're fine, thanks for coming. Do go through – there's an order of service just there, on the left.'

She turned away and looked beyond them, smiling more fully than she needed to at a couple she'd never met before, who were now walking up the steps. She was short of breath, her heart thumping. When Alice and Sharon had gone past, she glanced quickly after them, noticing there was a hole in the back of Alice's black tights and that she was in the same battered trainers she always wore when she came to walk the dog.

Patrick, standing beside her, had been talking to a man who used to work with Judith, a fellow teacher. He hadn't even glanced at Sharon or Alice, although he must have seen them walk past.

The vicar was signalling, suggesting they start. As Martha took her place in the front pew, between Simon and Patrick, she longed to turn around and take a proper look at the people behind her. It was gratifying so many were here, but she still hadn't worked out who most of them were. There were small groups who clearly knew each other – ladies from the WI, neighbours from Willow Road – and others who had come on their own, or arrived clutching the hand of a husband or wife who looked slightly awkward and probably hadn't a clue who Judith was.

Further along the pew, Patrick's wife, Helen, was sighing deeply and staring up at the ceiling. She had done little to conceal her boredom since earlier this morning, when they'd all gathered at the funeral directors to wait for the hearse. On the far side of her, their children were slumped back against the wooden seats; Max was eating a Crunchie, rustling the wrapper loudly and not bothering to close his mouth, while Samantha was playing games on a phone, giggling at the sound of tinny plinks and explosions. Martha wanted to grab it from her hands.

She flicked through the order of service, not really listening to what the vicar was saying. They sang a hymn, then there was a prayer. Then Patrick was getting up beside her, moving past Helen's neatly crossed legs and his fidgeting children, walking to the front of the crematorium, where he stood proprietorially beside Judith's coffin.

Martha had known she didn't want to say anything at the funeral. She couldn't have got up in front of all these people without bursting into tears, and today she needed to stay in control. But Patrick hadn't been fazed when she phoned to ask him. 'No problem,' he'd said. 'Just tell me what you want me to do.' Her suggestion that he might like to choose a reading himself, had produced a snort – she wasn't sure if it was laughter or derision. 'Not got the time, to be honest,' he'd said. 'Just find something suitable and I'll read it out.'

He did a good job; his eyes on the sheet of paper in his hands, his voice steady, pausing every now and then to look up and direct a few words into the room. Those gathered together here today would be full of admiration, thought Martha, bitterly. They'd think how well Judith's good-looking son had held himself together, would later discuss how proud his mother would have been of him on this most solemn of occasions.

By the time they filed out of the crematorium, the next funeral party was already waiting in the wings. Martha looked back and saw people lining up behind the plate glass windows, another monstrous black hearse pulling up outside the entrance. Sending the dearly departed on their way was like being on a particularly bleak production line.

The Hamilton Hotel, where they were holding the wake, was a half-hour drive away. She and Simon didn't speak in the car. They hadn't spoken much during the drive up to Surrey either, earlier this morning. Joe had been fractious when the carer, Jackie, arrived, and Simon had fed him breakfast while Martha showed the woman around and talked her through the lists she'd printed out. It had taken longer than planned and Martha – already feeling sick at the prospect of the day ahead – was jumpy and convinced she'd forgotten something. She went back into the house twice to make sure Jackie had noted particular points on the lists.

'It's not rocket science,' Simon had said, when they

eventually pulled out of the drive. 'You don't need to explain our life history to her.'

'I didn't!' Martha had said. 'But it's important she knows how we do things. Joe needs routine – it helps him stay calm. I hate leaving him with new people, you know that. I always worry more.'

'She'll cope,' Simon had said, dismissively. 'It's her job.'

Martha fumed and fought back tears as they sped down the dual carriageway. But by the time they got onto the motorway she'd stopped trying to pretend she wasn't crying. She had stared out of the side window as the grass verge flashed past, her cheeks damp, her eyes prickling and her nose running.

'It'll be fine,' Simon had said, glancing over at her, his tone softer. 'You'll feel better once today is over and done with.'

She nodded. But she wasn't crying about that.

They'd booked the largest of the hotel's meeting rooms. A waiter was hovering with a tray of Prosecco, and Martha took a glass and drank half of it immediately. She'd been intending to stick to water, but her resolve went of the window as soon as she saw the golden liquid bubbling in the polished flutes. Sod it, who cared? She didn't need to deprive herself of anything today.

There was a hubbub of chatter swelling around the room, a tinkle of laughter, voices rising as people greeted each other. Relief floated in the air, almost as palpable as the heady mixture of perfumes and aftershaves.

Martha moved through the room, smiling at people as she went, pointing towards the buffet table and indicating the food that needed to be eaten, resting a hand on an arm here, kissing a cool cheek there.

'I was in your mother's book group,' one elderly lady said. 'She was such a lovely lady! We did *The Testaments* just a few weeks ago, and Judith said it was one of her favourite books of all time – she told us some interesting facts about Margaret Atwood; she'd clearly read all her books.'

Martha thought back to the paperback she'd found on her mother's bedside table; the home-made bookmark with its drawing of a three-legged dog.

Turning away from the buffet table, she saw Sharon and Alice standing in a corner, their heads bent towards each other in conversation. They looked awkward and out of place. She shouldn't have been so abrupt with them earlier. She swapped her empty glass for a full one and walked over to them.

'Hello again,' she said.

'That was a nice service,' said Sharon. 'You've done her proud today, your mum. And all of this...' she gestured around her. 'Lovely venue, isn't it, Alice?'

The girl nodded. She looked drawn, riddled with unease.

'Must have cost a fortune,' Sharon went on. 'This is one of the nicest hotels in the area. Don't think I've ever been inside before, not the sort of place we'd usually get invited to.' She laughed and Martha bristled: the reference to money didn't feel accidental. Yet again, she wondered if these two women knew what Judith had been intending to do. But if so, why had they said nothing?

'How's Nipper?' she asked Alice, keen to change the subject.

'He's fine,' she said. 'Doing well. We can't stay long, actually. By the time we get back he'll have been on his own for a few hours.'

'Well, it's good to see you here,' said Martha. 'I appreciate you coming, I really do.'

'I'm glad to be here,' said Alice. 'It was important to me.'

Sharon was nodding, her head still tilted in faux sympathy.

'I liked the readings,' Alice went on. 'They were lovely. Very appropriate.'

'Thank you,' said Martha.

'It shows how well you knew her,' said Alice. 'Judith was a really clever lady. You could talk to her about almost anything and she'd have an opinion. She'd done so much travelling and she used to tell me such interesting things. Sometimes I'd come back from walking Nipper and we'd have a cup of tea together and chat for ages if Gracie didn't need picking up from playgroup.'

Martha could picture the two of them, perched in the upright chairs in Judith's sitting room, their cups of tea on the little table in between. It was how she always pictured herself, when she thought about visiting her mother. But somehow Alice seemed to fit better into the tableau.

'She was funny, too,' Alice carried on. 'Wasn't she, Mum? Really witty. She would make jokes about things she'd seen on telly or articles she'd read in the paper. I told her once that I didn't really understand how the European Union worked – there had been something on the news about Brexit. And she explained it all to me in such a clever way. I can't say I've ever been interested in politics, always thought it was a bit over my head, but that afternoon I was fascinated, listening to her. You can tell she would have been the most amazing teacher, fun but not preachy. I wish I'd had someone like her at my school; maybe then I wouldn't have dropped out! I'm not surprised she got that award from the newspaper – you know, the teaching medal thing they presented her with.'

Martha nodded, as if she knew this. As if her mother had mentioned it.

She sensed movement at her side and turned to see Patrick staring at the two women.

'Hi,' said Alice. 'That was a lovely service.'

'Thank you, Annie,' he said.

'It's Alice,' said Martha, glaring at him. He knew perfectly well what her name was. It was as if he wanted to unsettle the girl: put her in her place. 'Patrick, this is Sharon, her mother. She used to clean the bungalow, that's how Mum got in touch with Alice.'

He nodded curtly.

'Delightful to meet you,' said Sharon. 'We're so glad to be here today, we were both so close to your mother. She was a wonderful lady and a dear, dear friend to us.'

Patrick snorted. 'Whatever,' he said. 'Martha, can you spare a moment? The vicar wants to have a word.'

He walked away and Martha knew her face was colouring. 'Sorry,' she said. 'It's been a difficult day for all of us.'

29

Helen was so drunk she could hardly stand. She had collapsed into a chair with a bottle of Prosecco and was refilling her glass, not seeming to notice that the base was dripping, leaving a swathe of dark dots across her linen skirt.

'Thank God that's all over,' she was saying. 'What a bloody day. I hate funerals. At least there was some decent fizz at this place. Was that down to you, Patrick? Last time we came to stay with you, Martha, we had warm Pinot Grigio because your fridge had broken down or something. Do you remember?'

She cackled and slid to one side, jolting herself upright again and spilling more of her Prosecco. Martha glared at her. There had been nothing wrong with the fridge. Patrick and Helen had arrived one Boxing Day and spent the afternoon drinking so heavily and rapidly that they'd gone through all the white wine Simon had put in the fridge. They'd then sniffed at the expensive red he offered to open and started working their way through more – admittedly slightly warm – bottles of white in the wine rack.

'Daddy, I want to go. This is so boring,' whined Samantha,

not lifting her eyes from the screen of her phone. Martha could see now that it was bigger and newer than her own smartphone.

'Soon, princess,' said Patrick. 'Very soon.'

He had also topped up his glass. Martha had no idea how they were getting home, but hoped they were going to call a taxi. In contrast, Simon hadn't had a drink all afternoon, but he was in such a foul mood, she almost wished he had. Now the guests had left, he was sitting on a sofa by the window, glaring across at them all, his arms crossed, his foot tapping on the carpet. 'We need to go,' he'd hissed at her, just now. 'It's going to take bloody hours to get home, we'll hit rush hour traffic.'

Martha was desperate to leave too, the last thing she wanted was to be hanging around amongst the debris of her mother's wake. But they were waiting for the hotel manager to print out a copy of the invoice.

'That Sharon woman is trouble,' Patrick was saying now. 'I know her type. "Your mother was a dear friend" my arse. I can't imagine Mum giving the time of day to a woman like that. They had nothing in common. I wouldn't be surprised if she's the one behind all this. She probably encouraged her daughter to wheedle her way into Mum's life, make her think that they had this special friendship.'

'I don't think it was like that...' Martha started to say.

'I think it was exactly like that,' interrupted Patrick. 'Sharon knew there was money to be had – cleaning that bungalow made it easy for her to have a dig around and find out about Mum's finances. She also knew that girl, Annie or whatever she's called, was making herself useful with the dog. So, between the two of them, they hatched a plan to make themselves indispensable to a vulnerable old lady.'

'She's called Alice,' said Martha. 'You know perfectly well what her name is. Anyway, I think Mum honestly grew fond of her. She never really talked to me about Sharon...'

'But who would have benefitted if she'd got that house?' asked Patrick, emptying his glass and slamming it down on a table. 'Sharon, that's who. You said they're all living in her poky little flat at the moment – so Sharon would have got a good deal out of all this. She'd have the flat to herself and the girl and her child would have got to wallow around in a two-bedroom house with a garden, the kind of place they'd never usually have a hope in hell of living in.'

'Gracie,' muttered Martha. 'Her daughter's called Gracie. I really don't think that was the case. Sharon had nothing to gain from any of that.'

'How do you know?' said Patrick, his voice raised now. 'You have no bloody idea what they were intending to do with it. They might have talked about knocking it to the ground and building a block of flats!'

'Oh, for God's sake,' muttered Simon.

'Patrick, they don't even know about the codicil!' said Martha. 'They can't do, otherwise they would have said something! Anyway, can you please keep your voice down. Do we have to be discussing this here?' There was no one else in the room, but she was paranoid about being overheard.

'Judith must really have loved that girl,' slurred Helen, from the sofa. 'I mean, why else would you bypass your own flesh and blood and leave your home to someone like that? Even if that old bag of a mother encouraged her to do it, Judith made the decision herself. She must have looked on the dog walker girl like a daughter.'

The door opened and the hotel manager came back in with an envelope.

'Sorry about the delay,' he said, handing it to Patrick. 'That should all be in order, but please check it before you leave.'

Simon had stood up and was jangling the car keys in his

hand. 'Come on,' he said to Martha. 'We really need to get going now.'

'I mean, when you think about it, this isn't really to do with Patrick, is it?' said Helen, still slumped on the sofa. 'He was always her golden boy – he could do no wrong where his doting mummy was concerned. This is all about you, Martha. Judith found someone who did a better job, who spent time with her and kept her company and did all the things a proper daughter should do!' She cackled and put her glass to her lips, looking confused when she realised it was empty. 'So, however this happened, you're the one she didn't love enough. You're the daughter who was so easily replaced by a girl who only came in to walk the bloody dog!'

Martha stared at Helen, her mouth hanging open. There was a tightness inside her, as if something was squeezing her lungs and making it hard for her to catch her breath. She turned to look at Patrick, waiting for him to say something, expecting him to defend her. But he was smirking, swaying slightly as he tried to slide the envelope into the inside pocket of his jacket.

'Do you know, she has got a point,' he said. 'It does feel a bit like you've failed as a daughter, Martha.'

'Right, I've had enough of this,' said Simon. 'Come on, Martha, let's go. You two should be ashamed of yourselves – you're both drunk and you need to go home and sober up.'

'Oh, so high and mighty!' said Helen, pointing at Simon with her empty glass. 'Don't try and pretend you haven't been thinking about all this, too. You'd be just as pissed off as the rest of us if you weren't getting a share of the house.'

Simon shook his head in disgust. 'You're a selfish, money-grabbing bitch, Helen.'

'Hey, that's out of order,' said Patrick.

'And you're no better,' Simon said, turning to him. 'It doesn't sound as if you've been much support to Martha during all of this.'

'Well, how the hell would you know?' said Patrick. 'We haven't seen anything of you down here in the last few weeks, mate, offering to help us sort out this mess. Don't think you can just put on a suit and turn up to my mother's funeral to hang around looking miserable and playing the martyred son-in-law. Helen's right, all you care about is the money.'

'You're a fucking dick, Patrick,' said Simon. 'Always have been, always will be.'

Samantha raised her head from her phone, her eyes wide. 'Uncle Simon said the f-word!' she squealed.

Martha's heart was thrusting itself into her throat and she was suddenly burning hot, prickles of sweat bursting out across her forehead. 'Stop this, all of you,' she said. But it came out as a whisper and no one heard.

'Sod off back to your glass palace in the country, you bloody loser,' snarled Patrick. 'This is about my mother. It has nothing to do with you.'

'Don't worry, I've got no intention of wasting any more of my time here,' said Simon. 'You're poisonous, both of you.' He turned and grabbed Martha's hand, pulling her towards the door. 'Come on, we're getting out of here.'

Stumbling after him, Martha saw the stricken expression on the face of the hotel manager, who was standing outside in the hallway.

'I'm so sorry,' she managed, as Simon dragged her towards the front door.

'Goodbye and good-fucking riddance!' yelled Helen.

30

She was twisting the ring on the middle finger of her right hand, watching the diamonds sparkle, the sharp edges catching the sunlight that poured in through the window next to her desk. Simon had given her this eternity ring after Joe was born. It was perfect; exactly the sort of thing she would have chosen for herself, the tiny row of stones set in a band of gleaming white gold.

'I hope it's okay,' he'd said, as he stood beside the bed on the maternity wing. 'I wasn't sure if you'd like it.'

She had burst into tears, laughing through her sobs, as she saw the terrified expression on his face. 'I love it,' she'd wept. 'It's beautiful. I'm happy – honestly!'

She had worn it ever since, though it soon began to remind her of the stress and chaos connected with those first few days of Joe's life. Possibly because of that, it had felt like some kind of talisman that might keep them all safe, as they sat in consultants' offices and GPs' surgeries and heard yet more bad news. While they listened to a string of medical terms that rarely made much sense, she invariably found herself looking down at the ring, twisting it round and round. Simon had given her this because he loved her; together they would deal with whatever life threw at them.

The ring had stopped feeling lucky a long time ago, the protective qualities she'd given it disproved by years of adversity. But she couldn't bear not to wear it, because that would feel too risky: she was superstitious enough to believe that if she took off this ring she'd be throwing their futures off balance.

'Martha, can you get those spreadsheets finished by lunchtime?' called Clive, through the open door of his office.

'No problem,' she said. This was ridiculous; she needed to put everything else out of her mind and get on with work. The spreadsheets were almost done, but she'd been sitting here all morning struggling to focus. She tapped the keyboard and woke up the screen.

She had expected to feel relieved once the funeral was over, but nothing felt better today. It was partly because she was exhausted. They hadn't got home until after 10pm last night and, although Joe had been in bed for hours by that time, she had kept Jackie talking in the kitchen for longer than necessary, desperate to hear about every last detail of his day.

'Was he okay at bath time? He's sometimes overtired by that stage. Did he eat everything at tea? How was he with you in general? Did he seem worried at all, or upset that we weren't here?'

Over Jackie's shoulder, she had seen Simon grimacing at her as he pulled a beer out of the fridge, shaking his head as he flipped off the metal top.

'For God's sake,' he said, when the woman eventually left. 'You didn't need to give her the Spanish Inquisition! She was fine. Joe was fine. It was all bloody fine.'

He'd walked out of the kitchen with the beer, and Martha had collapsed on the purple sofa, edging her swollen feet out of her shoes, rubbing at an inflamed patch of skin on the back of her heel. She listened as he went up the stairs and walked across the landing above her head, then heard a thump as the spare room door was kicked shut.

When she got into work this morning, everyone had gathered around, asking about the funeral. Even Janey seemed genuinely concerned and interested.

'It all went surprisingly well,' Martha told them. 'The service in the crematorium was lovely and lots of my mum's old friends were there, people I hadn't seen in years. The hotel was great, where we held the wake.'

They had gradually drifted back to their desks, satisfied they'd made the appropriate noises and she'd supplied the right answers to their questions. Then Martha sat, staring at her computer screen, feeling as if someone had taken a knife and carved out a gaping hole where her heart used to be.

Everything she'd just told them had been true: but yesterday had been bloody awful – worse than she'd ever imagined it could be.

All she'd wanted was to give her mother a decent send-off. But it didn't feel as if that had happened. The service itself *had* gone well, and she'd been pleased with her choice of The Hamilton Hotel, from the quality of the buffet to the way the sunlight had streamed in through the windows as people chatted and mingled. It had all been surprisingly cheerful – or as cheerful as these things were ever going to be.

Even seeing Sharon and Alice hadn't been as difficult as she'd expected.

But the row with Patrick and Helen had left her feeling battered, almost physically sick. She kept remembering fragments of that final conversation: the snide remarks slipped in, the insults hurled, the venom in their voices.

'Do you think they're right?' she'd said to Simon, as he accelerated out of the hotel car park.

'What do you mean?'

'Is this all my fault? Did Mum feel like I'd let her down?'

Simon had sighed. 'They were so pissed they could hardly stand up straight. They probably won't even remember what they said in the morning.'

'But that didn't sound like it was just the alcohol talking – they really meant it. The two of them must have been discussing it, before today.'

'Who cares what they think?' said Simon. 'Your brother and his wife are vile, self-centred, vicious human beings. We've always struggled to get on with them and their bloody cocky kids. At least now, once probate is done and this whole business with the house has been sorted out, we'll never need to have anything to do with either of them again.'

'But those things they said were so hurtful.'

'Martha, let it go,' he said. 'They're not worth it.'

But she couldn't let it go. This morning, depression was creeping up and over her like an incoming tide. She was aching with hurt at Patrick's blunt fury, although in some ways that was the least surprising thing about yesterday. She was used to being undermined and bullied by her brother, and she and Helen had never had anything in common.

But the worst thing of all was that she'd failed her mother, yet again. She had let her down for the first time, three weeks ago, when she went home on that Friday afternoon, instead of staying beside Judith's hospital bed. Now she had let her down again, by not giving her the sort of send-off she deserved. There was always an excess of emotion at funerals – that was par for the course – but it had been Martha's responsibility to keep everyone on an even keel. She wasn't sure how things had gone so horribly wrong, but she should have done more to stop that happening. Judith would have been appalled at the way they all ended up shouting at each other in the hotel last night, humiliated that her children were capable of behaving so badly.

Martha twisted the eternity ring around on her finger, watching the row of tiny diamonds sparkle as they caught the light. And then there was Simon. Or rather, there wasn't Simon. She'd been relieved when he defended her, full of gratitude when he yelled at Helen and Patrick and told them what he thought of them. Once they got outside, she'd expected him to pull her close and hug her, to tell her that she wasn't to blame for any of this, that she'd done her best and he loved her. But he hadn't said a word. He'd stalked across the drive and unlocked the car, starting the engine before she'd opened the passenger door, then pulling away so quickly once she got in, that gravel spattered out in an arc behind the rear wheels. After their one brief conversation about Patrick and Helen, they'd driven home in silence.

The computer screen had gone blank again; she looked down at the keyboard and saw dots appearing on the grey plastic. It took her a moment to understand where they were coming from, to realise that tears were dripping from her cheeks and pooling on the keyboard below her.

31

'Why do you need to go into the office on a Saturday? You've never done that before.'

'We've never been in this kind of mess before.' Simon was eating a slice of toast, while pulling on his jacket. 'Where are my sodding keys? Why does nothing ever stay where you put it in this house?'

'Hall table?' suggested Martha. 'What time will you be back, do you think? If you can be home by lunchtime, maybe we'll take Joe to the park this afternoon. Or we could drive to that National Trust place with the big lake in front. The paths around there were really good, do you remember? We were able to take the wheelchair almost everywhere.'

'Not sure,' said Simon, walking out of the kitchen.

She stared after him, the spoon with Joe's mashed up Weetabix hovering in mid-air. 'What do you mean, *not sure*? You can't need to be working all day? Come on, Simon, we haven't been out as a family for weeks. It would be good to do something a bit different this afternoon.'

She heard a click as he unlatched the front door. 'Simon?'

Joe was squirming in his chair, his eyes on the spoon suspended in front of him.

Martha stood up and ran out into the hall. The front door was open and Simon was stepping through it. 'Come back here!' she yelled. 'Please don't just walk out on me when we're having a conversation!'

He turned and glared at her. 'We're not having a conversation, Martha. You're just telling me what you want to do later. As I say, I have no idea what time I'll be back. I don't know how long this is all going to take. If you want to go out somewhere, you'll have to do it without me.'

Behind her, Joe was beginning to wail in the kitchen and she could hear him knocking his feet against the legs of his chair.

'But I don't want to go without you,' she said. 'I want us *all* to go somewhere. That's the whole point! It doesn't matter where it is. I don't particularly care about going to the National Trust place, I just want us to be together. Like a proper family!'

He was looking back at her pityingly. 'Well, that's never going to happen, is it?' he said. 'We're not a proper family, Martha. We never will be. Why do you have to make such a bloody big deal out of this kind of thing? It's like you're trying to pretend there's nothing wrong and we can do all the stuff other people do. Well, we can't. I'm sorry – I know it makes you sad. It makes me sad too. But that's life. I've got to go. Everyone is supposed to be in by ten for a meeting.'

He turned and went through the door, slamming it shut after him. Behind her in the kitchen, Joe's wail had grown louder, the thumping on the chair more insistent.

Martha's pulse was racing, her head spinning with the effort of containing all the words she wanted to shout out after him. 'Great,' she said to the closed door in front of her. 'Bloody marvellous. Is that it then? You just bugger off to your office, and

I'll stay here and look after our son, again. As per usual. Thanks for nothing, Simon.'

She realised she was still holding the spoon of Weetabix out in front of her, her fingers trembling with rage. 'Fuck you!' she yelled. She flung the spoon at the door. It bounced off and clattered onto the tiled floor, leaving a brown stripe of congealed cereal across the paintwork, which began to slide slowly downwards.

Joe was screaming now, and she ran back into the kitchen. Putting her arms around him, she could feel his heart thumping nearly as hard as her own.

This was all so crazy. What were she and Simon doing to each other? Okay, so he was stressed by whatever was going on at work, but he seemed incapable of focusing on anything else – certainly not on her or Joe. All she wanted was for them to spend some time together. Was that really so impossible?

Joe was wailing in her ear, his fist bunched up against her, poking painfully into her chest as she tried to soothe him.

Maybe Simon was right – it was pointless them pretending to do the things normal families did. But if they stopped trying, they would be giving in, admitting they'd failed – and Martha wasn't sure she was ready to do that yet.

'Come on, Joe,' she whispered, his wails still shrill in her ear. 'Calm down now.'

It was his birthday in a couple of weeks – he'd be five years old. Martha realised she hadn't even thought about what they'd do to mark it. She usually made a big deal out of celebrating birthdays and anniversaries: those special dates were like a glue that bound them together, and it had always been important to her to mark that – even when things didn't work out as she'd planned.

Poor Joe: his birthdays invariably fell flat. When his first birthday came around, he hadn't been doing any of the things he ought to have been doing by that stage, but he was still their gorgeous boy, and she'd been determined to celebrate the fact that they'd made it through the first traumatic year. She'd planned a day trip to the seaside: they would walk along the beach and eat ice cream, holding Joe above the waves, so his toes could get tickled by the water. She'd been excited about it – he'd never been to the sea.

But then a letter arrived, from the hospital. It was an appointment on that day, for another brain scan – he'd had so many already, but in those early years her heart still leapt when the consultants suggested something like this. There was always the chance this would be the test that would show them exactly what was wrong and how it could be cured. By then, they were wise to the vagaries of the health system, and only too aware that trying to rearrange the appointment would lead to long delays.

'We can't cancel,' Simon had said. 'It's too important.'

'But what about our trip?' said Martha. 'I wanted him to see the sea.'

'It's no big deal,' Simon said. 'Joe doesn't even know or care it's his birthday.'

Maybe not, Martha had thought, *but I do*. Simon had been right, of course: Joe had no idea he was missing out on a treat, while they sat for hours on uncomfortable chairs in hospital waiting rooms. But she had felt so guilty. And now, four years later, it sounded as if she would still be the only one who cared about this latest milestone.

'Come on, sweetheart,' she murmured, resting her cheek against Joe's hair, her fingers cradling his forehead, the skin soft, despite the sheen of sweat that had broken out across it. 'Calm down now. It's all going to be fine.'

Was Simon really going to the office? The thought came out of nowhere, crashing into her mind, the shock of it making her catch her breath. Maybe there was no work crisis, and he was going to meet someone. Someone who wasn't always nagging him and asking where he was going and when he'd be home. Someone who wasn't always shouting at him and making him feel like he wasn't doing a good enough job as a father.

It was a possibility, wasn't it? Maybe more than a possibility. It would explain his irritability and bad temper; his lack of interest in anything she said or did. If there was another woman in Simon's life, it would explain why he could hardly bear to be in the same room as her, right now. It would explain why they didn't seem able to talk to each other anymore; why they hadn't made love in months.

Joe was calmer now, whimpering but no longer shaking. 'Good boy,' she whispered, stroking his hair, kissing his cheek. 'Good boy, well done. Mummy's here, you'll be fine.'

The awful thing was, the idea that Simon might have someone else in his life wasn't even making her particularly sad.

32

This was madness, but she didn't care. The roads had been quiet and Joe had slept for most of the journey anyway, exhausted after their fight over the unfinished bowl of Weetabix. As Martha pulled up outside the bungalow, she realised that, for the first time in the last few weeks, she was actually glad to be here.

As usual, it took a while to get everything out of the car, wake up Joe and move him into the house. She struggled to push the wheelchair across the small patch of lawn in the front, where the grass was long and full of weeds; she would have to drag Judith's mower around here later and sort it out. It was a fortnight since she'd been at the bungalow to meet the estate agents; there hadn't been any point coming here when they drove up two days ago; they'd gone straight to the funeral directors, then on to the crematorium and the hotel. Her stomach clenched, as she remembered the scene there with Patrick and Helen.

Before leaving home a couple of hours ago, she had grabbed some bread and a tub of soup from the fridge; now she put them in the kitchen and settled Joe into his chair, before walking around throwing open windows to air the musty rooms.

She'd wondered whether the bungalow would feel different, now they'd had the funeral; whether the sense of Judith in these rooms would be fainter after a line had been officially drawn under her life. But, if anything, the opposite was the case. Martha could still feel her mother's presence in everything: the pictures on the wall, the cushions on the chairs, the books lined up neatly on the shelves. She could picture Judith's liver-spotted hands drawing the curtains in the bedroom, flicking through the pile of post in the hallway, holding the heavy, old-fashioned telephone handset. She could see those hands putting on the blue and white striped butcher's apron in the kitchen and opening the fridge, her tattered slippers falling off her heels as she stood on tiptoe to peer up at the contents of the wall cupboards. Judith was still everywhere.

But that wasn't as hard as Martha had expected it to be. She missed her mother desperately, but being in this house was bringing back memories of happier times, which were strong enough to push away the mental image of Judith's body in a hospital bed.

'Your Granny would be pleased to have you here,' she said to Joe, as she spooned soup into his mouth. 'Although she'd probably be telling me I wasn't feeding you properly, that I was doing it all wrong!' She smiled as her son leant forward for another spoonful, then reached to push the brown fringe out of his eyes.

After they'd eaten, she took Joe into the garden, parking the wheelchair in a shady corner of the patio. It was nearly 2.30; would Simon be home any time soon? Probably not. Even if he did come back, he wouldn't think anything of the fact that she wasn't there; he'd presume she'd taken Joe somewhere for the outing she'd been so desperate for them all to experience together.

'Do you think your Daddy still loves me?' she asked the little boy, softly.

His head was tilted slightly to one side, his eyes focused on a sparrow that was flitting across the patio near the wheels of his chair.

'I'm not sure he does,' she answered her own question. 'Or not in the way he once did. I'm not sure I love him in the same way, either. It's all been too hard.'

Sometimes, in the middle of the night, when anxiety shook her awake her from a dream and then fluttered around in her head, making it impossible for her to get back to sleep again, Martha couldn't stop herself wondering what their lives would have been like now, if things had gone differently. Would she and Simon have been less angry with each other, less resentful, if Joe's birth had been free from complications and he'd come into the world as a normal, healthy baby?

By now, the Joe in that parallel universe would be at primary school, in the same class as Barney. He would have flashcards to help him learn phonics and would be able to write out the letters in his name. He would be painting big, colourful pictures and making models from discarded cereal boxes and margarine tubs. He would be able to count to ten and recognise different colours. He would be able to dress himself, feed himself and brush his own teeth.

She and Simon would definitely have had more children to fill their big, empty house – at least one, possibly two by now. When she was feeling strong enough, Martha sometimes allowed herself to imagine the rooms ringing with voices, plastic toys littering the carpet in the sitting room, small shoes carelessly discarded by the front door, rows of brightly coloured shorts, T-shirts and jumpers flapping in the wind on the washing line.

In that parallel universe, maybe she and Simon would still love each other, and she wouldn't have to live with this constant, exhausting sense that she'd let everyone down. He had never said as much, but Martha was convinced that Simon's disappointment after Joe's birth was directed as much at her, as at fate which had dealt them such a cruel hand. While she was pregnant, he'd been desperate for a son. 'I don't mind what we have,' he used to say. 'So long as he's good at football.'

'What if it's a girl?' she'd asked once, stretching out on the sofa, running the palms of her hands over her expanding bump, amazed at how her body was changing. 'I don't want you to be disappointed.'

'It will be a boy,' Simon had insisted. 'I know it.' He'd leant down and put his cheek against her stomach. 'But whatever happens, I won't be disappointed.'

They'd laughed, with the nonchalance of two naïve people who didn't know what was coming.

After the long, traumatic birth, it was extraordinary to set eyes on the tiny creature they'd been waiting to meet for nine months. They both fell in love with him with an intensity that was overwhelming. Exhausted, bruised, bleeding and in pain, Martha held the tiny scrap of a baby and realised that, until now, she had never understood what love meant. She and Simon had created this little person, then her body had looked after him until he was ready to make an appearance in the world. She was a physical wreck, but she felt superhuman.

But within days it was obvious their lives weren't going to be as straightforward as they'd anticipated. There were so many tests, so many machines, a constant stream of frowning specialists appearing at her bedside. Joe looked perfect, but it quickly became clear that something was wrong. He wasn't responding as he should, he wasn't feeding, he wasn't reacting to the sound of her voice, the touch of her hand. It was months before they got an official diagnosis but, long before that, Martha had started to believe this was her fault. She had let Simon down, and destroyed their plans for a future. She was responsible for what had happened, because she was the one who had given birth to this beautiful, wonderful – but ultimately damaged – little boy.

The sparrow had been coming nearer, now it suddenly flew upwards and landed on the arm of Joe's chair. She gasped and Joe's shoulder jolted beneath her fingers. The bird put its head on its side and stayed still for a few seconds, almost as if it was studying them. Then, in a flapping of wings, it was gone again.

'Come on, this way!'

The child's voice came from behind her. Martha turned as a little girl ran around the corner of the house. She stopped by the edge of the patio and stared, wide-eyed, at Joe.

'Hello!' she said, starting to walk forward.

Then Alice appeared, Nipper on the lead, dragging her forwards.

'Hi, Martha! I saw your car outside,' she said. 'I didn't know you were coming down today?'

The little girl had now walked right up to the wheelchair. She bent over, her hands on her thighs, staring into Joe's face. 'What's wrong with him?' she asked.

'Gracie!' said Alice. 'That's rude. You don't ask questions like that.' She came up and took the girl by the hand. 'I'm so sorry, Martha.'

The child looked at Martha, confused. 'But why is he in that chair...?'

'Come away,' said Alice, dragging her back towards the grass. 'You mustn't stare at people. Here, throw a ball for Nipper.' She leant down and took the lead off the little dog, which immediately ran down to the far end of the garden, the girl following, shouting out his name.

'So, this is Gracie?' said Martha. The family resemblance was extraordinary. The little girl had a mass of blonde hair streaming down her back, with the same high cheekbones as her mother, the same snub nose. She was going to be a beauty when she grew up.

'Yes, I'm sorry about that,' said Alice. She looked down at Joe. 'It's just the wheelchair. She was curious. She didn't mean to be rude.'

'It's fine, don't worry.' Martha was used to people staring and pointing. She was also used to embarrassed parents pulling inquisitive children away and telling them off for asking questions. 'This is my son, Joe. As you'll know, because you'll have seen Mum's photos inside the bungalow.'

Alice moved forward and squatted down in front of the wheelchair. 'Hi, little Joe,' she said, gently, putting out her hand and resting it on his arm. 'My name's Alice. You're a handsome boy, aren't you? Your Granny used to talk about you all the time. She was very proud of you.'

Martha's heart skipped a beat. 'Did she really?' she couldn't stop herself asking.

Alice looked up at her, surprised. 'Of course! She loved telling me about him. She was proud of you as well, for how you coped with everything. She said you'd had an awful time, during the delivery and then for ages after he was born, when you were trying to get a diagnosis. But she said you'd always been so strong and capable, and you never felt sorry for yourself.'

'God,' Martha said. 'I don't know if that's true.'

'Well, she believed it was. I think that sometimes, when you brought Joe down to see her, she felt a bit like a spare part, because you were so efficient. She would have liked to be able to help you more, but you didn't seem to need it.'

Martha's mouth fell open; she was amazed. 'I wouldn't have minded,' she said, almost to herself. But that wasn't strictly true. She *had* enjoyed coming across as efficient and capable – but why had she been like that with her own mother, who would have loved her whatever happened and would never have judged her? It seemed so ridiculous now.

'Sorry, I wouldn't have come over if I'd known you were going to be here today,' said Alice, standing back up again. 'We just came along to let Nipper have a run around in his own garden. I bring him here a couple of times a week. It seems like the right thing to do, to let him come home every now and then.'

'That's really thoughtful,' said Martha. 'Thank you. I would have let you know, but it was very last-minute. I only decided this morning. Just wanted to get away from it all, have a change of scene.'

Gracie had run back up to them and was standing behind Alice, grasping her mother's shirt in her fists, sticking out her head to look at Joe.

'How old are you, Gracie?' asked Martha.

'I'm three and three quarters,' said the girl. 'I'm going to big school soon.'

'That will be exciting,' said Martha.

'I go to playgroup now, but when I'm four I will go to school and wear a green skirt with a green cardigan. When I'm at big school, Mummy's going to a different kind of school too, to be a nurse.'

Nipper was suddenly back, yapping at Alice's heels. 'Can I go in and get him some water?' she asked. 'Would that be okay?'

'Yes, of course! There are bowls in the bottom cupboard, by the fridge. But you probably know that!'

Alice smiled and went inside. The little girl stood with her hands clasped in front of her, staring at Joe, then looking up at Martha. 'What's he called?' she asked.

'Joe.'

'Is he older than me?'

'Yes, he's nearly five now.'

Gracie nodded solemnly and stepped towards the wheelchair again. She reached out her hand and rested it on Joe's arm, stroking it gently, looking back up at Martha for reassurance.

Martha smiled and noticed how clear her eyes were: a pale, smooth cornflower blue, so different to Joe's eyes, which were a darker blue, his irises full of flecks and rotating shadows, like marbles.

The girl leant forward slowly until her face was close to Joe's, then kissed him gently on the cheek. 'Hello, Joe,' she whispered. 'My name is Gracie.'

She pulled away again, still stroking his arm. 'Will he talk to me?'

Martha shook her head. 'No, he can't do that.'

'Why not?'

'Well, when he was born, he didn't have enough oxygen, so his brain didn't grow properly and he can't do the things you and I can do.'

Alice came back out of the kitchen and put down a bowl of water for the dog. She stood beside Gracie.

'This boy, Joe, is like Uncle Billy,' the little girl said to her. 'He can't do lots of things.'

Alice smiled and stroked her hair. 'That's right,' she said. 'Joe is Judith's grandson. She used to tell us about him, do you remember?'

The girl nodded and turned back to Martha. 'Judith was Nipper's Granny too,' she told her, solemnly. 'We used to come and see her in this house before she died. I don't know if you knew her? She was a very funny lady.'

Martha smiled again and nodded. 'I did know her. You're right, she was lovely.'

'She always called her Nipper's Granny,' said Alice apologetically. 'I don't really know why.'

'Because it was her name!' said Gracie. 'Look, she gave me these!' She dug her fingers into the pocket of her skirt and pulled out something that clacked and rattled. As she opened her hand, Martha saw shells nestling in her chubby palm, seashells of various sizes and shapes, some white, some pink, some brown. They were like the ones Judith had kept in one of the many glass dishes she had on display, gathered decades earlier on a long-forgotten beach.

'I have them here, in my pocket, the whole time,' said the girl. 'They're my favourite thing. I'm going to take them with me when I go to big school.'

'They're beautiful,' said Martha. 'Were they the ones in the sitting room?'

Gracie looked confused.

'Yes, but your mum really did give them to her,' Alice said, suddenly. 'Gracie didn't just take them.'

'Of course not, I didn't mean that,' said Martha. 'It's fine. I'm glad she has them. Are you in a hurry, or shall I make a cup of tea?'

Alice looked surprised, then nodded and smiled. 'Yes please. That would be great.'

As she filled the kettle, Martha stared through the kitchen window at the three of them on the patio. Alice was wearing scruffy jeans and the same battered grey trainers she'd worn to the funeral. Martha was also wearing trainers today, but hers were Nike, pale pink with special support in the heel for trail running. They'd cost £120 in a sale and she'd only worn them a few times. She'd never run up a trail in her life, she'd just liked the colour. While the kettle boiled, she kicked them off and pushed them out of sight under the kitchen table.

Gracie had moved one of the plastic outdoor chairs next to the wheelchair and clambered up onto it, sitting herself beside Joe. She was chattering away, holding up the shells in front of him, one by one.

'This,' Martha heard her say, 'was Nipper's Granny's best shell, because she got it such a long time ago, and a little crab used to live in it.'

Joe's face was tilted towards the little girl and, if she didn't know better, Martha could have sworn her son was smiling.

33

She felt so much better after their afternoon at the bungalow yesterday, despite all the hours of driving and the disruption to Joe's normal sleeping patterns, which meant he got to bed later than usual, then woke twice in the night. Although Martha was tired today, she was calmer, somehow, as if going back to Surrey had allowed her to make some kind of peace with Judith – and with herself.

Over breakfast, she tried to tell Simon about Gracie, and how lovely it had been to watch her playing with Joe, but Simon was only interested in Alice.

'That must have felt a bit odd?' he said. 'Being there with her and knowing what your mum wanted?'

'It did at first,' said Martha. 'But we had a cup of tea and talked about the children, and Nipper. We talked about Mum as well, and things she and Alice had done together. She's going back to college in the autumn, to do a diploma so she can go to university and study nursing. She wants to work with children with learning disabilities. She said Mum had offered to look after Gracie for her, after school.'

She didn't add how much that comment had hurt, but this

morning she was still shocked that her mother had volunteered to care for someone else's small child on a regular basis. How come she'd never realised the extent of this relationship between the two women? It was a proper, mutually beneficial friendship. Martha had lain awake last night, telling herself it was pathetic to feel so excluded.

'So, you chatted about all this trivial stuff in your lives, but she never mentioned the house?' asked Simon. 'That must mean she had no idea what Judith was intending to do. Otherwise, she would have said something – particularly since it was just the two of you, there on your own.'

'I'm sure you're right,' she nodded. It *had* been strange to be sitting side by side in the sunshine, with this girl she hardly knew, but whom her mother had decided would inherit and live in the bungalow, a few feet behind them. There was some awkwardness initially, as they sipped their tea in silence, watching their children and listening to Gracie's easy laughter as she played with Joe. But then they had begun to talk: Alice had said how much more settled Nipper had been, Martha had asked about Gracie's new school. They'd agreed the garden needed some attention and Alice had offered to ask around and find someone to mow the lawns. The conversation between them had been easy.

When Simon took Joe upstairs to get dressed, Martha picked up her phone and tapped out a text.

Hi Alice, it was great to see you yesterday and to meet Gracie, she's gorgeous! I'm glad we got the chance to talk. Martha x

A reply pinged in almost immediately:

Me too! Thanks for letting G play with Joe. Hope you hear from that school soon x

Martha smiled as she read it: she could hear Alice saying the words.

As she put her phone on the kitchen table, it began to ring. Claudia's name came up on the screen; she'd left a message a couple of days ago, asking how the funeral had gone, but after the row with Simon and the last-minute trip down to Surrey, Martha hadn't got round to calling her back. She answered reluctantly; although she was feeling more positive today, she wasn't in the mood for Claudia. She didn't want to hear how well Barney was learning to ride a bike, or how successfully Adam was settling into his new role at work.

'Don't be a lousy friend, Martha,' she muttered to herself, before answering the call.

'Where have you been?' said Claudia. 'I've got so much to tell you. The main news is that we've booked a summer holiday – to Portugal – can't wait! We're going in July, as soon as Barney breaks up for the school holidays. Oh yes, and you'll never guess who I saw on Friday night, when I was out with Anna? We were in the wine bar, you know, the one on Compton Place...'

Martha began to tidy up the breakfast things, the phone tucked under her chin, letting Claudia's gossip wash over her.

'What's happening with that girl?' her friend asked, once she'd exhausted her own news. 'Have you had any more contact with her? Did she know your mum was planning to leave her something?'

'No, I'm sure she didn't,' said Martha, running a cloth around the hob, scraping away a bit of burnt bacon. 'I saw her yesterday though. I took Joe to Mum's and she came over with her little girl. We had a cup of tea together.'

'What?' Claudia sounded horrified. 'Do you mean you sat down with her – and talked to her?'

'Well, yes. That's usually what happens when you drink tea with someone.'

'But how could you do that?' asked Claudia. 'She might have ended up stealing what's rightfully yours! Are you seriously telling me you pretended everything was fine and sat there with her like a couple of mums in the park? God, Martha – that's a bit weird. I mean, I'm not criticising the way you're handling any of this, but you really don't want to encourage her. How do you know you can trust her? It sounds like you're being way too nice about it all.'

'So, actually,' said Martha. 'You *are* criticising the way I'm handling it.' She tried to keep her voice light, and laughed, to show Claudia she was able to take all this with good humour. But when the call ended, she slammed the phone down onto the worktop. It was none of Claudia's business if she chose to spend time with Alice. Maybe she *was* handling things badly; but she didn't know how else to do it. She had no game plan, no prearranged strategy to help her deal with what was happening. She was just getting through the days: it was all she could manage at the moment. It was unfair that everyone seemed to expect more from her.

34

'Right, the details are going up on the website tomorrow, and they want to stick up a board. I don't have a problem with that, but if you can't get down there, we may need to get a clearance company in?'

Martha was at work and, when her mobile rang, she'd been in the middle of writing an email about an outstanding payment to one of the suppliers. Her mind was miles away.

'Martha, are you there? Talk to me, for God's sake, I haven't got much time this morning. Going into an acquisitions meeting in ten minutes.'

It was six days since the funeral and that horrendous afternoon in The Hamilton Hotel, when everyone had ended up screaming at each other. Six long days – and this was the first time she'd heard from her brother. She hadn't expected an apology, but she had hoped he might make contact. Even the usual brief, impersonal text would have been welcome, because she couldn't believe they would just leave things like this, with so much anger simmering between them. Whatever their differences, she and Patrick were siblings, and she'd always believed the blood ties which bound them together were stronger than the personal differences which threatened to tear them apart. But, during the days after the funeral, her phone had remained silent, and it was clear Patrick wasn't going to be the one to end the stand-off.

'I think I ought to call him,' she'd said to Simon. 'We need to get past this because there will be so much to sort out – selling the house, getting rid of Mum's possessions. I don't want to do all that on my own.'

'Don't call him,' Simon had said. 'You shouldn't be the one to make the first move. Patrick and Helen behaved like total shits. The things they said were unforgivable. Have you forgotten how upset you were afterwards?'

'No, of course not. But he's my brother! We need to be on speaking terms.'

'They treated you really badly, so wait for him to call you,' said Simon. 'And when he does, don't apologise for something that isn't your fault.'

'You're making it sound so calculating,' said Martha. 'As if we're playing games with each other. But what's the point?'

'The point is, you need to show some self-respect and not let him treat you like that,' said Simon. 'He'll be in touch. When he needs to be.'

He was right: here was Patrick, on the other end of the phone. Finally. Although he clearly hadn't called to apologise, or even to ask how she was.

Martha hadn't got a clue what he was talking about. 'Sorry, Patrick – what do you mean a clearance company? I don't understand?'

He sighed heavily. 'To get rid of all the stuff in the bungalow of course. If the agents are going to start showing it to people, we need it to look a hell of a lot better than it does. I've sent in the probate form, so that's all underway, but you'll have to sort out the house.'

Martha slumped back in her chair and put one hand up to her face, closing her eyes and rubbing her forehead. 'Patrick, it's a big job. I was there last Saturday and I sorted through some of her clothes, but it'll take me a while...'

'You'd better crack on with it then, hadn't you?' he said. 'We need to get as much as we can for that place.'

Martha stared out of the window in front of her, watching the clouds race across the sky, morphing into each other as they moved. Had Patrick thought about their mother at all, over the last few days? In between the phone calls, meetings and machinations of his busy working life, had he found a couple of minutes every now and then to think about her, remember her – maybe even miss her? Probably not. As far as Patrick was concerned, Judith was dead, and there were now practicalities to be addressed. He had moved on – and would doubtless tell her she ought to be doing the same. God, if only it were that easy. Martha had been hoping the funeral would bring some kind of closure – wasn't that partly what these things were for? Her grief wouldn't suddenly come to an end once the curtains slid across the coffin in the crematorium, but she had subconsciously hoped that, having organised a ceremony to say goodbye to her mother, she'd be able to start the healing process. It hadn't turned out that way. Maybe it would have happened, had Judith's funeral been a normal one, with her grieving relatives gathered together to love and support each other.

'I've got to get into this meeting, so I'll leave that with you,' Patrick was saying.

'I can't just drop everything and go back to Surrey,' said Martha. 'I'm supposed to be working...'

'Me too, Martha,' he snapped. 'I've got a lot on my plate at the moment. It's a really busy time of year for me. But this is important, and we both need to compromise and make an effort to get things underway. I'm doing most of the legwork here, so the least you can do is be a little supportive.'

When he'd ended the call, she sat back in her chair and tapped a pen angrily against the edge of her desk. His arrogance was incredible. He clearly didn't feel that the way he and Helen had spoken to her after the funeral required any kind of apology. Or maybe he just didn't remember it: the pair of them had been drunk enough to have horrendous hangovers the next day. Even that thought didn't cheer her up.

'Coffee?' asked Janey, getting up and reaching across to pick up Martha's mug. 'It's 11.15; we're later than usual for our second one!'

'Please.' Martha tried to smile, but it felt awkward.

Eleven-fifteen. Right now, Dan and Johnny would be sitting in the hall, trying to get to grips with 'Five Little Speckled Frogs'. Having had to miss so much time at work, she'd offered to change Joe's nursery days and come in today without thinking what that meant. It was only afterwards, she realised it was a Wednesday, so she'd have to miss music therapy. A few weeks ago, she would have been delighted to have an excuse not to sit on those uncomfortable chairs, pretending to enjoy herself as she mimed along. But right now, she would give anything to be there. Who would Dan be sitting next to? Would he strike up a conversation with any of the other parents, in her absence? Possibly Chloe's mother, the one who laughed a lot. She was younger than Martha, and always friendly. Pretty too. Martha suddenly wanted to cry.

35

Simon had been a different person since the postman delivered the letter yesterday. He was communicating with her again, for one thing, sitting down and having proper conversations, meeting her eye, engaging with her. But he was also cheerful and full of energy, helping around the house. He'd wiped down the worktop after she'd cooked supper last night, then taken the bins out, without being asked. It was as if this man – who seemed to have the weight of the world on his shoulders just days ago – had been told he'd won a fortune on EuroMillions.

'Sunday's the best day to go down,' he was saying now, as he poured himself a coffee. 'Less traffic probably, and we can get an early start. We won't have to spend long there, I'm guessing they'll want us to drop him off, then head home again as soon as possible. Are you okay to sort out the packing? I can help, obviously, but you'll probably have a better idea of what he'll need.'

Martha didn't trust herself to do anything more than nod. When the envelope arrived, her heart had flipped as she saw the crested insignia on the front. Her hands were shaking as she ripped it open and her eyes scanned the sentences twice, three times, before she really took them in. Bile had risen in her throat and she rushed to the downstairs loo, feeling she might be sick. But there was nothing in her stomach. She'd put her hands on the basin and leant forward, studying herself in the mirror, noticing the wrinkles running down either side of her nose towards her mouth, the puffy bags under her eyes, the odd grey hair springing out at her hairline. She'd screwed her eyes shut to stop the tears welling up behind them.

A small part of her had secretly been hoping Greenways would turn Joe down; that they'd get in touch after his taster day to say they couldn't offer him what he needed. She wouldn't have been able to admit this to anyone, because it was such a selfish, senseless way to think. This specialist school was so important for her son: it offered him so much more than he could ever hope to get elsewhere. She should have been ecstatic about him being offered a place there, as excited and enthusiastic as Simon. For Joe, this was the start of something wonderful, hopefully the beginning of a new life.

But for her, it felt like the end.

The letter hadn't specified a start date. It just confirmed Joe could take up the place as soon as they could make arrangements to take him there. It was Simon who was keen to get things underway.

'No point hanging around,' he'd said, pinning the letter to the front of the fridge with one of the many primary-coloured magnets scattered across the door. 'I'll phone the nursery and give them notice. We might have to put it in writing, but that's not a problem – it's perfect timing because we've paid up until the end of the month. That's only next Wednesday, so it's no big deal if we lose three days' worth of fees – although they may refund it, if we ask nicely.' He'd stepped back and smiled at her. 'God, this is great news. It's going to make such a difference, Martha. Joe will thrive there, I'm absolutely certain of that. It's going to be fantastic for his development, and good for us too – so much less stressful, for you in particular. When he comes home at weekends, we'll have more energy to deal with him, and we'll be able to spend quality time together.'

Martha almost laughed out loud. She'd been begging Simon to spend quality time with his son for months, but there was always something more important that needed his attention. Now that Joe was going away, his father was suddenly looking forward to something which they could, and should, have already been doing.

Simon walked across to the sofa, where Joe was lying on his side, his eyes fixed on the television screen nearby, watching the brightly coloured cartoon play out.

'You're going to love this new school, Joey,' he said, leaning down and ruffling his son's fringe. 'Really love it. Right, I must get in the shower – going to be late for work at this rate.'

He walked out of the room, and Martha heard him whistling, taking the stairs two at a time. He hadn't called him that in years: Joey. It was what they'd called their boy when he was just a tiny baby, the name Martha used to joke that he'd hate when he grew up. She still used it every now and then, but it had been a long time since she'd heard Simon do the same.

She got up from the table and collected bowls and mugs, putting them into the dishwasher before wrapping up the bread and sliding it back into the bread bin, and closing the open box of cereal. All normal, everyday actions. Every one of them so hard to do right now.

But maybe the only way to get through this was to go through the motions and carry on as usual. If she did that, just putting one foot in front of the other, everything might start to feel a little easier. Of course Joe had to go to Greenways – the staff there could offer him so much. Simon was right: it would also make their own lives less stressful. But there was such a high price to pay. Right now, she was overwhelmed by the prospect of delivering him to the school, unpacking his things, adding small touches to a new bedroom to make it – for her at least – feel like home. She couldn't imagine how she would get back in the car afterwards and let Simon drive her away again, returning to this big, empty house. Just the two of them.

'I can't find my blue shirt,' Simon called down the stairs. 'The one with the thin stripe. Have you seen it anywhere?'

'In the airing cupboard,' she called back.

'Great, thanks!' He was whistling again, as he walked across the landing. She ought to be glad. Simon had been bloody hard to live with over the last few weeks; so hard that she'd begun to wonder where they could go from here. Whether they would be going anywhere. But the sullen, heavy-browed, snappy Simon had been replaced by an altogether different model now – one who reminded her of the man she'd first met, who'd had such a positive attitude towards life and a great sense of humour. The man whose eyes had sparkled when he talked, whose enthusiasm for everything always outweighed everyone else's. She should feel relieved – happy even – to see that familiar Simon re-emerge.

But she was furious. She wanted to slap him around the face, punch him in the belly, claw at his chest with her fingernails. She wanted him to feel the immense pain that had engulfed her, now Joe would be going away – a physical ache so intense it made every muscle in her body throb, as if she was coming down with a virus. Why did he not feel like that? Why had the news that their boy was going away been the one thing to lift him out of his misery and turn him back into the man she'd fallen in love with, all those years ago?

Joe had rolled onto his back, losing interest in the cartoons. She went across and pulled him up into a sitting position, tucking her arm around his waist and kissing his cheek as he squirmed away from her.

'God, I'm going to miss you,' she said.

36

There was a squawk of laughter from the sitting room, and the sound of glasses being clinked together. 'Happy days!' called out Claudia. Martha flinched as she pulled another bottle of wine from the fridge. If they didn't keep the noise down, they were going to wake Joe. She grabbed a bowl of olives from the worktop and hurried back along the hall.

'Then, she told him she wanted a full refund!' said Selina, who was lying along one side of the L-shaped sofa, waving her glass in the air as she talked. 'She threatened to put his photo up on Facebook, with a message about what had happened. You should have seen his face, he looked like he was going to have a heart attack!'

'I'm not surprised, that could ruin his business,' Claudia said. 'She's got about 800 friends on Facebook!'

'Oh goodie, more wine,' said Anna, holding out her glass.

Martha stepped forward and topped up her glass, forcing herself to smile. She was furious Claudia had invited Anna tonight. She was still smarting from the remarks she'd made at that dinner party a few weeks ago.

'She didn't mean anything by it,' Claudia had insisted. 'She was just a bit drunk. She's a honey when you get to know her.'

Martha didn't think there was anything vaguely 'honey' about this woman; what the hell did Claudia find to like about her? But, although she was the host, Martha hadn't had any input with tonight's guest list.

'I know Simon's out at football on Friday nights,' Claudia had said, when she called yesterday. 'Which means that if you're going to come for a drink with the girls – which you *really* need to do – you'd have to get a sitter. So how about we all come to yours? We'll bring wine, and I've got some canapé things in the freezer. You won't have to do anything, except relax and let your hair down.'

It hadn't quite turned out like that. The three women had turned up with two bottles of wine between them – which had disappeared in the first half hour – and Claudia had forgotten the canapés.

'If she really wanted to, she could make sure he never works as a personal trainer around here again,' Selina was saying. 'I mean, 800 Facebook friends! That's so impressive. She must know everyone.'

'Did you see that post she put up about the cat drinking from a champagne glass?' said Anna. 'That was hysterical. So clever.'

'God, yes,' said Claudia. 'Brilliant. Did you see it, Martha?'

'Nope,' she said. 'I don't really do Facebook.' She took a sip of her wine, her fingers tightening around the stem of the glass. Claudia knew that, so why was she even asking?

As they finished another bottle, Martha went into the kitchen for more. Simon would be furious: there was hardly anything left on the wine rack. This lot were getting through more in one evening than the pair of them drank in a fortnight.

The noise levels had risen again and Martha paused at the

bottom of the stairs, listening anxiously for signs that Joe was waking up.

'Truth or dare!' yelled Selina. 'Come on, let's do it. Claudia, you go first.'

'Truth!' giggled Claudia, who was now sitting on the floor, her back against the sofa, both feet resting up on the glass coffee table in front of her.

'Do you still enjoy sex with Adam?' shrieked Anna.

Claudia snorted with laughter. 'Yes, of course I do! Well, most of the time. When he's not being a total moron. Although we don't have it very often, to be honest. Too bloody knackered all the time! Your turn, Selina – truth or dare?'

'Dare!' screamed the woman, who was now lying on her back on the sofa. Martha could see dark patches on the cushions, where wine had splashed from her glass. Thank God they were only drinking white. ·

'Spoilsport!' said Anna. 'Okay, I've got one. Run around Martha's garden, singing something by Rihanna!'

'Oh no, please...' said Martha. But they were already falling off the sofas and staggering through into the kitchen. Claudia pulled back the sliding glass door and the outside sensor light clicked on as Selina stumbled across the patio and onto the grass.

'Shine bright like a diamond!' she shrieked, disappearing towards the fence at the far end. 'We're like diamonds in the sky!'

Martha went into the downstairs loo, splashing cold water on her face and grimacing at herself in the mirror as she heard them come back into the house. This was a bloody stupid idea. She should have told Claudia she wasn't in the mood. She thought of the piles of folded clothes on the spare bed upstairs, the open suitcase which already contained some of Joe's shoes and linen for his new bed. She'd picked the Thomas the Tank

Engine duvet cover: it was so bright and cheerful – she was sure it must be one of his favourites. She didn't want to spend too much time tomorrow packing – it was their last day together. But she needed to do a final load of washing, and she had to get Joe some new pyjamas. If Simon wasn't nursing too much of a football hangover, he might not mind if she sent him out to buy those.

Back in the sitting room, Anna had opted for truth. 'Who are you most jealous of, out of all your friends?' Selina asked her.

'Why would I be jealous of any of you?' laughed Anna. 'You're a bunch of losers!'

Someone put on some music and Claudia stood in the middle of the oriental rug, swaying her hips.

'Right, Martha, your turn!' she called. 'Truth or dare?'

'I really don't want to do this...' began Martha. But the women chorused their disapproval.

'Don't be a killjoy!' said Selina. 'Come on, which one?'

'Neither,' said Martha. 'Honestly, I've got an early start tomorrow and...'

'Okay, then I'm going to choose truth for you,' said Selina. 'I've got one. What's the thing you're most ashamed of doing?'

Martha shrugged. 'No idea,' she said. 'I can't think of anything.'

'There must be something?' said Anna. 'I bet you've cheated in exams? Or slept with someone else's boyfriend?'

Martha shook her head. 'No, I really haven't.'

'God, how boring,' slurred Selina.

'I know something she's done,' said Claudia.

Martha looked up and saw her friend staring at her, her eyes half closed. She was still swaying in time to the music, holding her wine glass against her rosy cheek.

'What?' asked Anna. 'Tell us!'

Martha's mouth was suddenly dry, despite the sip of wine she'd just taken.

'It's really bad, isn't it, Martha?' giggled Claudia.

'I don't know what you're talking about,' she said.

The others had turned towards her, their faces flushed with alcohol. For the first time this evening, they were all quiet.

'Go on,' said Selina. 'You've got to tell us, it's a truth!'

'This is ridiculous,' said Martha. 'We don't need to play these stupid games.' She stood up and grabbed another empty bottle from the coffee table. 'Who wants more to drink? I've got some cheese in the fridge as well.' She could hear the tremor in her own voice; hoping it wasn't obvious to anyone else.

'You'll have to tell us, Claudia, if she won't!' said Anna.

Claudia was still looking at Martha, a strange little smile playing across her lips.

Don't you dare, thought Martha. *Don't do this to me.*

'She's destroyed her mother's will!' said Claudia, in a stage whisper, turning to face the other two women. 'Her mother wanted to leave all her possessions to the girl who walked her dog. The house and everything! But Martha got rid of the evidence, so no one could ever find out about it.'

Selina's mouth had dropped open and Anna was staring at her. Martha opened her mouth to say something. Should she bluff it out? Maybe she could just deny it. The best thing would be to laugh at Claudia, turn the whole thing into a joke. But she realised she was taking too long to do anything at all. By her silence, she was proving that what Claudia had just said was the truth.

'Naughty, naughty!' said Claudia, in a sing-song voice. She was wiggling her wine glass in the air at Martha. 'What a bad girl you've been.'

Martha's heart was now thumping so vigorously, her entire body seemed to be shaking. Why was Claudia doing this to her?

The two women stared at each other, but Martha couldn't read what was going through her friend's mind.

'Jesus,' whispered Anna, from the sofa. 'That's awful. I mean, really bad. I can't imagine doing something like that.'

'To start with, she didn't even tell Simon!' slurred Claudia, turning to the others. 'Can you believe it? She couldn't admit to her own husband what she did.'

'Did she ever find out? The other woman, I mean?' asked Selina. 'Wow, no wonder you're ashamed of that. I always had you down as someone with principles.'

Martha stood in the middle of the room, staring at Claudia.

'You bitch,' she said.

There was an intake of breath behind her, she had no idea whether it was from Anna or Selina.

'Aw, come on, hon,' slurred Claudia, still swaying. 'Lighten up. You're among friends here! We won't tell anyone else your little secret.'

Martha stepped forward and reached out to grab the wine glass from her hand. Claudia stepped back, stumbling against the coffee table and dropping the glass, which hit the table with a crack, imploding and scattering hundreds of tiny fragments of glass across the carpet.

There was a stunned silence. Martha looked back up at Claudia.

'Get out,' she whispered. 'Get out of my fucking house!'

37

The room was larger than she remembered; once the wheelchair was parked in the corner, there was room for Simon to sit on the floor with Joe, while she put the carefully folded piles of clothes into drawers. She made the bed with the Thomas the Tank Engine duvet set and rested Fluff against the pillow, embarrassed at how filthy the teddy looked – even though she'd put it through the washing machine again last night.

'I hope all the staff will read the bit about Fluff,' she said. 'Joe won't be able to sleep without him.'

'It's ridiculous he's so dependent on that thing,' Simon said. 'He ought to be weaned off it.'

'Loads of children have favourite cuddly toys. It's a security blanket, there's nothing unusual about it.'

'But it's disgusting, Martha – the stuffing's coming out and it stinks!'

He was right, but she couldn't imagine looking down on Joe as he slept, and not seeing his arms wrapped around the mangled piece of brown fur.

They'd been asked to fill in an extensive form to hand in

when they arrived, answering questions about everything from Joe's favourite food to his sleep patterns, the clothes he usually wore, the cartoons he watched on the iPad and his daily routine at nursery.

'We do things our own way here,' said Carrie, the girl who would be his primary carer. 'But we need as much background as we can, because familiarity is essential while he's getting to know us all.'

They'd also been told that the initial settling-in period was going to last for a fortnight. Martha was shocked.

'So, we won't be able to take him home next weekend?' She tried to keep the wobble out of her voice.

'It makes sense,' Simon had said. 'It will be easier for him to adjust if he stays here for longer.'

That was probably true. But over the last few days – and particularly during the drive down earlier this morning – she'd been reassuring herself that all this wasn't so bad, because they'd be here again next Friday night to pick up Joe for his first weekend back at home. She'd been convincing herself that, although the weekdays would drag, she would throw herself into work and possibly join a gym so she could do exercise classes in the evenings; the time would pass quickly if she kept herself busy. But now she had to get her head around the fact that it would be two long weeks before she saw her boy again.

'He'll be fine,' said Simon. 'He won't miss us.'

That wasn't the point, but she didn't trust herself to say anything.

When Joe was ready to be wheeled away to have some lunch, Carrie suggested they head home. 'There's nothing else for you to do here, and it will make it harder, the longer you stay,' she said. Martha guessed she was in her late twenties, and it was unlikely she had children of her own, working such long hours. Yet she was standing here, confident and self-assured, waiting to take over the full-time care of someone else's son. There was suddenly so much Martha wanted to tell her.

'Please be gentle when you brush his teeth,' she said. 'He sometimes jerks his mouth away. And you need to play airplane games with the spoon when you're feeding him vegetables. He doesn't like having his hair washed either, so I sing to him while I'm rinsing off the shampoo.'

She felt Simon's hand on her shoulder. 'Come on,' he said, gently. 'Carrie knows what to do.'

'And don't let him kick too hard against the footrest of his wheelchair,' she said. 'He gets a bruise on the back of his heel.'

'We'll be going then,' Simon said. 'Thanks, Carrie.'

'You can phone any time,' the girl said. 'We'll send you an emailed report every evening for the first week.'

Carrie started to turn the wheelchair away from them, and panic jolted through Martha's body, like an electric current. 'Wait!' she whispered, and moved forward to grab the arm of the chair. 'I just need to say goodbye.'

'You've already said goodbye!' She could hear the irritation in Simon's voice, but didn't care.

She knelt down beside the chair and put her arms around Joe, pulling him towards her and resting her cheek against the side of his head, feeling the warmth from his body, smelling the shampoo she'd gently massaged into his scalp earlier this morning. He was limp in her arms at first, then began to strain against her, wriggling out of the hug.

'I love you,' she whispered.

'Come on,' said Simon. She felt his hand on her arm.

'I'm going to miss you so much...'

'Martha!' snapped Simon. 'Let's go.'

'I'm so sorry,' she whispered to Joe, just managing to touch her lips against his cheek before Simon dragged her back. They stood watching as Carrie pushed the wheelchair down the corridor, then the double doors slammed shut behind them and they were gone. Martha massaged her arm, where Simon's fingers had dug into the skin. She looked down, expecting to see a mark, but there was nothing: the pain was beneath the surface.

As they got in the car and drove up towards the main gates, Martha waited for tears to blur her view through the windscreen. But there weren't any; she was just empty.

'He'll be fine,' Simon was saying. 'He's going to do so well at this place. It's the best thing that could have happened. She's nice, Carrie, isn't she? Seems to know her stuff. We must try not to hassle her though. I know we'll want updates on how he's doing, every minute of the day, but we must try to step back and let him settle in.'

He was saying 'we', but Martha knew he was meaning 'you'.

She had turned back and taken a long look around the bedroom before they left; it was reassuringly cosy. She'd put some of Joe's picture books on the windowsill, and the new pyjamas were tucked under his pillow. She'd also put a framed photograph of her and Simon on the table and brought the small blue rug from his bedroom, which she laid on the carpet beside the bed.

'What's the point in that?' Simon had asked.

'It's to make him feel at home,' she'd said. The expression on his face told her exactly what he was thinking: their son wouldn't know or care that he wasn't sleeping in his own bedroom tonight. But she ignored it and turned away from him: she cared.

She wished she'd taken a picture of Joe in that new bedroom. She must do it next time, when they came to pick him up. God, that seemed like such a long time away. As they turned out onto the main road and Simon accelerated away from Greenways, she absently started flicking through the photographs on her phone. She had taken some yesterday, of their last proper day at home together. The sun had been shining and Simon had carried Joe outside and put him on the picnic rug under the willow tree. Martha had lain down beside him and run her finger across the smooth skin of his cheek, before turning onto her back and putting her head close to his, so they were both looking up into the network of branches overhead. The leaves were moving slightly in the wind and the sunlight seemed to scatter in different directions, sparkling as it passed through the gaps. It had been so beautiful, like a huge mobile created by nature and hung above their heads. She had held up her phone and taken a selfie of the two of them. In the photo, Joe's eyes looked even more blue than usual.

As Martha continued swiping back through pictures, she came to one she'd taken just over a week ago, at Judith's house. It was of Gracie, kneeling on the ground in front of Joe's wheelchair, holding up a shell. Her mouth was open, her brow slightly furrowed; she'd been in mid-sentence, thinking about how she was describing the pink whirled shell in her fingers. Joe was staring at her intently – almost as if he was listening to what she was saying. Of course, that wasn't possible, but Martha loved this photograph because it seemed to hint at the chance of something.

She ran her finger across the photo before closing the app and putting the phone away in her handbag. She wasn't kidding herself about Joe's future: he would never speak to her, never smile at her, never put his lips against her cheek and kiss her. He would always need to be washed, dressed and fed. She would be pushing her son in a wheelchair even when he was a grown man and several inches taller than her.

Whereas pretty Gracie had her whole life ahead of her; she was a bright little thing and would thrive at school when she finally got to go there in her green skirt and matching cardigan. Martha could imagine she would latch onto the other children with such enthusiasm that some would find it overwhelming. But she wasn't the sort of child who would care what other people thought about her; she would do everything with fire in her belly. A whirling little force of nature.

Had Judith ever made the comparison between the two children? It would be strange if she hadn't. She'd obviously seen a lot of Gracie, and possibly known more about the little girl who called her Nipper's Granny, than she did about Joe, the little boy whose granny she really was, but who couldn't communicate with her or properly receive her love. In that case, she must also have been very aware that the codicil she'd written to add to her will, was going to benefit this pretty little child much more than it was going to harm her own grandson.

As Simon accelerated down the slip road and they joined the motorway, her phone pinged. Before she'd even fished it out of her handbag again, she guessed who the text would be from. The first two lines were showing on the home screen of her phone, but she swiped to delete it without reading any further. By now she must have deleted at least a dozen texts from Claudia. The first couple had come through early on Saturday morning, and she read them still stunned at what had happened the night before.

I'm sorry! I was so pissed I wasn't thinking straight. Please forgive me? Xx

Then, an hour later:

I know you're mad at me but it was just a game! Please say you forgive me. Love you! Xx

The tone had changed during the day. By the time Claudia's

final text pinged in late last night, Martha had also rejected several of her calls.

M, this is crazy. You're my best friend! I know I behaved badly, but I'm paying for it. I've had such a massive hangover all day! Missing you xx

This most recent message today was shorter than the rest:

Where are you??? Don't ignore me xx

Martha shut off her phone and threw it back into her handbag. If Claudia was any kind of friend, she would know exactly where she was. She had known they were delivering Joe to Greenways today. She had also known how much Martha was dreading it. But in the fall out following her public shaming of her so-called 'best friend' on Friday night, it seemed to have slipped her mind.

38

'Hi, Martha, how are you?'

'I'm okay, and you?' It was strange for Patrick to actually start a phone conversation by asking how she was. He usually launched straight into whatever it was he wanted to say, barking out orders or telling her she'd done something wrong.

'Yes fine, all going well at this end.'

'Good,' whispered Martha, aware that this was yet another personal call she shouldn't be taking at work. She'd already called Carrie twice today, to check how Joe was getting on.

Listening to her brother's voice, she felt a stab of something that might almost have been love. Most of the time she found it hard to relate to this arrogant, hard-nosed man, but with Judith gone it was just the two of them now; they both needed to remember that. However much she hated the way he sometimes behaved and what he stood for, he would always be her brother.

'I was talking to a mate of mine last night, a lawyer. He thinks we need to be very careful about these women. I didn't tell him the whole story, about the note we found, I just mentioned they'd been worming their way into Mum's life and may try to make a claim against her will.'

The stab of something that might almost have been love, faded instantly.

'So, like I said to you the other day, I don't think we should be having any contact with that girl. I'm still concerned that she's going to ask if she's been left anything in the will. That's not an issue for me, obviously, but I know she has probably been calling you about the dog. From now on, you'll need to ignore her calls and texts.'

When he rang off, Martha sat staring at her laptop screen. She couldn't leave the office for another hour, but she'd lost all motivation to get any work done. Bloody Patrick: how dare he bark orders at her, telling her to have no contact with Alice? He'd be furious if he knew she'd not only seen her, the other week at the bungalow, but that they'd sat drinking tea together in the garden, chatting while Gracie played with Joe. Martha now wished she'd mentioned it; she would love to hear her brother's reaction when she told him she and Alice had been exchanging texts.

The most recent one had come in this morning.

Hi Martha, I just wondered if you'd decided what to do about Nipper? Gracie and I are so fond of him and getting used to having him around, so if you or your brother are going to take him, can you tell me soon? Before it gets too hard to hand him back! x

Martha hadn't yet answered her – because she wasn't sure what to say. She'd been feeling guilty about the dog – it was such an imposition on Alice, even though she seemed happy to have him. But Sharon, Alice and Gracie were already squeezed into a two-bedroom flat – it couldn't be easy having a yappy little Jack Russell there as well, however much they'd grown to love him. Every time Martha thought about them, it made her realise how lucky she was, to have such a big house with so much space.

Even though, with Joe gone, it was now the emptiest place in the world.

Thinking about it, since Joe was only going to be back home at the weekends, maybe she *could* offer to have Nipper? Simon would still hate it, but there was plenty of room and the garden was bigger than anything the dog had been used to. He would also be company for her, with Joe away. It was probably the most practical thing to do, but Martha wasn't sold on the idea; she'd never been a dog lover.

She would have asked Patrick what he thought, but he hadn't given her a chance to get a word in – as usual. He wouldn't particularly care what happened to Nipper, but – even if he didn't want the dog himself – Martha could imagine he'd insist they take him away from Alice, just for the hell of it. It would be another way in which he could exert control over the situation and remind the girl who was in charge.

Suddenly, Martha knew exactly what to do about this latest unanswered text. She picked up her phone:

Hi Alice, would you like to keep Nipper permanently? We'll contribute towards the cost for the next few months, but I'm sure he'll be happier with you. Besides, I know it's what Mum would have wanted x

She laughed out loud as she pressed *send*; this would really piss off Patrick. Good. It was definitely the right thing to do, Judith would have been pleased.

On the way home she pulled into a garage to fill up with petrol. There was a line of people in the kiosk, waiting to pay, while a woman up at the front had first one bank card, then another, declined. A toddler was clinging to her legs, screaming in frustration at not being able to get her mother's attention. The woman was pink with embarrassment, trying to quieten the child, while searching through her purse for a different card and apologising to the cashier. The people in the queue were shuffling from one foot to another, sighing loudly enough to make sure she was painfully aware how inconvenient this all was.

Martha wasn't in any hurry: there was nothing for her to rush home for nowadays. As she watched the woman frantically pushing her hair away from her face, she thought of Alice, although there was no obvious resemblance. Where was this woman going home to? How many other children were waiting for her there? She imagined a large family crowded into a small house, single beds lined up in a noisy bedroom full of clothes and toys and chaos. Then, out of nowhere, she suddenly pictured Gracie in the back bedroom of the bungalow. It was such a strange thought. What would that little room look like if the yellow walls were covered with bright finger paintings and drawings? How much space was there on top of the chest of drawers for rows of soft toys? The bed – where Martha had spent those two uncomfortable nights when Judith was rushed to hospital – wouldn't seem so hard and forbidding if it was covered in a colourful, patterned duvet.

God, she'd hated that bedroom and everything it stood for. The thought made her catch her breath. She'd hated the whole bungalow, in fact. There had been nothing comforting about being in that place: it was her mother's home and she had always felt awkward there.

The woman finally managed to pay for her petrol and dragged her screaming toddler back out to the car. But, as Martha moved forward in the queue, she was stunned by what had just occurred to her. She didn't want the bungalow, or anything in it – that wasn't such a surprise. But she suddenly realised she would rather it wasn't sold either. Judith had wanted Alice and Gracie to live there, so that was what must happen.

On the drive home and for the rest of that evening, she argued with herself. Even if she never wanted to see the bungalow again, she *did* need the money they'd get from selling it. When the estate agent's estimate had come through, Patrick worked out that – even after paying inheritance tax – he and Martha stood to gain about £300,000 each from the sale. It was a huge amount, especially considering how much she and Simon were going to have to find from now on, to pay Greenways' fees.

If she decided the money was the most important thing, she needed to do nothing at all. She could just sit back and let the smarmy estate agent do his bit, wait for a buyer to be found and look forward to the money eventually landing in her bank account. Financially that was the only sensible option, and Simon would think she was completely crazy if she suggested anything else. In fact, he'd be furious with her.

And yet. Was it really money she ought to have? Martha had always presumed it was, but her own mother hadn't thought so.

39

When Martha was about eight or nine, her mother fell out with a close friend. At first, she wasn't sure what had happened, but came across Judith sitting on the sofa one afternoon, sobbing. Horrified she ran up and threw her arms around her; she'd never seen her mother this upset before, and was shocked. She tried to wipe the tears from her cheeks, holding her mother's damp face between her small hands and planting kisses on it, desperate to make everything all right again.

'I'm fine,' Judith had sniffed. 'Honestly, it's nothing.'

Then, later that evening, there had been shouting in the kitchen and Martha crept down and sat on the bottom of the stairs, watching her father through the crack in the door. He was on the phone to someone, gesticulating with his free hand, his neck flushed.

When she was told they wouldn't be seeing Aunty Jean any more, Martha understood immediately that all these events were connected. Her mother's friend, Jean, had lived in the next road for as long as Martha could remember. The women shopped together, drank tea and wine together, went to the cinema together. Jean had spent Christmas with them, had gone on family holidays to Cornwall with them. Then suddenly, there was no more Jean. It left a gaping hole in their lives. Martha missed Jean's cackling laughter and the smell of her flowery perfume as she bent down and scooped her hair away from her face, kissing her on the forehead and telling her she was the prettiest princess in the world.

She asked her father where Aunty Jean had gone. 'We won't be seeing her any more,' he said. 'Don't speak to your mother about it, she's still very upset.'

So, they didn't mention Jean's name again. Martha caught sight of her once, a few months later, standing at the end of an aisle in the large Tesco superstore outside town. Jean had one hand on a trolley and was holding a packet of rice in the other hand, studying the label. For some reason, the sight of her had scared Martha. She'd moved away quickly, before Jean saw her. Years later she'd asked Judith what had happened, and her mother dismissed it with a wave of her hand. 'Oh that,' she'd said. 'Jean had a new boyfriend and we didn't take to him. It was something and nothing.'

It hadn't seemed like something and nothing at the time, and Martha knew Judith had been more upset than she cared to admit. Now, more than thirty years later, she had fallen out with her own friend, and she finally understood how devastating it was.

What had happened with Claudia last Friday night was still so raw, that at the moment she mostly felt nothing but fury when she thought about it. But every now and then, she'd remember something they'd done together – a trip to the seaside when the boys were just a couple of months old; a meal out with Adam and Simon to celebrate her birthday last year; a New Year's Eve party where they'd all dressed up as pirates. They had been so close and Martha hadn't realised how much she'd valued the friendship, and how special those memories were, until the person who featured most prominently in them let her down so badly.

Now, if Claudia's face flashed into her mind, it was like someone had punched her in the stomach. Martha had no idea why Claudia had done this, or what she'd been hoping to achieve. One thing was for certain, she didn't believe the texts, claiming she'd been so pissed she didn't know what she was saying. They'd all had a lot to drink, but when Martha stared at her friend across the shattered glass on the carpet, there had been something cold and calculating in Claudia's eyes. She had known perfectly well what she was doing when she told the other women about the codicil. So, it followed that she had deliberately set out to hurt Martha. For whatever reason, she wanted to humiliate her, bring her down a notch or two.

It was bewildering. Had she done something to upset Claudia? Had there been a sign their friendship had changed in any way? Maybe she'd said something thoughtless that had offended her, but she could think of nothing at all.

There had been no more texts since Sunday. Martha was relieved, but had also now – ridiculously – started feeling guilty for not accepting the olive branch. Maybe she'd been building this whole thing up too much? It had just been a stupid misunderstanding – Claudia hadn't meant to hurt her: she'd just shown she was hopeless at keeping a secret. They both needed some time apart now, but Martha was coming round to thinking this was probably something they could talk about at some stage, and try to put right.

Then, just as she was leaving for work on Wednesday morning, a huge hand-tied bouquet had been delivered by a girl from the local florist. As she held out her hand to accept it, Martha's heart leapt. Simon had already gone to the office, but these had to be from him. Beneath his newly cheerful façade, he must be missing Joe as well, so had ordered these to show he understood how she was feeling. What a sweetheart; she'd been too harsh on him.

Then she read the card: *How many more times do I have to say sorry? Please let's move on and forget all this x.* She took the flowers through into the kitchen, kicked open the bin and thrust them down into it.

'No more bloody times,' she muttered as the petals broke and stems snapped amongst the dirty food packaging. 'You don't need to say sorry any more, Claudia. I. Don't. Want. To. Hear. It!'

She hadn't told Simon about Friday night. It was yet another thing to add to the list of major events in her life she was keeping from him. Although none of it felt deliberate – there was just never the right time. With Joe safely delivered to his new existence in Wiltshire, Simon was still more cheerful than he had been a couple of weeks ago, but a different sort of distance had developed between them. Without their son to base their lives around, they'd already both settled into new routines – but it was as if they were operating in two separate bubbles which never came close enough to touch, burst and join together.

Although this was only day three of their new normal, Simon had been late back on Monday, then out at football training last night. Martha had no idea whether he'd be at home this evening, but she doubted he'd be waiting around to find out what her plans were. She still hadn't been to the gym after work, even though she took her kit with her when she left the house every morning. She couldn't face the idea of going somewhere new, exchanging pleasantries with strangers and pushing herself out of her comfort zone. Embarking on something so different seemed like too much of a challenge. She hated being on her own in the house, so much so that she'd volunteered to work every day this week, pretending to Clive she was keen to make up for the time she'd taken off before the funeral.

At precisely 5.25pm, Janey started tidying the papers on her desk and powering down her computer. 'Doing anything tonight?' she asked.

Martha smiled and shook her head.

'Rob's taking me out for dinner,' said Janey. 'He won't tell me where, it's a surprise. But I have a feeling it's that place out in Aldermere – you know, the pub with the Michelin star?'

'That will be lovely,' said Martha. Janey had had another blazing row with Rob on the phone yesterday morning, so this was clearly a make up meal. Poor Rob; she'd never met the man, but being married to Janey must be stressful and extremely expensive.

Martha was one of the last to leave. It was extraordinary: just a week ago, she would have been racing Janey for the lift, keeping to a tight schedule of picking up Joe from nursery and getting him home and fed. She wasn't used to having all this time on her hands and had no idea how to fill it.

They were short on milk so she pulled into Sainsbury's on the way home, picked up a basket and wandered aimlessly down the aisles. She found herself at the far end of the store, staring at the wine section, row upon row of red, white and rosé. She still hadn't replaced the wine the girls had drunk on Friday night, so put a couple of bottles in her basket. She would get organised and do a proper shop soon, but this would keep them going for now.

The prospect of opening one of these bottles when she got home and filling a glass with the cool, straw-yellow liquid, was enough to cheer her up, even though that wasn't a good thing. She generally tried not to drink during the week but, since losing her boy, she'd spent the last three evenings lying on the sofa, her hand curled around a glass, literally drowning her sorrows.

She felt so lost.

Waiting at the checkout, she pulled out her phone and began to flick through her emails.

'Hey, Martha! How are you?'

She turned, not recognising the voice. Dan was standing behind her in the queue, Johnny asleep in the buggy, a wire basket balanced on the handlebars.

'I thought it was you!'

'Oh, hello,' she said, her heart suddenly racing. 'How are you?'

'Good, all good,' he said. 'We missed you at music therapy this morning. It was quite a low-key session, that woman Liz wasn't there either and Suky had a cold, so she wasn't in the best mood.'

Martha stared at him.

'How's Joe? He's not ill, is he?'

She opened her mouth to reply, but found she couldn't speak.

In front of her, the smile dropped from Dan's face and he looked first startled, then horrified. There was a strange high-pitched wailing coming from somewhere, and she suddenly realised she was the one making the noise.

40

'Here, get that down you.' He put a mug of tea in front of her and slid into the seat opposite, taking his own mug off the plastic tray and pushing it to one side.

'I'm so sorry,' said Martha, blowing her nose again. She'd stopped crying, but knew she must look a sight: her eyes were puffy and the skin underneath her nose was raw. 'I'm sure you ought to be getting home. You'll need to be getting Johnny ready for bed.'

'That's fine,' said Dan, pulling the buggy closer to the table. Johnny was still asleep, his glasses pushed slightly to one side, his cheek squashed against the frame. 'He'll wake up in a bit and be bouncing off the ceiling until midnight. We don't keep regular hours I'm afraid. He's never slept well, so I just go with the flow.'

The woman behind the café counter was looking over at them, not even bothering to disguise her curiosity. Martha wiped her eyes again then picked up the mug with both hands and sipped at the tea. There was too much milk in it, but she didn't care. 'This is so kind of you,' she said. 'The last few days have been horrible and when you mentioned Joe, it just set me off.'

'When did you take him to this new school?'

'Sunday. It's ridiculous to be like this, I know. I should be happy about it. I *am* happy, because it's such an amazing place and we're lucky he's got in there. It's going to do him so much good.'

'But it's still hard,' said Dan.

She nodded. 'It's awful. The house is so quiet without him. I'm doing idiotic things like walking into his room and rearranging all the toys on the shelves, just so I can spend time in there. Do you know, every night I've gone in and drawn his bedroom curtains, then I've opened them again the next morning. How bloody stupid is that?'

'Oh, Martha, you poor thing. It's not stupid at all; any parent would be the same. I'd be devastated.'

Not every parent, thought Martha: Simon didn't appear to be in the slightest bit devastated. She could never have admitted to him that she was opening and closing Joe's curtains as if their son was still at home. He would have laughed at her.

'Is this school permanent then?' asked Dan. 'I mean, can he stay there long-term or are you just trying it out for a while, to see if it helps him?'

'I guess it's permanent,' said Martha. 'I've not really thought about it, to be honest. I haven't wanted to. The staff didn't make us any promises, but some of the sensory stimulation they use has had remarkable results, although mostly with children who have other issues – neuro-cognitive disorders or severe autism. Joe's disabilities are so advanced we've been told he may never be able to talk or understand what we're saying to him. We're not expecting miracles. I guess it just feels as if this place can give him such an amazing standard of care, and the therapy can't do any harm.'

She hadn't spoken in this kind of detail to anyone else, other than Simon. None of her friends really wanted to hear how extreme and untreatable Joe's disabilities were; if she did speak about what was happening, she soon became aware of their discomfort – they would shift in their seats, fiddle with their hair, play with their mugs of coffee on the table, look around for their own children. She knew part of that was guilt; they had healthy, happy, normal children – she didn't. But there was also a reluctance to find out more. Joe's condition and diagnosis were messy and awkward; he looked normal but he didn't behave in the right way. He made strange noises that scared other children; he moaned, his body sometimes shuddered involuntarily, his limbs jerking of their own accord. Other parents found him embarrassing to be with. They didn't understand, and they didn't really want to.

But Dan was different. Dan had a disabled son; he was a full-time carer. He had fewer expectations for his little boy, although he clearly loved him unconditionally. But he knew how it felt to go through the hurt and trauma of discovering his son would never fit in with so-called normal life. He knew how it felt to be stared at, pointed at, whispered about.

'Even though it sounds like a great place, that doesn't make it any easier for you,' he was saying now. 'Looking after him has been your life. I'm sure it's been bloody hard work and grim at times, but it's still been your reason for getting up every day. With him gone, you must feel as if someone's chopped off one of your legs.'

'That's exactly how it feels,' she said. 'But if you carry on being this sympathetic about it, you'll start me off again.' Although actually, she was feeling better. Just being able to talk about Joe and Greenways was helping – and being able to tell the truth. She spent so much time pretending life was enjoyable, and that caring for her disabled son was fulfilling, whereas it was actually one long, repetitive, physically strenuous, depressing grind. But she wasn't supposed to admit that to anyone, because it wasn't what a good, dutiful parent would do. She didn't need to say any of that to Dan, because he knew.

'Thanks for the tea, and for listening,' she said. 'I appreciate it.'

He smiled at her and she tried to work out what colour his eyes were. She'd thought they were blue, but even under the harsh strip-lighting of the supermarket café, she could now see they were green.

Johnny jerked himself awake and stared up at her, one fist rubbing his eye and pushing his glasses down his face.

'Hey there, matey!' said Dan, leaning over him. 'Had a good kip? Let me grab those, before they get broken. We go through glasses like you wouldn't believe. At least three or four pairs a year.'

'You must get him home,' said Martha.

'Yes, we've got macaroni cheese for tea tonight, haven't we?'

'Mac 'n' cheese!' yelled Johnny. 'Mac 'n' cheese!'

They both laughed. 'Thanks again, Dan,' said Martha. 'I'm so grateful.'

'Nothing to be grateful for,' he said. 'I'm really glad we bumped into each other.'

'I don't believe that,' smiled Martha. 'Your shopping trip was ruined because you had to buy tea for a woman you hardly know who turns out to be an emotional wreck.'

'And biscuits,' said Dan, pointing to the plate on the table between them. 'Don't forget I bought you biscuits too.'

'Biscuit!' yelled Johnny, leaning forward in the buggy and reaching for the plate. Dan grabbed it and pushed it back to the centre of the table.

'Seriously though,' he said. 'It's been good to chat to you. I've enjoyed it. I'm just sorry the circumstances aren't the best. But I tell you what, you can make it up to me by buying me a cup of tea next time.' He reached for the paper napkin beside his mug of tea and pulled a pen from his pocket. 'Here's my number. Give me a call or a text when you've got some free time.'

41

There was a loud rap on the front door. It was nearly 9pm – who the hell could it be at this time on a Friday night? Simon was out with the footballers, and wouldn't be back for hours. Martha suddenly realised it might be Claudia. She hadn't heard anything from her since the flowers had arrived, but maybe she'd left Adam to look after the sleeping children and come over to sort things out in person? Please no: Martha didn't have the energy to deal with that right now. She peered through the curtains in the sitting room and saw a car outside; it was too dark to make out much detail, but it definitely wasn't Claudia's white four-wheel drive. Thank God. She went to answer the door, her heart racing.

'Patrick! What on earth are you doing here?'

'Well, nice to see you too,' he said, walking past her into the hall. He threw a small holdall onto the floor, then turned back and kissed her on the cheek. 'Got a little something for us,' he said, holding up a bottle of whisky. 'Thought we could do with a proper catch-up.'

He turned and went through to the kitchen, leaving Martha staring after him, open-mouthed.

'Of course, it's good to see you, but– Why are you here?'

He had perched on one of the high stools around the breakfast bar and was shrugging off the jacket of his suit. 'God, the traffic was bloody awful. Should have thought about that, getting out of town on a Friday night. Plus, there were lane closures on the M4, usual story. Anyway, I'm here now. Find me a glass, there's a good girl, really need to make some headway with this. It's a sixteen-year-old single malt from a new distillery on the west coast of Scotland. Client gave it to me, a couple of days ago.'

She watched him open the bottle and pour out the liquid. He needed a haircut and his fringe was flopping into his eyes as he leant down and studied the glass. He looked uncharacteristically dishevelled tonight, as well as tired. The ceiling spotlights were accentuating the bags under his eyes.

'Look at the colour of that,' he said. 'Fabulous. You not having any?'

She shook her head. 'I'm on wine.'

'Okay, well cheers then. Happy days!'

She flinched. That was the toast Claudia always made. 'Patrick, I can't believe you're behaving as if nothing has happened. We've had a couple of abrupt conversations on the phone about selling Mum's house and, before that, the last time we spoke properly was at the funeral. Maybe you don't remember, but you and Helen were bloody rude to me at that hotel and I was really upset afterwards. It's bad enough burying your mother, without getting shot down by your own brother at the same time.'

'Yes, sorry about that.' Patrick had drained the glass of whisky and now refilled it. He didn't sound particularly sorry.

'Right. So that's it? You're just expecting us to move on and pretend nothing has happened?'

'Up to you.' He shrugged. 'If you want, I'll go away again.'

'For God's sake, of course I don't want you to go away,' said Martha. 'All I'm asking for is some kind of apology. But why *are* you here? It's a long way to come, and I might not have been in. Why didn't you call?'

'Spur of the moment thing,' said Patrick. 'Just thought it would be good to see you. God, can't a bloke act on impulse? Why do women always have to be so uptight about arrangements.'

'I'm not being uptight, I just...'

'You're all the same,' he carried on. 'Nothing we do is ever right. Don't do this, don't do that. It's fucking difficult being male, you know. We can't make you lot happy, however hard we work, however much effort we put into it.'

Martha stared at him; even for Patrick, this was unreasonable. She'd only asked why he'd driven a hundred miles to turn up with no warning on her doorstep on a Friday night.

'It would be nice to get a proper welcome,' he carried on, taking another mouthful of whisky. 'Hello, Patrick, how are you? What a wonderful surprise! How great to see you! But no, I just get moaned at for not telling you. Women! You're as bad as Helen. I just thought I'd surprise my little sister and come down to see how you are. But sorry that it doesn't fit in with your plans.'

'That's enough!' she said. 'Just shut up, Patrick.'

His eyes widened as he stared at her over the rim of the glass.

'Stop behaving like a shit. If you're going to be in my house, then the least you can do is show a bit of respect.' She could feel a muscle pulsating in the side of her neck. 'I'm sick and tired of you being so rude. You always treat me like an idiot and clearly have a very low opinion of me. But if you want to carry on like that, you'd better put your bloody designer jacket back on and get out of here.'

Patrick had slumped down, his fingers still curled around the glass of whisky, his elbows splayed out across the breakfast bar.

'Did you hear me?' yelled Martha.

He nodded and dropped his head onto one arm. He said something, but it was so muffled she couldn't make out what it was. She leant forward and pulled at his arm, trying to make him sit up, but his body was too heavy for her to drag up.

'Patrick!' she shouted.

He sat back up so suddenly that the glass jolted in his hands and whisky splashed onto the worktop.

'Sorry,' he whispered.

She looked at him, aghast. He was crying.

'I'm really sorry, Martha. You're right. I shouldn't speak to you like that.'

'Jesus. Patrick, what's the matter? What is it?' She moved forward and put her arm around him and he fell sideways against her, his shoulders heaving. 'Hey, it's going to be okay,' she said, putting her other hand up to hold the side of his face. 'Whatever it is, we can deal with it. Tell me what's happened?'

She was appalled and terrified at the same time. She hadn't seen this man cry for more than thirty years. She hadn't even seen him display any sign of weakness, uncertainty or self-doubt. Most of the time she had absolutely no idea what was going on in his head.

He sniffed and pulled away from her, wiping the back of his hand across his face. Martha fetched him a piece of kitchen roll, which he accepted with a wry smile.

'Thanks, God, sorry about that. What a fucking mess.' He blew his nose and picked up the glass, knocking back the rest of the whisky.

'Do you want to tell me what's going on?' asked Martha. She was desperate for a drink, but her wine was in the sitting room, and now wasn't the time to walk away.

He sighed and stared down at his hands. 'It's Helen,' he said. 'She's having an affair. It's been going on for a while now.'

'Oh no! I'm so sorry.' This was not what she'd been expecting.

'It's a bloke we both know, the father of one of the kids in Samantha's class,' he said. 'His wife has no idea.'

'That's awful,' said Martha. 'How did you find out?'

'Same way you always find out about these things. She left her phone lying around in the kitchen once and I saw a text flash up, when I was standing beside it. There was a lock on her phone so I couldn't read more than the first two lines, but I didn't need to see the whole thing, it was obvious what was going on. That was back in the autumn.'

'How long has it been going on?'

'Probably nearly a year now.' He laughed ruefully, not the usual brash Patrick laugh. 'She told me she'd finished with him, but I know she hasn't. I followed her one night and saw them together. I've tried to talk to him as well, fucking bastard. But that didn't end well. I threatened to tell his wife, but I don't think he even cares about that.'

'Will you tell her?' asked Martha.

Patrick shook his head. 'Probably not. She's a lovely woman and I don't think I can do that to her. If this thing ends at some stage, without causing too much damage and splitting apart two families, then there won't be any point putting her through what I've gone through.'

Martha stood in silence for a few seconds, her hand resting on his shoulder.

'The thing is, I still love Helen,' said Patrick. 'She's not just the mother of my children, she's my soulmate. I know the two of you have never really got on, and she comes across as being quite tough. But she's really kind and generous. She's got a soft side and she's funny too. We used to make each other laugh all the time.'

The picture he was painting of Helen was totally at odds with the one Martha would have come up with. She thought back to her drunken sister-in-law, slumped on the sofa at The Hamilton Hotel. That woman didn't have the slightest interest in anyone other than herself. Ironically, although Patrick wouldn't be able to see it, she was just like him – which was clearly why they'd fallen for each other in the first place. In some ways, none of this was coming as a surprise to Martha.

'That's why all of this business with Mum's will has been so awful,' Patrick suddenly said. 'I work like a dog to maintain our lifestyle. We have nice holidays and cars and the kids go to private school. You know all this. But there isn't a bottomless pit. I earn a lot, then Helen spends it again and it's a worry. When I thought we'd be coming into a bit of money, after Mum died, my first reaction was, thank God.' He paused and looked across at Martha. 'I'm sorry, I know how callous that sounds. I know I sound like a shit. But I hoped the money would help make Helen happy. I hoped it would save my marriage. After we found the codicil, on the way home afterwards I was shaking so much, I had to pull over for a few minutes because I didn't feel safe to drive. I'd been so scared when we found that note – then it was a massive relief afterwards when I realised it wasn't legally valid.'

He had started crying again, his face crumpling in a way that made tears spring to her own eyes.

'It shouldn't matter now,' he whispered. 'Because that girl isn't going to get the house. But I was so hurt. How could our own mother do something like that to us? Did she really hate us both that much?'

'No, of course she didn't,' said Martha, hugging him again.

'She loved us both very much, Patrick. Especially you! You were her golden boy, you know that.'

'Then why did she do this?' he asked.

'I don't know,' she said. 'I really have no idea.'

42

The silence was so strange. It was the first time in five years she'd not been woken at dawn on a Saturday morning. Her stomach muscles clenched as she thought about Joe. What would he be doing now? Was Saturday like any other day at Greenways, or did the pace of life slow down there, like it did everywhere else? She wanted to know whether he was sleeping well in that little bed, what he was having for breakfast, which clothes his carers had picked out for him to wear. She wanted to know everything, but was being told so little. She hadn't been able to stop herself calling every day this week – sometimes twice a day. Whenever she'd spoken to Carrie, she could hear the sympathy and understanding in the woman's voice, but by Thursday there had been impatience creeping in as well, and yesterday she'd been terse.

'Listen, Martha, I'm not working over the weekend, so it's best if you don't call. Let's catch up again on Monday. That will be easier than you trying to get through to the right person while I'm not here.'

'You've got to let them get on with it,' Simon had said.

'They're paid to look after Joe, not to answer endless phone calls from you.'

'I know that,' she snapped. It was fine for him, he didn't seem to be worried about any of this. But at the moment she still needed constant reassurance about how her boy was coping. Each morning she woke up missing him like crazy, but feeling relatively calm. Yet, as the day went on, she couldn't stem the panic that rose up inside her. The rational part of her knew Joe was being wonderfully well cared for, but a constant stream of 'what ifs' ran through her head. What if he was unwell? What if he didn't like the food? What if he had nightmares?

Now, she rolled over in bed and saw the back of Simon's head, half hidden beneath his pillow. She had no idea what time he'd got home last night. For once though, she was relieved he'd been so late; it had given her time to calm down Patrick, put a plate of food in front of him, try to counteract the whisky with some coffee. She had finally helped him up to the spare room just before midnight, dragging off his shoes as he collapsed face down on the bed and instantly began to snore.

She got up and pulled on her dressing gown, padding downstairs to the kitchen. As usual, Simon must have come back from the pub in need of food. Most of the cupboard doors were open, a plate and empty glass had been left out, alongside a packet of biscuits, a loaf of bread and a scattering of crumbs that trailed across the worktop and down onto the tiled floor. The end of the loaf, uncovered overnight, was now hard.

Martha filled the kettle and began to tidy up. It was so strange to be in here without Joe in his chair, or the television turned on in the corner, cartoons echoing through the tiled space. But – although it hurt to admit it – there was something therapeutic about the peace and quiet. She slid open the glass doors and stood staring into the garden, listening to birdsong. A squirrel was sitting on top of the fence, frozen in place having seen her, waiting for her to make a move.

'Morning.'

She spun round. Patrick was standing by the kitchen door.

'How are you feeling?' The answer was obvious: he looked bloody awful. 'Want a coffee?'

He nodded and walked towards the breakfast bar, running his hand through his tousled hair. He was still in the clothes he'd been wearing last night.

'I'm sorry about everything you've been going through,' she said, putting a mug in front of him. How much would he remember about last night? She'd never seen him so drunk.

He looked at her and nodded. 'I'm sorry too, for turning up like that,' he said. 'Not really how you wanted to spend your Friday night, was it?'

'Well,' she said. 'I had big plans, obviously. But it's not the end of the world.'

They smiled at each other and Martha suddenly saw so much of their mother in him. She'd always thought Patrick took after their father, but this morning he looked softer. He had Judith's deep brown eyes and their faces were almost exactly the same shape.

She sawed off the stale end of the loaf and cut fresh slices to put in the toaster, taking butter and marmalade out of the fridge and setting it all in front of him.

'You'll feel better once you eat something,' she said, pulling out a stool and perching on it. 'We also need to talk properly, now we're both sober enough.'

He buttered the toast and bit into it as if he hadn't eaten for days. 'I probably ought to get back to London, as soon as I've had this,' he muttered, his mouth full. 'Helen will be expecting me to look after the kids while she goes off shopping or to get her nails done, or whatever else is on today's busy schedule.'

'Are they all right, Max and Samantha?' asked Martha. 'Do you think they've picked up on what's happening between you and Helen?'

He shook his head. 'They're fine. In all honesty, we're quite far down their list of priorities, after social media and their friends and gaming.'

Martha was sure he was right. She topped up his coffee. 'Listen,' she said. 'About what you were saying last night. You were wrong – Mum didn't hate us. None of this was done to punish us. It was done to help Alice.'

He stiffened at the mention of her name. 'Whichever way you look at it,' he said. 'The end result is the same. She wanted that girl to get our inheritance.'

'That's true,' said Martha. 'But what's been upsetting me most, is not being able to understand why Mum made this decision. I felt like you, I didn't know how she could do it to us. But the more I think about it, the less I think it was personal. She knew Alice had no money and no proper home, and that she really needed the bungalow. She also thought we didn't. Look at us: we live in lovely big houses, we seem to lead comfortable lives, we don't want for anything.'

'We both know that's not exactly true,' said Patrick.

'Yes, but Mum didn't know that!' said Martha. 'She thought we were fine, doing well for ourselves. Neither of us ever let down our guard and admitted we had problems, with money or our marriages or anything else. So, she thought she could make this decision and help Alice, and it wouldn't be a big deal for us.'

'But we were her children!' said Patrick. 'Her flesh and blood, for God's sake. She had a duty to look after her family.'

'What's duty got to do with it?' asked Martha.

'Everything! Inheritance laws recognise the distribution of assets to direct family. Even if you don't have any family, everything then goes to the government first, before friends or bloody dog walkers!'

'But that only happens if you don't specify something else,' said Martha. 'Mum did. She knew exactly what she wanted to happen. Anyway, I don't agree that any of this is about duty. Just because she was our mother, it doesn't mean she was obliged to leave us everything. We expected it, but we didn't have any right to do that.'

Patrick was running his finger around the edge of his plate, scooping up the crumbs left by the toast. 'Well, that's very magnanimous of you,' he said. 'I'm not sure I can be so noble about it. But that doesn't explain why she didn't just tell us what she'd done.'

He was sounding calmer, less antagonistic. But Martha understood how much he was hurting; she was too.

'I think she probably would have told us,' she said, gently. 'When the time was right. She wouldn't have made a major decision like this, and left us to find out about it after her death.'

'But that's exactly what happened,' he said. 'She wrote that note six months ago. That's long enough to have found a time to talk to us about it.'

'Is it really?' asked Martha. 'How many times had you been down to see Mum this year, Patrick? Once – maybe twice at the most. I'm not saying that to make you feel guilty, I know life gets in the way. But neither of us went to see her as often as we should have done, and we were never with her together. I think she was probably waiting for the right time to tell us about the codicil, but she hadn't found it yet. She might even have been planning to introduce us to Alice, or involve her in our lives somehow. We'll never know now. But she didn't get the chance to do that, because she ended up in hospital.'

'She could have told us when we were both with her on the

ward,' said Patrick. 'That was the perfect time. Why didn't she do it then?'

Martha shook her head. 'God, for a bright man, you can be a real idiot sometimes. She didn't know there was any need to tell us – or any urgency. As far as she was concerned, she'd had a fall and needed a hip operation. She wasn't particularly old and she hadn't been ill. She had no idea she was going to die!'

They sat in silence for a few minutes, sipping their coffee, avoiding each other's eye.

'Maybe you're right,' said Patrick, eventually. 'It still hurts though.'

Martha nodded. 'I know,' she said. 'It hurts me too. But I don't want this to change the way I think about her. I miss her all the time and I'm so sad this has happened, because it's not how I want to remember my relationship with her.'

Patrick was nodding, still staring down at his coffee.

'There's one more thing,' said Martha, her own voice sounding loud in the echoing kitchen. 'I've decided I want to respect her wishes.'

He looked up at her, confused.

'I think Alice ought to have the bungalow.' Martha hadn't planned to say that. But now the words were out of her mouth, they felt right.

'What?' His mouth dropped open.

'I'm sorry, Patrick. But I think that would be the right thing to do. I realise I can't make it happen though, because half of the house is yours and, after what you've been saying, it's not fair for me to expect you to give that up. But in that case, once we've sold it, I'm going to give my share of the money to Alice, so she can think about getting a place of her own.'

43

'What the fuck are you doing here?'

Simon was standing in the doorway, one hand tugging up his pyjama bottoms, the other scratching his bare chest. He clearly hadn't expected them to have company.

'Patrick came down last night,' Martha said. 'He slept in the spare room.'

'Thanks for consulting me!' said Simon. 'I wondered whose car that was, outside. I can't say it's a pleasure to see you, Patrick. If I'd been asked, I would have suggested you bugger off and get yourself a hotel room.'

'Simon! For God's sake,' said Martha. 'We had things we needed to talk about.'

'Oh, that's great. So, the two of you are talking again now, are you? What good news. I'm surprised you dare show your face here, to be honest, Patrick. Have you forgotten the way your charming brother treated you at the funeral, Martha? I can't believe you invited him to come down, after you were so upset last week!'

'She didn't know I was coming,' said Patrick, getting off the stool and turning around to face Simon.

For a moment, Martha had an awful feeling the two men were going to launch themselves at each other. They stood six feet apart, radiating aggression and mutual dislike. She walked across and put her hand through Simon's arm, pulling him into the kitchen towards the purple sofa.

'Sit down, I'll get you some coffee.'

He shook off her hand and walked across to the kettle, shaking his head. 'I can get my own bloody coffee. You're a piece of work, Patrick. You were out of order at the funeral, and you haven't even bothered to get in touch with Martha to apologise for the things you and your pisshead of a wife said to her. Now you just turn up here and expect we'll all be happy to see you!' He took a mug out of the cupboard and slammed it down onto the worktop so hard, the handle came off in his hands. 'Fuck.'

'I know, you're right,' said Patrick. 'I have said sorry. Well, sort of. I am really sorry – both of you. I know what happened at the funeral was awful. We all said some things we shouldn't have said.'

'You did,' said Simon. 'I don't regret any of what I said. I think I just told you what an arse you were. I haven't changed my mind about that.'

'Okay, that's enough,' said Martha. 'This isn't getting us anywhere. Simon, thanks for standing up for me, but I can fight my own battles.'

He glared across at her, a muscle twitching beside his eye. 'Can you really? You've never been much good at standing up for yourself where your brother is concerned. He walks all over you.'

'Well, right now, I'd like to deal with this. Please.' Martha could feel her face flushing as she glared back at him.

'I'm leaving anyway,' said Patrick. 'I'll go and get my stuff from upstairs, then I'll be out of your hair. Thanks for breakfast, Martha. And for listening last night.'

He picked up his cup and drank the rest of the coffee, before setting it back on the breakfast bar. 'I need to think about what you said,' he said, looking at her. 'I don't know what to do, to be honest. I can't seem to think straight right now – I'm tired of the whole thing.'

Martha nodded. It was the same for her.

He started to walk away, then turned back. 'I am really sorry about what happened. Helen was out of order, and so was I. We shouldn't have said those things to you. None of it was true. You were the best daughter anyone could have asked for; you did so much for her.'

He walked over and put his arms around her. She breathed in sharply, taken aback. She hadn't been this close to her brother for years. He was hugging her properly now, almost too tightly, squeezing the breath from her. His cheek was warm and surprisingly soft against her forehead. He didn't smell great, his unwashed body stale in yesterday's clothes, but she hugged him back, equally tightly, swallowing away the lump in her throat.

44

T hey sat at opposite ends of the breakfast bar, staring down at their mugs. This new silence which had earlier seemed therapeutic, was now unsettling. The sun was streaming through the windows, throwing streaks of light onto the tiled floor, but there was a darkness in the room. Martha willed him to say something; she didn't want to be the one to start this conversation.

'Simon,' she said, eventually. 'We need to talk.'

She half expected him to look up at her, surprised, raising his eyebrows. She imagined him asking her what she meant, could almost hear the confusion in his voice. But he didn't look up at all. He just nodded.

'Help me here,' she said.

He sighed and sat up straighter, finally looking at her. 'What do you want me to say, Martha?'

'This isn't working, is it?' She had thought these words, so many times, but it was strange to hear herself finally saying them out loud. It made them brutally real. 'Us, I mean. You and me. We're not working anymore.'

He shook his head slowly. 'No, we're not.'

She waited for him to carry on, but the silence stretched between them, broken only by the gentle hum of the fridge in the corner.

'So, where do we go from here?' she asked. She hadn't taken her eyes off his face, waiting for some kind of reaction to flash across it. But there was nothing.

Eventually he sighed and slumped further down on the stool. 'To be honest, I don't know if we can go anywhere,' he said.

There it was. In an instant, everything was over. Her stomach flipped as if she'd been kicked.

They were still staring at each other. He looked exhausted this morning, drawn and pale, suddenly so much older than his years. She was aware she did as well. It had crept up on them without much warning, this onset of middle age. Simon's eyes hadn't changed though: they were the same deep pools of brown which had stared at her so intently the first time they met. The same eyes she had known and loved for years, but which now seemed to be studying her with the impassivity of a stranger. The expression on his face was so blank, she had no idea what he was thinking, but sadly this was nothing new. She was beginning to realise that she hadn't been able to work out what was going on in his head for a long time.

She looked down at her fingers, twisting together on the breakfast bar in front of her. This was the moment that would change everything. She could almost imagine herself, balanced on the edge of a cliff, staring over into an abyss: a voice in her head was telling her to step forward and plunge into the unknown, because this was the end and there was no point dragging things out any further. But it was terrifying: the acknowledgement their marriage had failed, with all the potential heartache and stress that would cause.

She took a deep breath; her hands were trembling.

There was an alternative: she could step back from the brink and sort this out. It wasn't too late. She had been reckless in starting this conversation: what the hell had she been thinking? She must tell Simon he was wrong and suggest ways they could smooth this over. If she got off her stool right now and walked across to where he was sitting, she could talk them away from the edge. She imagined putting her hand on his arm and curling herself around him, telling him they would work this out and they'd get through it. But she couldn't move: her body was like lead.

'You're right,' she whispered. 'There's nowhere for us to go from here.'

Blood was pounding through her veins, taking her breath away and crashing in her ears like waves on a beach. There was a scraping sound as he pushed back his stool. She looked up, thinking he might come towards her, but he went to the kettle, lifting it to check it was full of water, then putting it on to boil. He turned around and leant back against the worktop, his arms folded in front of him.

This was really it, then.

'Is there someone else?' she asked.

He shook his head. 'No. There never has been.'

She believed him; it had never felt like she had a rival for his affections.

'What about you?'

'Me?' she laughed. 'No, of course not. God, when would I have found the time to get myself a lover!'

He wasn't smiling.

'Sorry, Simon, I didn't mean to joke about it. But no, there's never been anyone else.'

The kettle had boiled but he carried on leaning against the worktop, staring out through the windows to the garden.

'Is there any point in us... I mean, should we go for counselling or something?' She hadn't thought of this before now, and wasn't sure it would do any good. But it seemed like the right thing to say. 'It all feels pretty final, but there's no point in rushing things. We need to work it out properly. For Joe's sake, maybe we should go and see someone.' She could hear herself gabbling. 'We do need to think about Joe, how he'll cope with all of this.'

'You know that's not true,' said Simon, gently. 'It doesn't matter. It won't affect Joe because he doesn't even know us, Martha. He won't know or care that we're not together anymore.'

'He does know me,' she whispered. 'He really does.'

'Well, you tell yourself whatever you need to hear. But you know I'm right. This isn't about Joe, it's about you and me and we need to decide what will be best for us.'

Her heart had slowed slightly, and she was able to breathe again, although her head was pounding.

'There's no point pretending we can sort things out,' said Simon. 'It's all gone too far for that. I'm sorry, Martha, but I don't love you anymore, not in the way I need to. And I know you don't love me like that, either.'

The words should have been like a slap in the face, but they weren't. Now that this was actually happening, none of it was as awful as she'd expected.

'I'll move out,' Simon said. 'Find somewhere else to live. You should stay here for the time being, until we sort out what we're going to do about this place. We'll have to put it on the market, but there's no urgency.'

Her house: her beautiful house. Her stomach contracted at the thought of leaving this big, stylish place she loved so much and had worked so hard to turn into a home for the family she never had. But he was right; that is what would need to happen.

'You don't have to go straight away,' she said. 'We can stay here together. There's enough space for the two of us to live here and keep out of each other's way.'

Ironically, that was what they'd been doing for a long time anyway. She couldn't remember when they'd last sat down in the evening to watch a film, or cooked together in the kitchen, chatting about their days while they chopped and mixed and stirred.

'I'm not going to walk out on Joe,' Simon said. 'Don't think that. I'll always be there for him. I'm not expecting you to become his full-time carer, when he's back for the weekend.'

She nodded. Although, with the best will in the world, there was a possibility that would happen. How would they cope with Joe's complex needs if they sold this house and moved into two smaller places? Even if he was only back at weekends, they would need to adapt two separate homes for a wheelchair, pay for two separate stairlifts, two adapted beds, buy two cars that could transport their son and all the equipment they needed for him. The process they were embarking on had such immense consequences for all three of them, but she couldn't face thinking about any of that right now.

'It's going to be hard,' she said.

'I know.'

'Let's try to be kind to each other, while we're sorting it all out.'

He nodded and, finally, walked across to where she was sitting. They put their arms around each other and she closed her eyes as she rested her cheek against his bare chest.

'I'm sorry we haven't been able to make it work,' he said. 'Nothing went as we'd planned. I know life isn't meant to be easy, but too much went wrong.'

She nodded too now, her cheeks damp against his skin. He was right; there had been too many disappointments.

45

Finding out where they lived wasn't a problem. Judith's address book had been sitting amongst a pile of paperwork in Martha's kitchen ever since she'd worked her way through it to contact people about the funeral. There were only three entries under G, and it was the last one, written in her mother's familiar forward-slanted writing: *Sharon Gordon – Flat 3, 14 Prospect Court.* Then, in a different coloured pen, after Sharon's name, Judith had later added *Alice & Gracie.*

Martha had no idea where Prospect Court was, but it didn't take long to find on Google Maps. It was more than a mile and a half from the bungalow, and it didn't look as if there was a direct bus route. That meant Alice would have been walking three miles every day just to get there and back – and that was before she even took Nipper out.

Martha left home at 10am and two and a half hours later turned into Prospect Court. It was one of a dozen roads on a seventies estate; the buildings were a uniform brown brick and number 14 was a small block with neatly tended shrubs growing in a flower bed beside the front door.

She parked across the road and looked at the building. Her

palms felt sweaty on the steering wheel. She'd only decided to drive back here last night, and her main concern had been to get this conversation over and done with. She'd been practising what she might say in the car, talking out loud to herself. Whichever way she did it, the words seemed inadequate.

But this was the right thing to do. Three weeks ago, grieving and in shock, she had let her brother bully her into doing what he wanted. As usual. She was still grieving now – that wouldn't change for a long time – but she was thinking more rationally. During the lowest moments, usually when she woke in the darkness before dawn and her mind started going over everything again, it all seemed too much. She had lost her mother, her son and her husband, and the pain was overwhelming. But when daylight started streaking through the curtains and she dragged herself out of bed, life didn't feel quite so bad. Martha got dressed every day, ate breakfast, went to work, sent texts, went to the gym, met friends, went shopping, thought about Joe almost constantly. And through it all, she was generally managing to stay positive. These recent changes in her life had been immense, but they didn't need to be devastating: she constantly reminded herself that she would get through them. Most of the time, she believed it.

But this conversation was long overdue.

Someone had put a string of solar fairy lights across the top of the door frame of the block of flats. There were six bells and Martha pressed the one with 3 scribbled beside it in biro.

'Oh! What are you doing here?' Alice was wearing a baggy green T-shirt and holding a plastic spatula. 'Sorry, that's really rude!' She stepped back and opened the front door. 'Come on up.'

The smell of bacon was wafting through the open door of the flat.

'Is this a bad time?' asked Martha. Why hadn't she called to let them know she was coming, rather than turning up unannounced? She hated it when people did that to her – they always seemed to catch her half-dressed, without any make-up on, or in the middle of trying to shovel food into Joe.

'No, it's fine,' said Alice. 'It's good to see you. Mum, look who's here!'

Martha's heart sank: she'd been hoping Sharon would be at work.

'Hey, this is a nice surprise.' The older woman was sitting at the kitchen table with Gracie, the pieces of a jigsaw spread out in front of them. Nipper was lying in his basket underneath the table and he lifted his head to look at Martha, before flicking an ear and lying back down again.

'Sorry to just turn up like this,' said Martha.

'Where's Joe?' asked Gracie, jumping off a chair and coming to stand in front of her.

'I'm on my own today, Gracie. Joe has started at a new school so he couldn't come.'

'But I want to show him these!' said the girl. She ran back to the table and picked up a pile of stones. 'Look! I found them on our walk last week, and they've got fosses in them.'

'Fossils,' said Alice.

'Tell him he has to come next time.' Gracie rattled the stones together in her open palms.

'Gracie, why don't you go and put the telly on,' said Alice. 'How's Joe settling in?'

'Fine,' said Martha. 'I Facetimed yesterday while the physios were helping him in the hydro pool. It was wonderful to watch, they're such amazing people.'

'I bet you miss him though?'

'God, yes. So much. But I know it's going to do him good, and he'll be home for the weekend soon.'

She hoped she sounded casual and laid-back about her boy;

she certainly didn't feel it. She'd been counting down the days – sometimes the hours – until she would see him again, putting a cross through each date on a chart she'd printed out and pinned to the kitchen wall at home. After she'd broken down in front of Dan in Sainsbury's she had gone home and lain on Joe's little bed and cried again. She'd curled her legs up under her and breathed in the – now so faint – smell of him from the pillowcase, which she couldn't bring herself to wash.

She hated herself for being this weak: she ought to be coping better and was embarrassed about it, and definitely not ready to admit how much she was struggling.

A few months ago, she might have confided in Claudia, knowing she'd smile sympathetically and give her a hug, saying, 'Ah, bless you.' But even that wouldn't really have helped, because her friend would then have gone back to her perfect life and her flawless, able-bodied children, with no real understanding of the enormity of the emotional overload Martha was dealing with. So, for the last few days she'd been answering questions about Joe like this: with lies, a smile and a brave face. But speaking to Dan had helped and, strangely, it suddenly occurred to her that, if there was anyone else she might feel able to talk to about it right now, it would be Alice. She didn't seem like the type to judge.

'I'm glad you decided to come down,' the girl was saying. 'I've been wondering whether you wanted me to do anything in the bungalow, but I didn't want to offer in case it sounded pushy.'

'You could have done,' said Martha. 'I would have been grateful, to be honest. So much has been going on at home, I haven't really thought about anything else.'

Gracie was shrieking with laughter in the room next door and Sharon had started to pack away the jigsaw. 'Kettle's just boiled,' she said. 'Cup of tea?'

'Thanks,' said Martha. She really wanted to speak to Alice on her own, but it didn't look as if Sharon was going anywhere, and she couldn't ask the woman to leave her own kitchen. She stared around the cramped room, embarrassed to be here, wishing she'd done this differently. There was a big corkboard on the wall next to the table, drawing pins skewering letters, flyers, photos and several of Gracie's colourful paintings. One looked familiar: it was like the dog she'd drawn on Judith's bookmark – this time with four legs – and underneath was written *My Nippa.*

'So, how are you feeling?' asked Alice. 'I know it's only been a few weeks, but has life settled down a bit?'

'Without Mum? Yes, I think so. I still miss her, obviously, and I have good days and bad days. But none of it is as brutal.'

'I know what you mean,' said Alice. 'At first, it would catch me unawares. I'd be doing something else, then I'd suddenly think about Judith and it would all flood over me again – even though I'd thought I was fine. It's a strange thing, grief.'

'You're right,' agreed Martha. 'Very strange.' She pulled out a chair and sat down. 'Alice,' she said. 'I hope you don't mind me coming here. But there's something I want to tell you.' She clasped her hands tightly together on the table. 'It's about the bungalow,' she said. 'About Mum's will.'

'Oh, okay.' The girl looked puzzled.

'After Mum died, we started going through all her documents,' said Martha. 'And we found something.'

Alice had pulled out a chair and was sitting a couple of feet away. If Martha stretched out her hand, she would have been able to rest it on the girl's skinny forearm.

'It was a piece of paper – a note Mum had written – and in it, she said she wanted to leave the bungalow to you, after she died.'

'I don't understand, why would she do that?'

'I'm not sure. She never spoke about it to us, but I think she thought that you needed it more than Patrick and I did.'

Alice turned to stare at Sharon, who was looking equally dumbfounded. Martha was suddenly certain Patrick had been wrong. Neither of them had had any idea about what Judith was planning.

'This is extraordinary. I can't believe it!' said Alice.

'The thing is, there's more,' said Martha, staring down at the table and running her forefinger up and down a crack in the wooden grain. 'This is going to sound awful, Alice. It *is* awful. But Patrick said the note wouldn't stand up in court, because it hadn't been witnessed. We were both so shocked by it, and we weren't really thinking clearly. He suggested we just get rid of it.'

The two women were silent. Martha couldn't face looking up from the table to see the expressions on their faces. She could feel her own heart beating forcefully in her chest. 'We didn't do it straight away. I held on to it and took it home with me. I didn't know what to do. But...' she paused, her pulse thundering in her ears. 'In the end, I did destroy it.'

No one said a word. American cartoon voices shrieked from the television in the room next door.

'I don't know what to say,' said Alice, eventually. 'So, what does all this mean?'

'It means Judith left you her house, but there's no way you can prove that,' said Sharon, quietly.

Martha could hear the accusation in the woman's voice. She plucked up the courage to look at her and nodded. 'That's exactly what it means,' she says.

'So why are you here, telling me this?' asked Alice. 'If you've stopped this happening, what's the point in coming to tell me about it now?'

'Because what I did was wrong,' said Martha. 'I shouldn't have destroyed that note. It doesn't matter if it was legal or not, it was what my mother wanted and over the last few weeks I've come to realise that Patrick and I should have respected her wishes. So, although the note itself is gone, I know it existed, and so does he. I came here today to tell you about it, because I need to put things right. When we discovered this, I was shocked and hurt. I couldn't understand why Mum had done this to me. To us.'

She picked up the mug of tea Sharon had put in front of her and took a sip, wincing as she burnt her top lip.

'I can't pretend it's not a big deal,' continued Martha. 'Because financially it really matters. Patrick and I both have families and commitments and I'd be lying if I said we didn't need what we'd get from the sale of the bungalow. There's some other money in savings and investments, but that may be swallowed up by inheritance tax.'

Alice was nodding and looking down at the table, twisting her fingers together.

'But what I've started to realise,' said Martha. 'Is that this isn't our decision to make. Mum wanted you to have the place. She wanted you and Gracie to make it your home, and I don't think we have a right to argue with that.'

Sharon was a few feet away, leaning against the sink. Martha heard her take a sharp breath in. Alice looked up, her eyes wide.

'So, do you mean you're not going to stop it?'

'No,' said Martha. 'I'm not. But I'm not quite sure how it's all going to work. Patrick isn't happy about what I've decided, but there's a lot going on in his life as well. I don't think he's up to a fight, but it's unlikely he'll just agree to us giving you the house. So, I think what will happen is that it will get sold and then, once all the details are finalised, I'm going to give you my share of whatever we get for it.'

They sat in silence, listening to Gracie in the room next door, singing along to something on the television.

Alice was shaking her head. 'You can't do this, Martha. It's not right. That was Judith's home and you ought to have the money from it, as her daughter.'

'That's what I thought too, at first. But I've changed my mind now. I've had a lot of time to think about it and none of it is as important as Patrick and I thought it was. We don't have any right to anything. You can't choose your family, but you can choose your friends, and Mum chose you.'

Alice looked as if she might be about to cry. 'I don't know what to say. I really don't. I can't believe she thought that much of me. I mean I loved her, and I know she loved us too. But to leave us her home?'

'You were a good friend to her,' said Martha.

'Whatever Judith wanted, you must have fond memories of that house,' said Sharon.

Martha shook her head. 'It doesn't mean anything to me. I never lived there – when Mum bought it, I was in my early thirties, I had my own flat. So, it never felt like home.' She turned back to Alice. 'There are a few things I'll want to keep, but if there's anything else in the bungalow that you'd like, I'd be happy for you to take it. Maybe you can come along one day, when I'm sorting things out.'

Alice smiled. 'I'd love some of her books, if you don't mind. She lent me a few, but there are loads I'd like to read.'

Martha smiled. 'Of course. I'm sure there will be other things as well. Having this money may mean you can get a place of your own, so you might want to think about taking some of the kitchen stuff or even bits of furniture. But we can talk about all of that when we're there.'

'Wow,' said Alice, turning to look at Sharon. 'Martha, I don't know what to say. I mean this would all be amazing, for me and Gracie. But I know it's the opposite for you. It must be really hard.'

'You don't need to say anything,' said Martha. 'There will be a lot to sort out, paperwork to draw up, documents we'll all need to sign. I'm sure it will take some time, but at least we won't be at each other's throats while that's happening.'

'Even Patrick?' asked Alice.

'Yes, even Patrick,' said Martha, although she wasn't entirely sure that was true. The Patrick who had broken down in front of her last Friday night and wept into his sixteen-year-old single malt, was a very different man to the one who'd aggressively suggested Alice and Sharon had been influencing Judith to change her will. But he was still straggling way behind Martha on the path towards accepting their mother's decision, and she doubted he'd be big-hearted enough to make any of this easy for either of them.

She took another sip of her tea, staring at the corkboard on the wall in front of her. There were several photos pinned down one side: some black and white, most colour. She recognised Sharon as a much younger woman, and there were several pictures of Alice holding Gracie as a baby and a toddler. Right in the middle was a large head shot of a little boy in a white shirt and grey V-necked sweater, sitting sideways and turning his head towards the camera. It had clearly been taken by a school photographer – one of those posed photographs Martha had always pretended to be slightly cynical about, but which she would have loved to be able to pin to her own wall. The boy was grinning, the tip of his tongue sticking out to one side of his mouth. He had a mop of dark blond hair, falling across his wide, flat face. His features were unmistakably those of a child with Down's syndrome.

'Who's that?' asked Martha.

Alice turned to look at the board and grinned. 'That's our Billy,' she said. 'My little brother.'

Martha stared at her. 'Your brother?'

'Yes. He was five years younger than me. He died when he was seven.'

Martha's mouth fell open and she looked back at the photo.

'He was our little angel,' said Sharon. 'Such a happy lad. Bit of a monkey too, mind you, when he didn't get his own way.' She was still leaning against the sink, smiling as she looked at the photo. She turned to Martha. 'We don't always have them for long, these children of ours,' she said. 'But we were lucky to have Billy.'

Martha suddenly remembered Gracie talking about Uncle Billy, the afternoon she met Joe at the bungalow. At the time she hadn't even wondered who that might be.

The door crashed open and the little girl came running in, her hands cupped in front of her. 'I've got a bug!' she said. 'It's like the one in that book.'

She opened her hands and pushed them towards Martha, who flinched as a brown beetle inched its way across the girl's palm. 'Well, look at that,' she said, trying to sound interested. She loathed anything that crawled.

'Mummy! You look too!'

Alice smiled and put her hand on Gracie's arm. 'That's great, he's a beauty. Shall we put him outside?'

'I'll do it,' said Sharon, holding out her hand to the little girl. 'Come on, love.'

As they went out of the front door of the flat and down the stairs, Martha turned back to Alice. 'I'm sorry,' she said. 'I didn't know about Billy.'

Alice shrugged. 'Why would you have?'

'Did my mum know about him?'

'Yes, of course,' said Alice. 'We talk about him a lot. He's not a secret.'

'I wasn't suggesting he would be. I'm just a bit surprised, that's all. It didn't occur to me you had a brother.' She was embarrassed by how lame that sounded; they both knew what she meant. 'Did she ever meet him?'

'No,' said Alice. 'He died a year or so before mum started cleaning for Judith.'

'That must have been so awful,' said Martha. Those words were nowhere near enough, but she didn't know how else to put it.

'I helped look after him,' said Alice. 'He could be a bit of a handful. It was hard work for Mum, but we managed it together.'

There was so much more Martha wanted to find out, but it felt intrusive to ask any more questions. She sat cradling her mug between her hands, listening to Gracie's high-pitched squeals, drifting up through the open window.

'Don't be too angry with her,' Alice said suddenly. 'With Judith, I mean. I know you must be upset – your brother too. But your mum never meant to hurt you. She really loved you.'

'Alice,' said Martha. 'Can I give you a hug?'

Alice laughed, her chair scraping against the floor as she stood up and moved towards Martha. 'I'd like that,' she said.

46

When she let herself into the bungalow, letters were scattered across the carpet, catching on the bottom of the front door as she pushed it open. Most were junk mail, but there were a couple of bills and Martha was surprised to see an envelope addressed to her, the handwriting spidery. Inside was a card, a painting of peonies on the front, the message thanking her for organising the funeral and telling her Judith would have been so proud. It was signed *Margaret*. Who on earth was Margaret? It must have been someone she'd spoken to at the crematorium. Kind of her, to get in touch.

There was also an envelope addressed to Patrick, with *Moretons* branded across the top. She ripped it open and skimmed through the letter inside. It was written confirmation of the valuation Jeff Daniels had already given to Patrick over the phone a couple of weeks ago. Martha had no idea why he'd bothered sending a letter to this address – the details had been agreed and finalised by Patrick and the For Sale sign was already up outside. As she read the words the man with the highly polished shoes had written, Martha could almost hear him saying them: *At Moretons, we pride ourselves on offering a professional but personal service. We would be delighted to be given the opportunity to market this delightful property on your behalf, and look forward to hearing from you.*

'Bollocks to that,' she said, ripping the letter in half. 'You hated the place.'

The bungalow smelt musty. It was less than three weeks since she'd brought Joe here, but seemed like longer. So much had happened since then. She wasn't intending to spend the rest of the day here, just an hour or so, starting to go through Judith's things. At some stage she'd have to come back to pack up all the clothes and shoes, and empty the drawers and cupboards. Maybe Alice would want to keep the pretty dressing table in the bedroom – although it might be too old fashioned. As she wandered from room to room, Martha made mental lists – she and Sharon might find the pots and pans in the kitchen useful, along with the microwave, which was almost new.

On top of the bookcase in the sitting room, was the framed photo of herself and Joe. She picked it up and studied it again, although she'd looked at it so often over the last couple of years that it was ingrained on her memory: every line, every shape, every shadow. She ran her finger across the picture of her little boy. It was so wonderful to see his face screwed up like this with laughter: his eyes half closed, his mouth open, the remembered shrieks of what sounded like happiness. This photograph was special because usually there was nothing on this little face – it was a blank canvas that showed no emotion, other than frustration when he wanted food or drink. The only time he looked like he did in this picture was when he was being tickled – but even then, it wasn't actual happiness, or even proper laughter. It was an involuntary response to her fingers searching out the soft skin on his tummy.

Simon constantly reminded her that Joe didn't know her. He didn't recognise the sound of her voice or the shape of her face or the smell of her skin, even though he'd grown inside her body and she was the person who spent most time with him – or had done, until recently.

Was he right? In some ways it was immaterial. They would never know for sure, so what was wrong with her believing she had a special connection with her boy?

'You know who I am,' she whispered to the laughing face in the photograph. 'I'm sure you do.'

She carried the frame across to the armchair on the right – the one Judith had always sat in, her legs crossed, her reading glasses sliding down her nose as she tapped a pen on the newspaper, frowning as she tried to work out a crossword clue. Alice definitely wouldn't want these awkward, uncomfortable chairs, although Gracie wouldn't care. Martha imagined her running into this room, Nipper at her heels, clambering up onto the chairs. With an innocent child's disregard for convention, she must have yelled and laughed, exclaimed and chattered – filling this musty old bungalow with new life.

'Bring Joe next time!' the little girl had insisted, as Martha left the flat earlier. 'We can play in the garden at Nipper's Granny's house. Please?'

'I'll bring him,' Martha had laughed. 'I promise. We'll come down and see you one weekend.'

She would look forward to doing that.

It was incredible how much better she felt, having spoken to Alice; it was as if a weight had been lifted from her shoulders. It wasn't just that she'd passed on good news, and seen how surprised and overwhelmed the girl had been – although that had been wonderful – it was more that Martha's own guilt now felt so much less significant. Patrick and Simon would both tell her it was ridiculous to feel bad about what had happened, but nonetheless she had, and now it seemed like she'd done the right thing. She had stopped fighting her mother over this and, for the first time in many years, finally felt like a good daughter.

47

Simon carried Joe in from the car and put him in his chair in the kitchen, while Martha followed with the wheelchair and his small overnight bag. It had been packed by Carrie; when Martha put it in the boot of the car, she hadn't been able to stop herself looking inside, to check there was everything they'd need. She was being paranoid: it went without saying that Carrie would have included all his medication, and he was only home for one night, so wouldn't need many clothes. But it was strange someone else was now in charge of doing these things.

The traffic had been heavy on the way back, so they were later than planned and hungry. Joe was whining and banging his hand against his leg, so Martha put some pieces of banana in front of him, while she reheated the food she'd prepared last night. She stopped to kiss the top of his head each time she walked past the chair, running her fingers across his cheek, not even minding when he jerked his head away and reached for more banana. There was something subtly different about him, but she couldn't work out what it was. Then, as she bent towards him for the third or fourth time, running her fingers across his back, she realised his clothes smelt of someone else's washing powder.

'It feels like he's never been away, doesn't it?' she said to Simon, as she pulled the dish out of the microwave. 'Now he's back here again, in his chair.' That wasn't strictly true; it was wonderful to have her boy home, but it was also a little strange. Over the last two weeks she had started to get used to this big, quiet kitchen, and to walking down the hall to the front door without scraping her ankles against the wheelchair. She had even got used to walking past the empty bedroom at the top of the stairs, with its clown patterned curtains and piles of primary-coloured toys, stacked neatly on the shelves. She didn't like this new normal, but she had begun to adapt to it.

She and Simon ate their lunch at the breakfast bar, on either side of Joe.

'His hair has grown,' she said, reaching out her hand and stroking his fringe away from his face. 'I'll need to trim it before he goes back.'

'He looks well though, doesn't he?' said Simon. 'He's obviously eating properly.'

Martha nodded. Carrie had sent a typewritten report back with them, which was still in her handbag. Although she'd been given regular updates by phone and email and knew Joe was making good progress, she was excited at the prospect of seeing something more detailed, learning about every aspect of her boy's new life.

'We can look at that report after lunch,' she said. 'Maybe read it while he has his sleep?'

'Okay,' said Simon. 'Good idea.'

They were stepping carefully around each other, being overly cautious and courteous: at times he was like a stranger, rather than the man she had loved so much and spent the last nine years with. But, ironically, since deciding they could no longer be together, things had been so much easier between them: there was unspoken relief that decisions had been made. She had no idea what the future held, and it was going to be very different to the one she'd so carelessly assumed they would all have. But she was telling herself that different didn't have to be bad.

The estate agent had sent through the rough draft of the marketing brochure this week, and the photographs – taken on a glorious sunny day – showed off the house at its best.

'I don't think we'll have any shortage of interest in this property,' the woman had said. 'Someone will snap it up.'

Martha had smiled and nodded, determined not to show this stranger how much it was hurting to have to give up her beautiful home. The board was going to be hammered into the front lawn on Monday – that would give the neighbours something to gossip about – and details had already been sent out to buyers on the agency's books, for whom this was going to be 'exactly what they're after'.

This morning, on the drive down to Greenways, Simon had told her he was moving into a work colleague's spare room. He would pack his bags and head over there after they'd dropped Joe back, tomorrow afternoon.

'You don't have to do that,' she'd said. 'It's not a problem you being at the house.'

'I know, but it's better if we have a clean break,' he'd said. 'Greg has plenty of space and he's away a lot for work, so I won't be getting under his feet.'

'Okay,' she'd said. 'If that's what you want.'

Even though this would make little difference – they'd already been leading separate lives while living under the same roof – his words had shaken her. Simon moving out would make the finality real. Stretching out in their big bed on her own at night had become easier, but knowing Simon was doing the same in the spare room, just a few steps along the landing, had softened the impact of what was happening. How would it feel, with him gone?

Simon was now feeding Joe his lunch, making big swooshing motions with the spoon to keep his interest. 'Come on, Joey,' he said. 'Just a couple more. This is your favourite. You know Mummy makes the best macaroni cheese in the world.'

She laughed as she watched them enact the mealtime pantomime, clapping as Joe accepted another mouthful. The other day, Dan had said he and Johnny were having macaroni cheese. Had he made that himself, or had his wire basket in Sainsbury's contained a couple of ready meals? At the time she'd been so overwhelmed by her own grief, she hadn't noticed or even thought to ask. But now she wanted to find out. She wanted to find out about a lot of things: where they lived, what Dan had done before his son was born, why Johnny's mother wasn't part of their lives. She'd sent him a text last night:

Hello again, thanks for rescuing me the other day. Can I buy you a pint when your mum next looks after Johnny? Martha x

As soon as she'd pressed send, she regretted it, but the reply pinged in almost immediately:

I'd love that. You free this Thursday? x

Even if she'd had something planned, she would have rearranged it. Every time she thought about Thursday evening, her heart gave that mad little flip again. She'd already thought about what she would wear, laughing out loud at herself as she stood in front of her wardrobe. She was behaving like a love-struck teenager – and it felt great.

As she began stacking the plates in the dishwasher, the doorbell rang.

'I'll go,' she said to Simon. 'Are you expecting anything?'

She pulled open the front door and caught her breath.

'Hi, Martha.'

'What are you doing here?'

Claudia's face was tanned, she'd clearly been spending time in the sun. 'I know you probably don't want to see me,' she said. 'And I can understand why. But will you please just let me come in and explain?'

Martha could hear Simon talking to Joe in the kitchen, his laugh echoing around the big space.

'I'd rather you didn't come in, we're in the middle of lunch,' she said, her hand still resting on the handle of the front door, her body blocking Claudia's view down the hallway. 'What do you want to say?'

Claudia sighed and looked down at the paving slabs by the front door. She was wearing a pair of Chelsea boots Martha hadn't seen before: brown, shiny, clearly very new. 'Listen, I know what you must think of me, and I don't blame you,' said Claudia. 'What I did was awful.'

She paused and looked back up. Martha didn't say a word, she wasn't going to make this easy for her.

'If I'm being totally honest with you, I have no idea why I said what I did, when we were here that night,' Claudia continued. 'I'd had a lot to drink – we all had – and it just seemed quite funny.'

'Funny?' said Martha. 'What the hell was funny about it?'

'Nothing, you're right. It was just... I didn't think they'd all take it seriously,' said Claudia. 'When Selina started talking about the thing you were most ashamed of, it just popped into my head, and I couldn't think about anything else. We were daring each other to say things, that was the point of it all. I thought you were going to tell them yourself, but then you seemed to be backing away from the whole thing, which I thought was a bit pathetic, so I started to prompt you.'

Martha could no longer hear Simon's voice from the kitchen. 'Pathetic?' she said.

'Well, you know – it just seemed cowardly. I mean, that's the point of the game. You're meant to be put on the spot and made to own up to stuff you've done.'

'Really, Claudia? Why would I *own up* to something like that?' she hissed, stepping out and pulling the front door closed behind her. 'I'd done something I was really ashamed of, and you were the only person I'd told about it – which, by the way, I regretted afterwards, because it didn't make me feel any better, it made me feel a whole lot worse. But it was a secret, Claudia! That's the whole point of secrets – you sometimes share them with people who are close to you, but then you expect those people to keep them!'

Claudia's expression had changed; she was now sheepish, hugging her handbag closely to her chest. 'I know,' she said.

'Is that it? You know. You know you shouldn't have told them? You know friends are supposed to keep secrets? You know you bloody let me down?' A vein was pulsing in her neck now, heat flushing through her body.

Claudia finally looked up at her again. 'All of those things,' she said. 'I'm sorry.'

Martha felt disarmed. What was she supposed to do now? She should go inside and slam the door in her friend's face. Yet she also wanted to step forward and throw her arms around her. Claudia had betrayed her – and that was what it had felt like, a huge betrayal – but... this was her closest friend. They had shared so much over the last five years: hopes, fears, laughter, tears, frustration, excitement, good news, and very, very bad news. That was why this was so hard: Claudia was important.

She had been at Martha's side during the most traumatic time of her life; nobody else really knew what she'd gone through and how hard it had been to keep going.

But looking at her friend now, standing near enough to hug, Martha couldn't decide whether any of that was enough. 'Thanks for coming to apologise,' she said. 'I know this must have been hard for you to do, and I appreciate it.'

Claudia looked back up at her, starting to smile. She put out her hand. 'Well, I wasn't sure how you'd react, but it seemed like the only way to get to see you! I got fed up with never getting a reply from you – it was all a bit ridiculous.'

She put her beautifully manicured hand on Martha's forearm, squeezing it. Martha stared down at it; that really was an impressive tan. 'The thing is,' she said, slowly. 'I don't think that you coming here like this is going to do it.'

Claudia was now looking confused. 'But, what else do you want? I've tried to text and call you so many times, and I sent you flowers – I know you got them because I checked with the florist. Come on, Martha. This is crazy. You've made your point: I did a stupid thing. Let's put it behind us and move on. Life's too short to be petty about something like this.'

Martha laughed. 'You're right!' she said. 'Life is far too short. And I agree with you, we both need to move on. I can't see any point in us staying in touch, Claudia.'

Claudia's mouth fell open. 'But... we've been friends for so long.'

'Yes,' nodded Martha. 'We have.'

'What about the boys?' said Claudia. 'They've known each other their whole lives, they've grown up together. You can't just cut off contact like this. Barney won't understand why he's not seeing Joe anymore. He'll really miss him.'

Martha shook her head. 'No, Claudia, he won't. You know that's not true.' She opened the front door and stepped back inside the house, before turning around again. 'On the other hand, I *will* miss you,' she said. 'But not as much as I always thought I would. I think my life is better off without you in it. Good luck with everything.'

Closing the door, she turned and walked back along the hallway into the kitchen. Simon was by the sink, cleaning the empty macaroni cheese dish.

'Who was that?' he asked.

'No one important,' she said, bending down to kiss the top of Joe's head. 'Right, lovely boy, what are we going to do with you this afternoon?'

THE END

ACKNOWLEDGEMENTS

At the risk of sounding like an overwrought Oscar nominee, I hadn't realised how many people had helped me with my writing in general - and this book in particular - until I began to make a list. Going way back, it all started with support and constructive feedback from my Faber friends, then mentoring from Amanda Saint, followed by an award from Katie Fforde at the Stroud Book Festival, which encouraged me to believe in my writing and keep going.

Fellow writers are some of the most supportive people in the universe and I owe so much to Hannah Persaud, Rachel Joyce, Kerry Fisher and Chloe Turner, who have always dropped everything to advise, read and encourage. More recently it's also been great to have the writerly support and friendship of Kirsten, Gem and the rest of the 'Nanos'.

I wrote 'A Thousand Tiny Disappointments' during the first lockdown, when the world was a strange place, so I felt lucky to be able to slip away and immerse myself in someone else's life. My mentor Alison May did a brilliant job of helping me knock the plot for this book into shape, then my first readers - book group buddies Amanda, Liza, Sarah and Anne – looked at an early draft, hashed it out with me on Zoom and suggested ways to improve it. I'm also so grateful to Caroline Hutchins for ensuring I handled everything to do with Joe with sensitivity.

Finally, a big thank you to everyone at Bloodhound Books, particularly Betsy for bringing me on board, Tara for patiently answering my inane questions about the publishing process and Clare for her editing skills. It's great to be in the kennels with you all.

And of course, none of this would mean anything without the love and cheerleading of the fabulous Lingards – Mat, Sam, Maddy and Jess. You're my everything x

DISCUSSION QUESTIONS FOR BOOK GROUPS

- What is the significance of the title 'A Thousand Tiny Disappointments' – did you think it was relevant and/or meaningful?
- Inheritance is a subject that elicits strong reactions and emotions. Do you believe children have a right to inherit from their parents, whatever the circumstances? Similarly, do parents have a 'duty' to ensure their children are provided for, after their death?
- How does Martha's relationship with Patrick influence what she does with Judith's handwritten codicil?
- Martha and Simon's marriage is in crisis from the start of the book. A floundering relationship is never just one person's fault, but how much of Martha's behaviour is influenced by the guilt she feels about Joe – and the fact that she believes she has let Simon down?
- It was only after her mother died, that Martha began to realise that the recent distance between them, may

have been partly her fault. Did she damage their relationship by being too proud to ask for help?

- When Martha discovered how close Alice had been to her mother, it played on all the insecurities and inadequacies she already felt as a daughter. How would you have reacted in a similar situation?
- Were there times when you disagreed with Martha's actions? What would you have done differently?
- Martha felt let down by Claudia, but they had been close friends during a hugely important time in their lives. Should Martha have found it in herself to forgive Claudia?

A NOTE FROM THE PUBLISHER

Thank you for reading this book. If you enjoyed it please do consider leaving a review on Amazon to help others find it too.

We hate typos. All of our books have been rigorously edited and proofread, but sometimes mistakes do slip through. If you have spotted a typo, please do let us know and we can get it amended within hours.

info@bloodhoundbooks.com